DEAD

OF

NIGHT

ISBN-13: 9781636960388
ISBN-10: 1636960383

Cover design by: Damonza.com
Printed in the United States of America

BLAKE BANNER

A HARRY BAUER THRILLER

DEAD
OF
NIGHT

R

RIGHT HOUSE

ONE

U nder a black sky, pierced by icy stars high above the Sulaiman Mountains, we lay shivering, waiting. Then the soft crackle in my ear and the quiet, gravelly voice of Sergeant Bradley, the Kiwi.

"All right, move in. Move in for the kill, boys."

There were four of us in the patrol. We pulled down our night-vision goggles, the world turned a strange, eerie green and black and we scrambled at a crouching run, moving fast and silent across the sand and loose stones. I was at the back. Ahead of me, scattered at irregular distances, with their C8 Carbines across their chests, were: The Sarge—the big, bearded New Zealander —at the head. Behind him, fifteen feet to the left, was Jones, six foot six of solid black, Welsh muscle; then Skinner, ten paces to his left, small, wiry and lethal, from the East End of London. As at home in a tavern in Senegal as he was in a pub in Whitechapel, as long as he was drinking beer, he didn't care who he had to fight.

And then me, Bauer, the Yank. I had their backs.

We moved silently, with startling speed over the cold sand, driving uphill, over loose gravel and rocks, among the boulders and the small shrubs. Soon the vast wall of the mountain had blocked out the sky and the small stars ahead, and we were clambering, more slowly now, up a narrow path forged over centuries by cloven hooves and sandals.

After fifteen minutes of climbing we came to a small plateau where scattered, gnarled cypress bushes stood, twisted, tortured silhouettes among the stunted rosemary bushes and the thyme. Here Jones and Skinner peeled off and vanished noiselessly among the shadows. Bradley and I continued along, half-crouching beside the path, keeping low.

Soon, at the northern end of the plateau, the terrain on our right began to climb again, steeply toward a jagged system of ravines and peaks. Bradley dropped on his belly and began to crawl. I followed suit. My own breathing was loud in my ears, and just ahead I could hear the soft slither of Bradley's camouflage on the dust. A nocturnal bird cried out and from far off came the howl of what might have been a wolf, or a dog.

And then we saw it and froze: the tiny, green glimmer of light from a flame.

Bradley's voice crackled softly again: "We have eyes on the cave. Light visible. Do nothing. Either they are not expecting company, or this is a trap. Please confirm you are in position."

Jones came back.

"Affirmative, Sarge. We see the light."

Bradley signaled me over and I crawled up beside him. He pointed at me, pointed to a small copse of gnarled bushes fifty or sixty feet from the cave and directly in front of it, and touched his eyes with his two fingers in a victory sign.

I moved off at a crouching lope, taking irregular steps and occasionally dropping to a crawl. The air was freezing, but I was sweating with the exertion and the weight of the Bergen on my back. I kept my mouth covered with a thick, woolen scarf, not so much because of the cold, but to conceal the telltale clouds of condensation that could give a sniper a target.

I came to the crop of twisted cypresses and crawled in among the trunks. I raised my goggles, pulled the C8 from my shoulder and peered through the nightscope. Six guys in Taliban dress sitting around a fire, eating and talking. They were at the entrance to a large cave. I spoke softly into my mic.

"Six Taliban at the mouth of the cave, eating. I see assault rifles against the rocks. Looks like we are not expected. I see more light inside the cave."

Bradley's voice came back: "OK, boys, close in to ten yards. Bauer, on my word, you open fire. Jones, Skinner, we close in from the sides. Bauer, fuck's sake don't shoot us."

There was no acknowledgment. It wasn't needed. We all knew what we had to do.

I began to crawl, easy, relaxed, keeping my limbs loose, keeping my head and my shoulders down. At thirty feet I stopped. Now I could see the targets clearly, sitting cross-legged, gesticulating at each other as they spoke. I took my scope and focused on the nearest weapon leaning against a rock. It was an AK47. At that distance, with the scope, I could see the selector set high to the safety position. By the time its owner reached it and flipped to full auto, they'd all be dead. These men were not expecting to be hit tonight. This was not a trap.

I breathed into the mic: "Bauer in position. Nearest weapon six feet from nearest guy. Safety on."

Bradley's voice came back without hesitation.

"OK, Bauer, kill them. Repeat, kill."

Nine times out of ten spraying an area with fire is wasteful and ineffective. Slugs from an assault rifle spray wide, and after a few yards your bullets are passing harmlessly between your targets. Short, concentrated bursts of two or three slugs are more effective. That is, unless your victims are in a small, confined space. In which case, due to ricochet, your thirty rounds are multiplied by ten and become three hundred rounds bouncing unpredictably in all directions.

The stone nook in which they were sitting, to get shelter from the icy desert breeze and keep in the warmth of the fire, was just one such confined space. I aimed at the head of the nearest guy, sitting with his back to me, and muttered, "Just not cricket, old chap," in a fair imitation of a British officer. Then I opened up.

After the fifth round had exploded from the barrel the weapon was dancing in my hands like a hooked fish and I was struggling to keep it centered on the target. After a couple of seconds the magazine was empty and the small stone alcove was strewn with badly injured, dead and dying men. To the right I could see Sergeant Bradley sprinting toward the fire, and on the left Jones and Skinner closing in.

I pulled out the magazine and rammed in a new one, scrambled to my feet and ran the ten paces to the scene of the slaughter. A couple of cracks, like firecrackers, rang out in the night: one of the guys finishing the job, confirming the kill.

By the time I got there they'd taken up positions, on one knee, covering the deeper entrance to the cave proper. I knelt beside the Sarge and he signaled me forward with his left hand.

I ran four steps to an outcrop of boulders and peered around it. I could see a large opening in the cliff face, ten feet high and about twelve feet across. Orange light wavered on the left-hand wall. I signaled Bradley to follow. He came up beside me and had a look, then pointed to a cluster of rocks beside the mouth of the cave. I made a dash and ducked in beside them while he covered me.

Now I couldn't see the inside of the cavern. All I could see was the black sky above, the narrow passage of sand I had just crossed and the cluster of rocks fifteen feet away, where the bodies lay. Soft, flickering amber light touched it, and in that light I saw Bradley turn back and gesture. A couple of seconds later Jones and Skinner had joined him. Then, with a brief scuffle of boots in the dust, one by one, they crossed the sand and joined me.

For a moment we remained motionless, listening. We exchanged looks that said none of us could hear anything. The Sarge got on his belly and wormed his way to the edge of the entrance. After a moment he rolled on his back to look at us and gestured me and Skinner to the far side, and Jones to join him.

In that configuration, we moved into the cave. The floor seemed to have been largely cleared of rocks and gave the impression of being frequently used. The firelight we'd seen was coming from a couple of flaming torches that had been wedged into cracks in the rocks. They were positioned at a dogleg where the passage turned left and disappeared from view.

We moved, quickly and silently to the bend where the torches were, and Sergeant Bradley dropped on his belly again, wormed his way along and peered around. I followed suit, keeping in the shadows.

It was another long passage, ascending slightly. The midsection was in shadow, but at the far end you could see light spilling from some kind of cavern, and we could just make out the soft murmur of voices. Bradley pulled us back and spoke quietly.

"If the intel is good, that's Mohammed Ben-Amini in there, the fuckin' Butcher of Al-Landy, plus three mullahs and maybe a dozen men. Her Majesty's MoD has politely requested, if it's at all possible, we bring Ben-Amini back in one piece so they can give him a fat pension and a big house in Surrey, and spend the next ten years pumping him for information. So, if you can take him alive, please do. If it gets too hot, plug the bastard. Let's go." He held up three fingers. "Flashbang, grenades, carbines."

We spread out and moved down the passage at a silent run, avoiding the few rocks that littered the sand. At six feet from the end, where it turned right and opened out into the firelit cavern, Bradley stopped and raised his left hand. He dropped to his belly for the third time, crawled a couple of feet and peered in. He grinned malevolently, pointed at me and jerked his thumb. I pulled a G60 stun grenade from my belt, yanked out the pin and hurled it into the cavern.

There was a metallic clank, a second of silence, then sudden shouts and an almighty flash of three hundred thousand candles of light and one hundred and sixty decibels of detonation. We were ready; four grenades followed and exploded in rapid succession.

Then we moved in, carbines at our shoulders and goggles to protect our eyes from the dust. It was carnage, a charnel house. Six men lay partially dismembered around a large fire. Two were mullahs, the other four were Taliban fighting men. A seventh man lay beyond the fire, clutching at his belly, his lips pulled back over his teeth, weeping and crying out. Skinner shot him in the head. We moved on, walking quickly, scanning left to right, following a narrow path among boulders. Two men in white robes, one on his knees, vomiting, the other lying facedown with his hands over his ears. I double-tapped twice and shot them both.

Voices up ahead, crying out, shouting and weeping. The cave was growing darker as we moved away from the fire. We switched on the flashlights under the barrels of the carbines. The Sarge began to run. We kept pace. Nine men came into view. They were sitting and kneeling in the dirt, waving their arms and shouting at us. A couple struggled to their feet. Most were holding their hands up. The beams of light from our weapons played over them. They looked confused, scared, concussed from the explosions.

Bradley shouted at them in Arabic to drop their weapons. A couple of them dropped and prostrated themselves facedown in the dirt. One of them, dressed different to the rest in a red jacket, was on all fours trying to walk away. The other six were variously on their knees or trying to get to their feet, shielding their eyes with their hands. I knew they'd gone deaf and couldn't hear what Bradley was shouting at them. He shouted again, louder, and a couple of the guys getting to their feet took aim at the lights they could see bobbing toward them. The cave exploded with automatic fire. It was over in two seconds. They were all dead. All except Mohammed Ben-Amini, the Butcher of Al-Landy, who, dressed in his red jacket, had adopted the fetal position and was weeping convulsively.

I slung the carbine over my shoulder, pulled my sidearm and stepped over to him. He squealed like a stuck pig as I grabbed his collar and dragged him to his knees. The Sarge, Jones and Skinner gathered around and I shoved his face toward his dead comrades.

"Hey, Mohammed, you speak English?"

His face was screwed up and he was babbling incoherently. Jones stepped forward with his canteen and poured a little water over his face. Mohammed spluttered and looked up. Jones offered him the canteen.

"Here you go, boyo, have a drink. Relax."

His terrified eyes swiveled to Bradley and then to me. I jerked my head toward the canteen. He took a swig and wiped his mouth with his wrist. I repeated, "You speak English?"

He nodded. "I speak some. Little."

He showed me what a little was with his thumb and index.

I nodded. "We saw what you did to the village of Al-Landy. We were there..." I gestured at the four of us. "And we saw..." I put my fingers to my eyes and moved them around. "We saw what you did."

He made a crying face and spread his hands. "It was will of Allah! They were *kafir*, bad, not good believers. My men..." He gestured at his dead men. "My men had God's anger in their hearts..."

"You murdered fifteen children. Five of them were babies. You cut off one man's head in front of his wife and his kids. You raped the women and the little girls, and then you killed them..."

He leaned forward, appealing to me. "That man, he taught blasphemy. *Sharia* demands justice."

I roared, "*Blasphemy? He wanted to buy a TV for the coffee shop!*"

It was like he didn't hear me. "And the women..."

He reached up toward my face, "...they had been with men..."

"*They were raped!*"

"They allowed themselves to be raped, they did not fight... All of them, the whole village was touché! Touch by *shaitan!*"

There was a moment of silence. Skinner broke it by speaking what we were all thinking. "And this bastard is going to live out the rest of his fuckin' life in luxury in Surrey, in a five fuckin' bedroom house, while my mum and dad live on a basic pension in Essex." He looked around at us, one by one. "That seem right to you?"

Jones shook his head. His voice was deep, quiet and melodious, and full of menace. "My brother, Ewan, still works at the mine in Blaentillery. It's bloody hard work, I can tell you, backbreaking, and he barely makes enough to feed the kids and pay the mortgage. So no, not really..."

I looked at Bradley. He sighed, "Come on, lads, this is the British Army. We're soldiers, not judges or executioners. We do as we're told. Let's get this bastard back to base and send him off to Kabul."

I didn't move. I could still see the terrified eyes of the little four-year-old as this son of a bitch took aim at him. Every moment of the massacre was moving through my head in slow motion, every blast of automatic fire, every slash of the blade, every scream, every child. I held Bradley's eye, but he couldn't hold mine. Jones and Skinner didn't budge either. They just watched him, until Jones finally said, "Hey, Sarge, don't you need to piss or something?"

Bradley growled, "I can piss in the cave, Jones."

"Ah, no, but it's not healthy, see, Sarge? Too much ammonia in a small, cramped place, without appropriate ventilation, see? Best to piss outside. More healthy."

Bradley knew what he was being told—to piss off, as Brits like to say. He didn't like it. He was old school, and I'm pretty sure that if it had been anybody else but this son of a bitch he would have stood his ground. But he wanted this bastard punished as much as we did. So he sighed, pointed at us in turn and said what he had to say, even if he didn't mean it.

"But I want this man alive and well when I get back, you understand?"

I nodded. "Don't worry about it. We won't do anything you wouldn't do."

Skinner spat elaborately on the ground. "Not unless he does son-fink really stupid, like."

Jones nodded. "Yeah, boyo. Not unless he does something really, like, stupid."

There was a footfall. We all turned at the same time, weapons cocked and in hand, beams of light playing over the rock walls.

A voice rang out, loud, an American voice, edged with malice and with humor.

"The British Army does not make war on women and children, or on prisoners. It is reassuring and rewarding to hear the voice of the British trooper on the ground upholding those great values of civilization."

He stepped into the circle of light from our flashlights. I knew him: Captain Bill Hartmann, currently attached to Delta Force, but nobody knew where he originated. Most assumed he was CIA. Right now he had four men behind him in full battle dress, armed with HK416s.

He smiled at us each in turn. "Hail, dear allies," he said. "Well met. I have to congratulate you on a superb job. But you guys look tired. Why don't you let us take it from here?"

Bradley stepped in front of Mohammed and squared his massive shoulders.

"This man is our prisoner and he is coming back to London with us."

Hartmann's smile was a thing you wanted to stamp on. He shook his head and said, "No, Sergeant, he's not. We are taking him back to Washington." He pointed a finger at Mohammed. "I suggest we get this piece of shit outside and you talk to your colonel on the phone. He'll give you your new orders. We have a couple of choppers waiting. One of them will take you back to your base. Think of it as a small thank-you, for services rendered."

I still had my P226 stuck to the back of Mohammed's head. I said:

"This man has to face justice for what he did."

Hartmann narrowed his eyes at me. "You're an American."

"I said, this man has to face justice for what he has done."

"And so he shall, son. Good old American justice. We'll see to that back home, don't you worry. Now hand him over and quit being an asshole."

Nothing happened, except that I could feel my finger tightening on the trigger.

"I know what you'll do with him. He won't stand trial and he won't be punished."

He took three strides and came up close in front of me. He cupped the back of my neck with his left hand and looked into my eyes.

"This guy's brother is a Saudi prince, boy. He plays golf with three different presidents from two different parties. One of his sons is at Harvard and another went to

Sandhurst, and that's just the tip of the iceberg. So grow up, son. This is the real world, and down here bad shit happens all the time. So hand him over before I have my boys shoot your boys."

I pulled Mohammed to his feet and we all marched outside. There was an icy wind and a frosted moon was riding a few inches above the eastern horizon. Bradley made the call, said, "Yes, sir..." a few times and hung up. He looked at me and jerked his head—I should hand him over.

I grabbed the bastard by the scruff of his neck and rasped at him in Arabic.

"*Sawf ajduk!* I will find you, and you will pay for what you did to that village. I swear!" Then I thrust him toward Captain Hartmann.

They both stared at me for a moment and Hartmann wagged a finger at me.

"I don't like you, boy. You're in the wrong army, doing the wrong stuff. You ain't heard the last of me." He turned to Bradley. "You got a chopper waiting at the plateau. You should report this son of a bitch." He pointed at me. "He was going to execute a valuable prisoner, an unarmed man. I'm going to talk to my people, and they will talk to your people. You'd better be on the right side when the shit comes down, Sergeant Bradley."

They walked away, along the path, toward the plateau where the choppers were waiting. I turned to Bradley. "I'm sorry, Sarge."

He shook his head. "You should have shot him when you had the chance."

Jones slapped a huge hand on my shoulder. "We'll back you up, boyo. If it comes to that."

Skinner spat again and slung his rifle over his

shoulder. "Ain't nobody saw what went down here tonight 'cept us, right? Our word against his."

I nodded. I knew guys like Hartmann, and so did they. And they knew that Hartmann's word carried more weight than the four of us put together, and then some.

We made our way back toward the plateau and the waiting chopper in silence. We knew it was over. It was over for me, at least.

TWO

They gave it the works. They wanted to make it stick, and even though the Brits—and especially the Regiment—don't like being told what to do, they knew that the "special" part of the Special Relationship meant that Washington looked after Westminster's interests because Westminster no longer had the military might to do it herself. So while Washington would usually ask nicely, because Britain was an essential ally, Westminster would usually say "Yes" to whatever Washington asked. That was the way it was in post-imperial Britain.

We were flown to Bagram, to the small, unofficial HQ the SAS still had in what was left of the airbase there. I was allowed to shower, eat and sleep for four hours, and then I was summoned to Brigadier Alexander "Buddy" Byrd's office for a "chat."

The office was functional, military green steel and melamine. The venetian blind was raised and the window showed a view of dilapidated, empty barracks and desultory soldiers and officers trying hard to look like they were doing a job instead of thinking of going home.

The Regiment doesn't stand on ceremony, and there is a tradition of officers and troopers using first names. It's an unspoken recognition that if you made it far enough to become a "blade," you're worthy of respect. I stepped through the door and Byrd watched me close it and sit down on the beige and chrome chair opposite him at his desk. At sixty, he was handsome, lean and strong, and probably the most dangerous man I had ever met. Yet he had a bland, amiable face and spoke with the quiet, deferential manner of the English upper-middle classes. He smiled, then turned it into a wince.

"Spot of bother up at the caves, ay?"

I nodded. "Yeah. It got a bit out of hand."

"Shame Mohammed didn't defend himself, really. Would have saved everyone a lot of bother."

"Yeah. He's not that kind of man."

"Whitehall wanted him rather badly, of course."

"Hartmann was right behind us. They let us do the dirty work, then they came in and claimed the prize."

"He says you were going to execute Ben-Amini."

"I was. The Sarge was telling me not to do it. I couldn't get the memory of the massacre at Al-Landy out of my head. The kids, the children..."

I stopped myself and looked out at the bright glare of the desert day. When I had my breath under control again I went on.

"But that wasn't why he reported me. He was mad at me because I wasn't going to hand over Ben-Amini. None of us were. But the Sarge spoke to brass and we got our orders, which we obeyed."

Byrd sighed and pulled open a drawer. He pulled out a bottle of Glenlivet and poured us a shot each. He'd never done that before and I knew it was a farewell.

"For my part," he said, "I couldn't be less interested in Whitehall's political maneuverings. But we are soldiers and we must obey orders. On the other hand, we can't go around executing prisoners without trial, because then, however justified that execution may be on a personal level, as an institution we become no better than them. I hope you understand that, Bauer."

"Yeah, I do, and I agree. What I was about to do was wrong, but the thought of that man living in a mansion, while the lives of those children, those women and those innocent men..." I shook my head, not satisfied with how I had said it. "Not their lives—their torture, the horror of the last minutes of their lives. All of that is forgotten, because that bastard can be useful. And his punishment for murdering those children and those women is to be given a mansion in Surrey, and a yearly income most working men can't even dream of."

He sipped his whisky and set it down carefully on the desk, like setting it down wrong might have consequences.

"I know, and between you, me and the bedpost, I actually agree with you. But, as soldiers, we can't do anything about it. If you want to do something about it, you should get a different job."

I snorted. "Like a politician?"

"Well." He smiled. "I haven't known many politicians to do much of any use, with some notable exceptions. But look, I have been instructed to make you an offer. It isn't much of an offer, I'm afraid, but it's the best we could get for you."

"Resign or face a court martial."

"That's right. If you face the court martial I'm afraid the best you can hope for is a dishonorable discharge, which would be a shame, because you have served well and with honor."

"And if I don't?"

"You will simply resign and we'll give you your discharge papers."

"Is that all? What kind of reference am I going to get when I apply for a job?"

He held my eye. "A bald statement that you served with the Regiment for eight years and saw active service."

"And every major security company in the UK and the States will know exactly what that means."

"I'm afraid so. But it's better than a dishonorable discharge, or a prison term for attempted murder."

"Is that a threat, sir?"

"Don't be stupid, Bauer. I am as unhappy with this as you are, but I have my orders and I have to follow them. This is the choice they are giving you. And if they are offering it to you it's because somebody in the brass is looking after you. They could simply court-martial you, but they have chosen not to do that, but to give you an option. My advice is to take the offer, because if Hartmann and the Firm bring pressure to bear at trial, things could go very badly for you."

I examined the whisky in my glass. "Sure sounds like a threat."

He blinked a couple of times. For "Buddy" Byrd that was a major display of emotion. "Look, Harry, you can't afford to be emotional about this. Not least because you'll wind up turning on your friends, and right now you need all the friends you can get. We stick together in the Regiment, you know that, and you need to remember it and trust it. I want things to work out for you, but clearly what I can't do is go up against Whitehall and the MoD, or the Pentagon and the CIA, for that matter."

I studied the whisky a little longer and decided I could allow myself to drink it. I threw it back and swallowed it, then set the glass on his desk. I looked him in the eye and nodded once.

"Eight years. It's a lot to let go of."

"I know, Harry, and I'm sorry."

"You got the papers there?"

He opened the file and slid them across the desk to me. I read them through. They were neutral: a simple resignation. I took my pen and signed them, signed away eight years of my life, signed away the only family I had ever had, signed away my friends, my comrades, my clan.

I went to stand but he stopped me.

"We'll fly you back to London..."

I shook my head. "I can do that myself."

He paused, hesitated. "Fair enough. But my advice to you, Harry, is to go back to New York. If you want to work in security, I am sure you'll find a good job there. It's a big, rich market in the States. They need men like you."

"Thanks."

He stood and reached out his hand. "It has been an honor and a privilege. Look after yourself and, if you need anything, you have friends here. Remember that."

We shook and I left.

I took his advice. When somebody like Buddy Byrd gives you advice, it's because he knows what he's talking about. So I took the next available flight back to London. It was summer, so it was raining and sultry. I have a theory that, as climate change takes hold, the British archipelago will become tropical, with large rainforests and huge, man-eating insects.

I spent two weeks sorting out my place in Hammersmith. I gave away everything I could, and what I couldn't give away, I sold at what the Brits call "boot sales," where you sell junk from the trunk of your car at a parking lot, a church hall or village green. After two weeks my house was pretty much empty; the rooms were bare and had that soulless, lifeless echo. The few bits and pieces that were left I gave to a charity shop, put my house on the market through a realtor and bought myself a ticket back to New York.

I hadn't been in the USA for almost ten years, most of my adult life. I had left behind an unhappy childhood, an adolescence of violence and rebellion against injustice, and a pregnant wife. If she had been my wife I would have stayed, but she was the wife of a local pillar of the community, and she begged me to leave and not contact her ever again.

I had done as she asked and, pretending to myself I didn't care and I wasn't hurt, I got on a ship and sailed across the Atlantic to start a new life in what was then still Europe.

During my teens, searching for meaningful ways to rebel, I had picked up a black belt in tae kwon do and an instructor's level in jeet kune do. When I got to the UK and applied to join the Special Air Service, it turned out I was in better shape than I thought I was. I managed to claw my way through the first phase of selection, known as "endurance" or "the hills," which is designed to break down normal people's physical and mental resistance.

Less than ten percent of candidates make it through that phase. I believe I only managed it because the thought of giving in to authority was worse than dying of exhaustion. But when I told Buddy that, he laughed and told me it was what they all said, and that was the very quality they were looking for.

The second phase was jungle training in Latin America, near Mexico, and the third was escape and evasion techniques, and the hell of resisting interrogation. They are months of training that shape you, and live with you for the rest of your life.

Somehow I survived them and went on to spend the next eight years on active duty in Central and South America, the Middle East and other places I wouldn't name if I could.

In all that time, the one place I never returned to was the one place I should have called home, but never did. The USA, New York.

And now was time to return: to what, I had no idea.

Nobody lives in Manhattan, unless they have inherited property, or they are millionaires. I explored the Village, Queens and Brooklyn, but they weren't much more accessible than Manhattan. So finally I wound up with a pale blue, clapboard cottage on Shore Drive, just beside the Throggs Neck Memorial Post, with a head full of memories, an almost empty house and a rapidly dwindling bank balance.

I started a systematic round of all the major security companies, handing in my resume and applying for interviews. Some never bothered to answer, others politely declined. A small handful invited me along and told me they could not offer me work in the States, but they always had a need for high-caliber mercenaries.

After a week I had run out of security companies to approach. The only ones that were left paid so little I would barely be able to afford a rental on a small apartment, let alone a mortgage on a house.

Another week and I was getting worried. So I began spreading my net wider to large, five-star hotels and exclusive clubs, but always I received the same polite refusal.

On the Friday of the third week desperation was beginning to set in. I was at the offices of Allied Security Solutions, at 260 on East 161st Street, between Walgreens and Checkers. The company was on the ninth floor, and the view from their personnel department's window was depressing, like a painting by a dispirited Cubist who had nothing left on his palette but gray, beige and a nameless mixture of the two.

The guy across the desk from me, Dick Van Dreiver, was big and hard, with a platinum crew cut and pale blue eyes that had looked at death and seen it as an opportunity. He wore an expensively vulgar double-breasted Italian suit that whispered cruel things every time he moved.

When he'd finished looking at my resume, he dropped it on the desk and smiled like we were about to share a joke. His accent was South African.

"You know what I'm gonna say, right? You know, if it was up to me I'd snap you up in a second. I know how valuable guys like you are. But I am gonna be straight with you, chum. You are not going to get the kind of work you want in this city, or any major city, for that matter. I mean..." He picked up the resume and waved it at me. "You're an amazing guy. But you resigned, and they won't write you a letter of recommendation beyond, 'Yuh, he was in the regiment.' Where is your commanding officer's reference?" He leaned forward. "You left under a cloud and they gave you the option of resigning rather than an expensive, embarrassing court martial. What did you do? Shoot somebody you oughtn't?"

I didn't answer and he sighed. "I know, it sucks. Eight years of devoted service and this is the thanks. But look." He dropped the resume on the desk. "There is a lot of highly paid work out there for a man with your skills and talents."

"Yeah, I know, but I don't want to be a mercenary. I know what happens out there and I don't want to be a part of it."

"Fair enough. I get that. It's part of the reason I am sitting behind this desk. But you don't need to go that far. I can give you a private recommendation for a job I happen to know pays damned well, and doesn't involve raiding small villages and murdering innocent people."

I frowned. The slight flippancy of his tone grated on me. "What kind of job?"

He raised his palm and gave me a warning look. "Now, hear me out. You'd start as a doorman at a club." I laughed and made to stand, but he stopped me. "It pays a grand a week as a starting salary, rising to two grand if you pass the probation period of a month. And the employer's creative with the way he approaches tax, so most of your pay goes where it belongs, in your pocket."

I sat and scowled at him. "A grand a week, for a *doorman?*"

"Yuh, well, I'm guessing we are neither of us naive, Mr. Bauer, and obviously what we are looking at here is a position as a bodyguard. Your potential employer, Peter Rusanov, recently purchased a club, here in the Bronx. The previous owners attracted what we might call a very varied clientele. You had Hollywood actors, judges, the mayor..." He shook his head. "I even saw a senator in there once, and they are all rubbing fucking shoulders with drug traffickers and gang members with skulls tattooed on their foreheads. To say the club is lucrative is the understatement of the century. The *declared* turnover is in the millions. The *actual* turnover is a hundred times higher, because they are not selling just champagne, right?"

He shrugged, spread his hands and sat nodding for a while.

"Now, obviously a joint like that carries a risk element, and the last owner was killed. So, along comes Russian businessmen Peter Rusanov and he sees the potential of this place, but he also sees the risk. So he plays it smart. He leaves the running of the place in the hands of the local gang, an outfit that goes by the name of the *Chupa Cabras,* but he also gets himself a praetorian guard composed of ex-special forces veterans, whose loyalty he knows he can rely on, provided he pays them well."

I stared at him for a long moment. "You're offering me a job as a bodyguard to a Russian Mafia boss."

He shrugged again and pulled down the corners of his mouth. "I have no idea if he is Russian Mafia or not, and frankly, I don't give a shit. You're not in the army now, Mr. Bauer, and they will not look after you anymore. They betrayed you and these are the options they have left open for you. Take it or leave it."

I sank back in my chair. My house in London was nowhere near being sold. My bank account was approaching critical numbers and I was nowhere close to finding a job that paid anything like the kind of salary I needed. And Van Dreiver was right. The bottom line was that, even if Byrd, Bradley, Jones and Skinner had stayed loyal to me, the army had betrayed me, stabbed me in the back and hung me out to dry. I was out of options.

But even as I said the words to myself, in my mind, I could see Bradley's diabolical face, bathed in firelight under the black sky of the desert, his eyes reflecting the dancing flames, his mouth twisted into a daemon smile.

"You're never out of options, boy. You're just out of

imagination."

And then the idea came to me and I smiled.

"OK, Van Dreiver, you have a deal. When do I go and see this guy?"

"You don't. First you'll see the manager of the bar. It's called the Mescal, on Park Avenue, in South Bronx, Mott Haven. You know it?"

"Yeah, I know it."

He picked up the phone. "I'll make the call, you go over right now."

THREE

The Mescal Club was located just where East 135th Street becomes Park Avenue. It's no secret, at least not to me, that the super rich and powerful in this world have a dark side. They like to get down and dirty sometimes. They like to slum it and flirt with the squalid and the dangerous. The Mescal Club was the ideal place to do just that.

It was essentially a converted warehouse, set back from a dirty road, in a large parking lot beside the railway tracks. In stark contrast to the filthy street, the graffiti, the dumpsters and the chain-link fences, the club itself sported a purple awning trimmed in gold, a gold logo representing a peyote bud, two large potted palms flanking the door and a short strip of red carpet. There was no Renaissance fountain depicting Poseidon with a bunch of dolphins, but you felt there ought to be.

When I got there it was six PM. The door was open, but it was quiet. I stepped into a lobby carpeted in red, with a small mahogany counter on the right. There was nobody behind it right then, but I could see a door to a cloakroom that had no cloaks in it. On the left there was a short flight of stairs, also of mahogany and also carpeted in red. Ahead there were heavy, padded doors. I went to them and pushed through.

It was a large space with a high ceiling. A long, shiny bar made a dogleg from the left wall to the rear. There was a lot of booze behind the bar, and something told me they sold most of it most nights. To the right of it, six broad, wooden steps rose to a lounge area with sofas and big padded chairs. And against the right-hand wall there was a stage with steel poles where I figured the girls danced.

The rest of the floor area was taken up with tables, each with a lamp and a flower, and sofas, armchairs and low tables flanking the walls and making cozy nooks in the corners.

Sitting at the bar, at the far end of the room, were three guys. They were all looking at me. The guy in the middle was big, about six-six, with massive arms and legs and a back like an aircraft carrier. He swung slowly round on his stool to watch me. His head was big but his eyes were small and close together, making him look simian.

On his right was a man in his late thirties. He had short hair, tattoos on his face and a pencil mustache. He had that look about him that some men get when they've lived a long time with violence, like they could have grown wise, but instead they'd gone bad, poisoned by all the hatred in their souls.

On his left was a guy in a suit. He was tall and lean and his clothes were expensive. His hair was cut real short, the way Buddhists and ex-Russian military wear it. I figured him for the latter.

The gorilla said, "We are closed."

"I'm here from Allied Security, Van Dreiver sent me."

"We're still closed."

"I'm not here for a drink. I have an appointment to see Joe Chamorro."

The simian, who I figured was Joe, jerked his head at the pencil mustache. Mustache slid down from his stool and crossed the room to stand in front of me, looking up into my face. He'd had acne when he was a kid and his skin was pockmarked and oily.

"You don't hear so good? The man said the place is closed."

I felt a small pellet of hot anger in my gut. I spoke quiet and calm.

"I hear fine. But repeating that it's closed doesn't change the fact that I have an appointment to see Joe Chamorro at six PM. Right now it's six PM. Are you Joe Chamorro?"

He cocked his head to one side. "I ain't Joe Chamorrow, but..."

I didn't let him get any further. "Then get out of my face and get Joe Chamorro for me."

He closed his mouth and looked back at the gorilla. I jerked my head at him and said, "You, you're Chamorro, right?"

He nodded once. His face was impassive. I pushed the mustache aside and crossed the room to stand in front of the ape-man.

"We have an appointment, at six. I'm here. You want to offer me a job or you want to measure dicks?"

If he didn't like my tone his face didn't show it. "Dick said you been in special ops. That true?"

"For the last eight years, Special Air Service, Iraq, Afghanistan and other places I can't mention."

Mustache had come up beside me and was looking like he wanted to gut me right there. I ignored him and

Joe asked: "You ever kill anyone?"

I narrowed my eyes at him like he was stupid. "That was my job."

He grunted. "How many, one, two?"

"I lost count, Joe. Ask your barman how many drinks he's served in the last eight years."

There was a trace of a smile on his fat face, and his small eyes seemed to sneer. "We get fights here sometimes. People pull knives, break bottles. I don't want no exhibition martial arts. I need a guy who can finish it fast and put the brawlers on the street. Can you do that?"

I sighed. I was getting bored. "Yeah, I can do that."

Mustache gave me a shove on the shoulder. "Eh, you watch your tongue, gringo. You talkin' to your boss. You watch your fockin' mouth!"

Joe was still watching me. The pellet of anger in my gut was getting hotter and I was running out of patience. I spoke quiet.

"Tell your pet monkey that if he touches me again I'll break his hand. Now, I am about through with this piss-ass interview. You have a job for me, make me an offer. You want to play tough guy, go play in the sandpit, boss."

Mustache stepped toward me, planning to thump me with both hands on my chest. I took his right wrist in my right hand, seized his fingers with my left and made like I was breaking kindling for the fire. I heard three of his four knuckles crack. His mouth opened to let out a scream. I took a small step with my right foot, and smashed him in the jaw with my right fist. I heard that crunch too.

As he went down I stepped behind him and supported his weight long enough to pull the Glock from his waistband. Then I let him drop. I could see the alarm now in the Russian's face and in Joe's simian eyes. I ejected the magazine and put the pistol on the counter.

"Are we done with the bullshit? Or do I have to put you two in hospital too?"

Joe turned to the Russian, who gave a small nod. He turned back to me.

"OK, you got the job. You start tonight, nine o'clock. Be on time. First week you man the door. After that we see."

"Yeah?" I shifted my gaze to the Russian. "So do I get paid, or am I doing this because Joe is such a nice guy?"

The Russian spoke for the first time. "One thousand bucks a week. We declare five hundred. The other five is tax free bonus. You on probation for one month. After that we see about promotion. Tonight we sign contract."

"Agreed." I showed him the magazine and set it next to the Glock. Mustache was beginning to moan on the floor. "Be advised, next time one of your clowns comes at me, I'll break more than his fingers."

He closed his eyes and gave his head a small shake. "We must make small test. Now you are in family and Mr. Rusanov will make sure you are treat with respect."

The next week was a drag. Not much happened and Joe's men stayed largely out of my way. Most of my work consisted of standing at the door watching for people with average bank accounts who were going to be a pain in the ass for people with above-average bank accounts. Occasionally there was a bit of pushing and shoving, but there were no major incidents, until Saturday night.

Saturday night Mr. Rusanov showed up at twelve midnight in a black Bentley. He had three girls with him whose combined ages probably almost equaled his. His car was preceded by a dark blue Audi and followed by another. Two guys in suits climbed out of each Audi and stood around the Bentley while the chauffeur opened the door for Rusanov and his harem. Then the whole entourage proceeded across the parking lot to the door. There the girls went in with two of the bodyguards and Rusanov, and the other two stopped to talk to me.

He was sixty or sixty-five, in good shape, with big shoulders and hard blue eyes under a three-hundred-dollar haircut. His voice was the kind of tectonic disturbance that causes tsunamis. He rumbled, "Bauer."

"Yes, sir."

"I hear good things about you. I like."

"Yes, sir."

"Tonight maybe I have visitor. I don't want visitor. He is Mexican motherfucker, Gregorio McDonald. He want my club. You make go away. OK?"

"Yes, sir."

"Good," he rumbled a laugh and repeated, "Good."

He went inside and for the next two hours did the kinds of things rich bad people do when they don't feel like watching TV or playing Scrabble. Then at two AM a red Ferrari pulled into the lot, followed by a Chevy van. I knew what the van meant, and suddenly felt acutely the loss of my C8 Carbine and my P226.

The growl of the Ferrari died and a man in a cream suit with elaborate cowboy boots climbed out. From the other side emerged a perfect woman who had apparently been lobotomized shortly before having her face pumped full of Botox. They approached at a relaxed pace, he stroking his thin mustache, she clinging to his arm, watching the night with empty eyes. I blocked the door with my body. His face hardened. Before he could say anything I asked him:

"Are you Gregorio McDonald?"

"What the fock? Who the fock…?"

"Are you Gregorio McDonald?"

"I am Gregorio McDonald! Now get the fock…"

"You can't come in. Please leave, and tell your boys in the Chevy to get out of the parking lot."

"You get out of my fockin' way, gringo. I wanna see Peter. He expectin' me and when I tell him…"

"You have to leave."

His face was crimson by now and he waved a finger in my face. "I gotta see Peter Rusanov! I got a business proposition for him! You let me in! Nobody tell me I can't…"

"For the last time, Mr. McDonald. You have to leave."

He screamed and screwed up his eyes. "*Step aside or I fockin'*…"

He got no further. He had come too close. I slammed the heel of my right hand into the tip of his jaw. He staggered one step back and fell, but by that time I was past him and running.

I knew I had three, maximum four seconds for the boys in the van to react. I got there as the side-panel door was sliding open. I could just make out a guy in denim with bare arms and an AK47 climbing out. I didn't stop to think. I grabbed the door and put all my two hundred twenty pounds into slamming it closed again, biting deep into his forearms and his knee. He screamed with pain and dropped the assault rifle. I caught it before it hit the ground, took a large step to my right and emptied a short burst into the cab. Another step to my left took me back to the side door, which was six inches open with a denim leg and a disfigured bare arm hanging out. Inside I could hear raised, panicking voices. I shoved the cannon in and emptied the magazine. It took about three seconds, which when you count them out is a long time.

Like I said, you can do that in enclosed places.

When I was done I wiped my prints off the weapon and used the man in denim's hands to smother it in his prints. Then I pulled him out and dumped him on the ground beside his rifle, and walked back to the entrance. The Botox Babe was standing by her man, rigid with terror and botulinum toxin. I hauled McDonald to his feet by the scruff of his neck and snarled at his woman, "Go away. Now."

She reached in McDonald's pocket, grabbed the keys to his Ferrari and ran. I dragged him inside and shoved him through the padded doors into the throbbing, flashing nightmare that was the bar. I escorted him through the manic, shouting, grinning crowds and up the wooden stairs to where I knew Rusanov would be sitting.

He watched me approach with McDonald and scowled.

"I toll you, no disturb. No let this piece of Mexican shit in."

I nodded. "Yeah, but I thought you'd like to know that his boys just committed mass suicide in their Chevy van in the parking lot. One guy with an AK47 killed the five in the back, the two in the front and himself. This clown tried to force his way in and I had to break his jaw. I thought you might want to talk to him."

For a long while Rusanov was as expressionless as

the Botox Babe downstairs. Then he said, "All dead? In van?"

"Yeah."

"Fingerprints?"

"All his."

If volcanoes could laugh they'd laugh like Peter Rusanov. He roared, then exploded, turned to the guy on his right and spoke to him in Russian. Two of them got up and took McDonald away. Rusanov gestured at me.

"Sit! Sit here, near me, have drink, woman, you want coke? We talk. We talk about future for you. You have big future."

He laughed a lot again and I sat beside him and told a girl with no more than a tray and a G-string that I'd have a whisky, straight up, no coke. He leaned forward and slapped my shoulder with a huge hand and glared at me.

"Tell truth, detail, what happen?"

I told him truth with detail and he listened carefully. The naked waitress came and placed a tumbler of whisky in front of me and went away with blushing cheeks. When I'd finished and pulled off half of my drink he signaled to one of his boys, said something in Russian and sent him away. Then he leaned over to me and spoke above the noise of the music.

"You are good boy, Special Ops. I like this. I have good job for you. You go home now. Take Clara if you like, or Zoe..." He laughed. "Or both! Have some party, relax. You been good boy tonight. Tomorrow you come back six PM. No more door for you. I have nice job for you. Nice job."

"What about my pay?"

He looked away from me, like he wasn't going to answer. I followed the direction of his gaze and saw his guy in the suit returning. He handed Rusanov a manila envelope. Rusanov looked inside and handed it to me.

"Special bonus, my thanks for your services tonight. Ten grand. Now go, rest, relax, have fun. I see you here tomorrow, in my office upstairs. Go. I go talk to Señor McDonald."

I drained my drink and left, with ten grand in my pocket and a sick hollow feeling in my gut. I had no problem with killing the guys in the van, or what was going to happen to Gregorio McDonald, for that matter. I was pretty sure it was no worse than what he had done to many others. What was making me sick was my employer. I was working for evil, and that was bad.

FOUR

I didn't take Clara or Zoe home. It's not that they weren't cute. They were. But I like to choose my own sleeping partners. And when I do, I like them to have a slightly wider vocabulary than, "Yes baby, right there, just like that baby." Clara and Zoe were sweet kids, but I had a feeling that was about the reach of their conversation. Who knows though? Maybe they had complex views on world peace.

I drove my beat-up VW Golf home, slept four hours and rose at seven thirty. I spent the day training and doing some research into Bronx gangs, Russian and Albanian mobs and offshore accounts. At four PM I showered and changed my clothes, and drove back to the Mescal Club, thinking about something Sergeant Bradley had said to me one night in the Lacandon Jungle, on the border between Mexico and Guatemala.

We'd been lying among ferns on the banks of the Usumacinta River, eight miles northwest of *Frontera Corozal*. We were waiting for a riverboat. We had intel it was loaded with five hundred K of pure coke, a wholesale value in the States of about ten million bucks, but a street value of five times that.

We were there because Her Majesty's MoD was

doing a favor for their friends in the Pentagon, and their friends in the Pentagon were doing a favor for *their* friends in the *Distrito Federal.* We had no legal status there and what we were about to do amounted to murder, discretely sanctioned by governments who believed themselves above the rule of law.

When I said this to Sergeant Bradley, he'd snorted something like a laugh and said, "There are two things you need to remember in this world, Bauer: one, the most valuable commodity on this planet is not oil and it is not heroin. It is violence. He who has the most violence available to him, is the most powerful man on Earth. And the reason for that is the second thing you need to remember: the law we hold so dear is nothing more nor less than rules supported by the threat of violence. He who controls the violence, makes the law."

Five minutes later we had strafed the decks of the riverboat with automatic fire and breached its hull with RPGs, killing a dozen men and sending fifty million bucks worth of cocaine to the bottom of the river.

That day, we were the law.

I got to the Mescal Club at five minutes before six and climbed the steps to the office upstairs. I knocked on the heavy mahogany door and it buzzed open. The office was an oblong, thirty-five feet long and maybe fifteen or twenty feet wide. The walls were bare redbrick and the floors were polished wood. There was a desk at the far end, in front of a large, plate-glass window. In the middle of the floor there was a nest of armchairs and a sofa around a coffee table, and against the right wall there was a large, wooden dresser with a tray of bottles and glasses.

Rusanov was sitting in an armchair with a glass of cognac in his hand, smiling up at me. On his right was the tall guy I'd met before, during my interview. Rusanov gestured me in.

"Close door, Special Ops. Get drink. Sit here beside me."

I went to the tray and poured myself a ten-year-old single malt, then sat in the chair opposite the tall guy in the suit, with Rusanov on my right. He was still talking in his staccato, article-free bursts.

"Igor has contract for you. You sign. Make you manager of club. We can this way explain big increase in income, huh?" He laughed like he'd said something real funny. "Also bonus sometimes, yuh? Now you sign contract and I tell you nice job. You make fat money."

Igor reached down for an attaché case he had beside his seat, opened it on the coffee table and pulled out a three-page contract. I took it and read it carefully. I was surprised to see it was a standard contract of employment. I signed it with a signature that wasn't mine and handed it to Rusanov. He initialed it and gave it to Igor who witnessed it, rose and left. It was a bizarre, law-abiding ritual that allowed me to commit crimes on Rusanov's behalf.

"Now, we talk business. I am Russian, Special Ops. You know this. I have good friends in Russia, powerful people. Good friends, bad enemies." He leered and made one of his tectonic rumbles. "Here, in Bronx, we can make much money. *Much* money. With drugs, with prostitutes, with protection." He shook his head like a grizzly bear who has become aware for the first time of the beauty of the Rocky Mountains. "So much money here. But money is like shit. It attract many bugs. Flies all coming to shit. Here we have Mexican flies and *Albanian* flies."

He made an elaborate shrug with his big shoulders

and pulled down the corners of his mouth.

"Mexicans no such big problem. Some are useful friends. Mexicans only want sell: sell coke, sell heroin, sell new shit that is killing everybody, driving crazy..."

He made a crazy face and laughed real loud.

"We can work with Mexicans. They make product, we sell product. Good deal." He sighed a sigh that was heavy and loud. "But Albanians, Rudaj Gang, the Albanian Boys, big problem. Good organized, *tight!*" He clenched his fist to indicate what he meant by tight, and repeated, "Very tight. Family, clan, Albanian government very close with Mafia. Big problem."

I raised an eyebrow at him. "Not like the Russian Mafia, then..."

He looked about as amused as a polar bear with a zit on its ass. Then suddenly grinned and rumbled a laugh.

"Albanian flies motherfuckers and must die. Rudaj Organization receiving big shipment from Mexico. Coming in big RV from Arizona. We gonna take shipment, fifty kilo heroin, fifty kilo cocaine. Same time we gonna kill Aleksio Marku, new head of Rudaj Organization. We hit so hard, they never gonna get up again."

I nodded once, letting him know I was not impressed. "That's the plan, what's the strategy?"

He grinned and nodded.

"That plan, what strategy? I like. I like this. Yes. That plan..." He shrugged, nodded, spread his hands. "But what strategy? How we gonna make it happen? Good..."

He was quiet for a while, studying his glass of cognac. When he finally spoke, it was to the glass. He had become sour, like the glass had let him down badly.

"Lunchtime, corner of Waterbury Avenue and

Commerce Avenue, by Hutchinson River. There is big parking lot. Two men bring RV and park there. Four men from Rudaj go in Mercedes SL 550. They parking beside. In trunk is about three and half million bucks. Maybe little more. Plan is, Marku's boys, from Rudaj Organization, take RV and boys from Arizona take Mercedes. Simple."

"Where do Marku's men take the RV? It's not an easy thing to hide."

He shrugged again. "Simple. Other side of river, East Tremont Avenue, Marku's Used Car Mart. Put RV at back of lot for sale. That night take out the stash and distribute, one kilo here, two kilo there, thirty, forty distributors."

I nodded. "You want me to kill three of Marku's men after the guys from Arizona have left. I keep one alive and find out where Marku is. Your boys take the RV and I go and visit Marku."

He leered. "Is good."

"Yeah, is good, but to be really good you need to hit all his operations at the same time. You need to send boys to every operation he has."

He shook his big head. "He has twelve operations around Bronx. Maybe fifty men. I cannot..."

"Bullshit. We select which operations to hit on the day. The night before we place bombs in the others, synchronized to go off at the same time. You run protection in the building trade?"

"Of course."

"Then you can get dynamite. We can rig them to be detonated by a simple phone call. I'll carry a burner. As soon as I kill Marku, I make the calls and we blow the guts out of the Albanian Mafia. After that you order your men to make any remaining hits."

His eyes were wide, his mouth slack. He gurgled with pleasure and said, "Yes, oh yes. That is good."

"When is the delivery due?"

"Day after tomorrow."

"How many men have you got that are well trained and you can rely on?"

"Twenty, maybe twenty."

I thought for a moment. "OK, I need to meet with them, five at a time. We'll annihilate the Albanians from the Bronx. The Bronx will belong to us."

He liked that.

I spent the rest of that evening, and the rest of the night until two AM, in Rusanov's office, talking to his men in small groups and discussing the plans for the following days.

The next day I returned to the club at noon. I had selected a couple of guys to work with me. I didn't want a squad who could become a problem. I just wanted two guys who were used to taking orders and who I could deal with. They were Fjodor and Dima, both Russian Special Forces and both with experience of active service. Fjodor was an easygoing lunk with a big mustache and an easy laugh, who had seen action in Chechnya and somehow survived. According to Dima it was because he was too stupid to know when he'd been shot. I thought maybe that was true.

Dima was tall, lean and a wiseass. He had also seen action in Chechnya and had survived by either murdering or raping everyone he came across who wasn't in Russian uniform. Sometimes he had done both and thought it was funny when he said, "But not necessary in that order, right?"

He smoked Russian cigarettes and drank prodigious amounts of vodka, like he thought being a stereotypical asshole was a smart thing to do. The two of them suited me just fine.

I taught them how to make detonators from a bunch of burner cells I'd told them to buy, and we rigged five bombs, concealed in kids' rucksacks. Finally, at one thirty AM I gave them their final briefing and loaded four of the rucksacks into the trunk of my VW.

It took me three hours to distribute them and place them in places where I was satisfied they could not harm civilians, but would cause maximum damage to the Albanian gang's infrastructure and personnel. After that I allowed myself four hours' sleep and rose at nine thirty AM. I had a pot of strong, black coffee but passed on breakfast, and made my way to Commerce Avenue. I spent the morning reconning the area, including the used car mart which was just a mile away, on the other side of the river.

By ten minutes to noon I was in my old Golf at the corner of Waterbury and Commerce, wrapping Scotch tape around my fingertips and watching the entrance to the large parking lot. I knew Fjodor was parked just outside the gate in his Audi, ready to block the exit, and Dima was inside, in his all too predictable black BMW, prepared to move in close when the RV arrived. That was what they thought the plan was.

As things turned out luck was on my side, and at twelve thirty a black Mercedes SL 550 sped past and pulled into the lot, ahead of the arrival of the RV. I had planned on the RV arriving first, but adjusted my plans fast and followed the Mercedes in. It had parked, with its trunk backed up to the wall, on the far left of the lot, where there was plenty of space on either side for the camper to move in next to it. They had the tinted windows raised and they hadn't emerged from the car. I pulled up a few spaces away from them and climbed out, then walked over to the Merc and rapped on the glass.

After a second it slid down and an ugly face looked out at me the way Cain might have looked at Abel when he suggested they could resolve things with a meaningful dialogue. I smiled sweetly and said:

"I have a message for Mr. Marku."

His expression didn't change. "Go fuck."

"No, I am serious. You came for the RV, right?"

I saw his hand reach inside his jacket and had the confirmation I needed that these were the guys. I didn't want to go killing a guy just because he parked his Mercedes in the wrong place.

It's hard to pull a gun fast from a shoulder holster in the confines of a car. So I gave him a moment, and when he had it out from under his arm I seized the barrel with my left hand and levered down. Simultaneously I rammed my Swiss Army knife through his carotid artery and his jugular vein, in the side of his neck. I left the blade in so most of the bleeding was internal. His pal on the far side of the car was still goggling when I levered the gun back and pulled the trigger. I hit him square in the head. He must have had a thick skull, because there was no exit wound.

I took a moment to pull the weapon from the driver's dead hand and examined it. It was a Walther PPK, .38. I never did believe that Bond would use a girl's gun like that. I shrugged and slipped it into my waistband behind my back, under my jacket. Then I signaled Dima to come over. He pulled up beside me and stared through his open window like I was out of my mind.

"Back her up and pop the trunk," I said, indicating

the maneuver with my finger.

He did as I said and brought his trunk up to the driver's door of the Merc.

"Get out, give me a hand with this guy."

He climbed out and came and stood by me, staring with narrowed eyes at the dead driver with my Swiss Army knife still protruding from his neck. "You crazy fuck," he said.

"Yeah, save your opinion for when you write your essay at school tomorrow. Now grab his legs and help me dump him in the trunk before anyone sees us."

The Albanian was big and heavy, and we struggled to fold him into the confined space. When we were done I recovered my knife and had Dima back in on the other side. We dragged the other guy out too, and crammed him in beside the driver while Dima muttered about the blood and the mess.

"All over my fuckin' trunk, man."

I had a quick look around. There was no sign of the RV yet so I pointed to the far side of the lot and snapped, "Go park over there. Stay put unless I call you. Just stay in the car. Don't get out!"

He shook his head. "I cannot see Fjodor from there."

"Just do as you're told, Dima. Do it now. The RV must not see you here."

He sighed, "You crazy, Special Ops. I hope you know what you're doing. My car a fuckin' mess."

"I know what I'm doing. Quit griping. Now get the hell out of here."

He drove away and parked at the far end. I called Fjodor on his cell.

"Yuh."

"Fjodor, get your ass over here to the Mercedes. Leave your car there. *Fast!*"

I saw him climb out of the Audi and come over at a trundling run. As he approached I jerked my head at the Merc and said, "Get in."

He climbed in the passenger side and slammed the door. I got in the driver side and beckoned him close, like I was going to whisper in his ear. I said, "Listen, this is what we're going to do…"

And I did to him what I'd done to the driver of the Mercedes SL 550. I severed his carotid and his jugular with my Swiss Army knife, through the side of his neck. He looked astonished, but only for a couple of seconds. He soon bled out internally and I eased him back into a normal sitting position in his seat. Then, with that taken care of, I settled down to wait for the RV.

FIVE

The RV rolled in half an hour later. It paused a moment at the gate. The glare of the sun on the windows made it impossible to see the driver, but after a moment it turned toward where I was sitting in the Merc, executed a slow and cumbersome maneuver, and reversed in beside me. I popped the trunk, climbed out and walked around the hood. Through the windshield of the camper I could now get the measure of the guys inside. I knew I was going to have to kill them, and I wanted some idea of how hard that was going to be.

They were rednecks. Big, tough and amiable. They smiled easy and swung down from the cab, a six-two blond who looked like he'd been raised on mom's apple pie while riding rodeos, and a smaller guy who looked half Mexican. I returned the easy smile and held out my hand.

"No names," I said. "You had a good drive?"

The blond answered. "Easy as pie. All in the back. You wanna have a look?"

"Yeah. Let's get out of sight. Any police attention?"

He pulled open the side door and I followed him and the Mexican inside. The Mexican was shaking his head.

"No, we was invisible, man. People see an RV and

45

they see an all-American family on vacation."

The blond got on his knees and started easing out the panels on the side of the couch.

"We kept our eyes peeled. Don't do to be overconfident. But we wasn't followed. There it is."

He stood and revealed a wall of black plastic bags bound up in duct tape. "Fifty K of premium quality coke and fifty of H. You wanna test it?"

I shook my head. "No."

Then I pulled the PPK and plugged each one of them in the chest. When they were down I confirmed the kills with a shot to the head. Because it don't do to be overconfident.

I swung down from the side door of the van, slammed it shut and went to lean on the near window of the Merc, like I was talking to dead Fjodor. After that I walked at a calm, steady pace over to where Dima was waiting in his black BMW. I stepped up to the passenger side and knocked on the window. The door latch clunked and I opened the door to get in. He looked at me with ill-concealed contempt.

"You finish being crazy yet?"

I smiled like he was funny and we were pals and said, "Nearly." Then I shot him once in the head. He also had a thick skull—the .38 stayed inside what brain he had.

Finally I removed the sports bag from the back of the Merc and had a quick look inside. It made me smile. I had never seen three and a half million bucks all together like that before. I slung it in the back of my old VW. I was nearly done. I just had a couple of things to see to before I was all finished.

I took Fjodor's keys from his pocket and drove my

car to St. Peter's Episcopal Church on Westchester Avenue. It wasn't far, only a quarter of a mile or so. It took me five minutes to walk back. Then I climbed into Fjodor's Audi and took another two minutes to relax my heart and steady my breathing.

So far everything had gone better than planned. But I was aware I was on a knife edge and things could turn really bad at any time. I pressed the ignition and the big engine hummed into life.

I drove at a slow, steady pace up Commerce Avenue, right onto Westchester and right again onto East Tremont. From there it was a half mile drive to Marku's Used Car Mart. I pulled onto the forecourt, killed the engine and climbed out into the bright afternoon sun.

I took some time to look at a few cars, then made my way into the three-story office building. It was a lot of office for a used car mart, but I guess few people questioned that. There were two guys there in suits, one sitting behind a desk, the other leaning with his back against the wall. Neither of them smiled.

"I'm looking for Aleksio Marku," I said. "You guys know where he is? It's important."

The guy behind the desk had greased hair and a five-o'clock shadow at two in the afternoon. I decided I didn't like him. He said, "Important to who?"

I showed him my teeth and said, "To him, and also to you. See, I have a hundred K of his dope and three and a half million bucks of his money. So, I think it's important for him to talk to me. And, on the other hand, if you fail to take me to him, I wouldn't like to be your balls in the next twenty-four hours."

He reached for the phone on his desk and I smashed my fist into the middle of his forehead. He collapsed and as his pal came at me off the wall, I slipped my left arm inside his arcing right and grabbed the back of his head. The heel of my right hand smashed into his jaw and I felt the joint snap and crunch under his ear. His eyes rolled up and I stepped behind him, hooked my elbow under his chin as he went down, gave a firm squeeze, pull and a twist, and felt his vertebrae snap.

I dropped him behind the filing cabinet and flipped the closed sign on the door. Then I returned to the desk and slapped the guy in the chair till he woke up. As he opened his eyes I yanked his head around to look at his dead pal. Then I pressed the muzzle of the PPK against his right knee.

"Listen very carefully, because I will not repeat myself. Every time you lie or hesitate I am going to blow one of your joints off. That means you only have to hesitate four times to be totally incapacitated for the rest of your life. Three times and you will only have the use of one arm. Am I getting through to you?"

He nodded feverishly at his knee, with bulging eyes, like it was his knee asking him the question.

"Where is Aleksio Marku?"

His jaw worked, tears sprang into his eyes, he licked his lips. I pulled the trigger.

The explosion was loud in the confined space. The slug punched through his knee joint and ripped a grapefruit-sized hole in the back of his leg. He screamed. I took a handful of tissues from a box on his desk and stuffed them in his mouth until he'd stopped.

Then I said, "Pay attention. You will bleed out and die in about five minutes. Get a doctor and you can go the rest of your life with one prosthetic limb. Keep stalling and you'll be lucky if you live the rest of your life with no arms and no legs. *Am I getting through to you?*" He nodded through his whimpering. I repeated, "Where is Aleksio Marku?"

He pointed up at the ceiling. I took the tissues out of his mouth. He said, "Third floor." Then he pointed to a fire-door in the wall behind him. I broke his neck too and pushed through the door in the wall into a narrow stairwell with an elevator at the far end. I ignored the elevator and sprinted up the stairs three at a time.

There was a landing, synthetic pale blue carpeting, double glass doors ahead of me onto a large room with lots of empty desks. On my left, johns, on my right a door: Manager. I took three long steps and kicked the door open.

Plate-glass windows overlooking East Tremont Avenue and the St. Raymond Cemetery. A large steel desk. A man behind it, astonished, gray hair, a gray suit. Beside him, on his right, a hat and a coat on a stand. A sofa on my left. Cabinets on my right. Blue synthetic carpet under my feet.

I snapped: "Aleksio Marku?" Terror in his eyes. "Are you Aleksio Marku?"

He swallowed like he was swallowing a golf ball. "I...what...who are you?"

I snarled, "I need to talk to Aleksio Marku."

"I am..."

I double-tapped him between the eyes. His brains sprayed over the window and he slumped back, staring at the ceiling like he had never seen a ceiling before and he couldn't believe it.

I turned and ran down the stairs, pressing the speed dial on my burner four times. I didn't hear it or see it, but I knew that around the city—around the Bronx —rucksacks were exploding, ripping the guts out of the

Albanian Mafia. And within half an hour, Peter Rusanov would be getting the news. I needed to get back to the club.

I left the Audi where it was, spent a couple of minutes looking around the cars in the lot outside, like I was thinking of buying one, and then walked away, peeling the adhesive tape from my fingers.

It was a little less than a mile to St. Peter's, where I had left my VW, but I took it easy, like I was strolling, and used the time to relax my heart rate and think through what came next. I got there after half an hour, climbed in the VW and called Peter.

"I hear news. Is good. Where are you?"

"On my way to the club."

"Everything good?"

"No problems. Everything went according to plan."

"And the money?"

"I'm bringing it with me. I'll see you in the office."

I hung up before he could answer and made a slow, three-quarter-hour drive to Mott Haven via Shore Drive on the Eastchester Bay, watching my mirrors more than I watched the road ahead. Nobody followed me.

I finally made it to the club at three PM and climbed the stairs to Rusanov's office. When I pushed through the door he was sitting behind his vast desk. He was smiling but looking cautious, and raised an eyebrow at the small kid's rucksack that I had in my hand.

"You take long time to come back. Where is Dima and Fjodor?"

I smiled like he was worrying about nothing and dropped the rucksack on the sofa. Then I went over to his desk.

"They're downstairs. Did you ever see three and

three-quarters of a million bucks before, in cash?"

He nodded. "Yes, and much more. Why down-stairs?"

I walked around the desk, still smiling. I knew he had a button he could press to call for help. I didn't want him to press it.

"They said they needed a drink. I could use one my-self. Look, I want to show you something..."

Now he was frowning and I saw his right hand twitch toward his alarm button. I moved fast, faster than him, and delivered a right hook hard on the tip of his jaw. The chair spun and rolled. His eyes rolled too, up into his head as he lost consciousness. I took a handkerchief from my pocket, grabbed the letter opener and rammed it hard down behind his left collarbone, severing his ca-rotid artery and his jugular vein. It's one of the fastest and cleanest kills there is. The bleeding is profuse, but it is all internal. He never knew he'd died.

I left quietly and trotted down the stairs like a guy whose world is in perfect order. There was nobody at the cloakroom yet, so I stepped into the bar. Chavez was pol-ishing glasses. He was a member of the *Chupa Cabras* and watched me as I crossed the room, like I didn't belong and he'd like to put me where I did belong. I smiled at him.

"Who's here?"

He finished polishing the glass in his hands before he answered.

"*El Patron* is upstairs. Benny and Oscar, and the other boys in the back room." He narrowed his eyes. "Where are Dima and Fjodor?"

"They're with Peter," I said, and reflected that it was probably true—they were all in hell. I turned and left, got back in my beat-up old VW and accelerated fast toward the Grand Concourse, to take the Deegan Expressway. As I was picking up speed, heading east, I pulled the burner from my breast pocket and pressed the last speed dial number. I heard the explosion, and felt the rumble through the road.

I figured that had been a good day's work, even a good week's work. There was significantly less trash on the streets, and also less significant trash on the streets. Peter Rusanov and Aleksio Maku, both gone, and their organizations broken. If the cops and the Feds, and the mayor, took the opportunity and used it, that could make a difference. It could save lives.

I followed the Bruckner Boulevard as far as Hollywood Avenue and crossed the bridge onto Layton, then turned right into Shore Drive. As I approached my small, blue clapboard cottage, I noticed a shiny Chevy SUV parked outside. I pulled up just in front of it and climbed out, looked around. There was nobody looking back, so I let myself in the house and closed the door behind me.

There was a small hallway, a kind of enclosed porch, with a coat rack and a hat rack screwed to the wall, and a small table with an empty fruit bowl for keys. Through there, on the left there was a door that led to my open-plan living room and kitchen. I knew they were there before I went through. It might have been intuition, or maybe I had picked up unconsciously on a handful of small things that were wrong; maybe I smelt them. Whatever it was, I went into the living room with my hand on my newly acquired Walther PPK .38, knowing they were going to be there.

One of them was sitting at the breakfast bar, sipping coffee. The other was sitting in an armchair, reading a *National Geographic*, which he dropped on the table as I came in. He also had a mug of coffee on the small lamp table beside him.

The one at the breakfast bar was in his late forties, with very short hair and a good but inexpensive blue suit. The one in the armchair was closer to sixty, thin and craggy, with a gray crew cut and an expensive gray suit. He said:

"Our conversation is being monitored right now from the SUV outside, and relayed to the field office in Manhattan. If you shoot us, you will be dead within thirty seconds. I assure you it is not worth it."

I put the PPK back in my waistband, but stayed standing in the doorway.

"Field office in Manhattan? You're Feds?"

The older guy reached in his jacket and pulled out a badge. His pal at the bar did the same. I examined the older guy's one. He said, "Special Agent Butler, and this is Special Agent Levy." It looked genuine, plus they smelt like Feds.

"What do you want? And why shouldn't I have you prosecuted for breaking and entering?"

He smiled, but it was devoid of humor. His pal just stared at me without expression. Agent Butler said, "Because we are here to arrest you on multiple counts of murder, drug trafficking and theft. I have a warrant if you really want to see it."

I shrugged and shook my head. "Bullshit."

"We've been tailing you since you arrived in New York, Mr. Bauer. We know your background and we've been watching you closely for the past three weeks. We know about your association with the late Peter Rusanov, and we have audio and video records of everything you did today."

I shook my head again. "Bullshit."

Butler laughed. "Not a very compelling defense, Mr. Bauer. Is that what you intend to rely on in court? Bullshit?"

"I don't need a defense. You're pissing in the wind. Get out."

Levy finished his coffee and set the cup carefully down in its saucer. Butler sighed.

"We can arrest you if you want, Mr. Bauer. But I think that when I invite you to come with us to Federal Plaza, to see the video evidence and listen to the audio of your conversations with Rusanov and Maku, you will come voluntarily."

He wasn't wrong. I knew I was screwed. But I figured that if all they wanted was an arrest, they'd have done that by now. Obviously they had something else in mind. So I did the only thing I could do. I played along.

SIX

T hey took me to the twenty-third floor of the Federal
Plaza, on Broadway, and locked me in an office with
a beige carpet, dark wooden walls and a picture of Trump
beside a stars and stripes. There was a black leather sofa
which I sat on for about an hour, and then stretched out
on to sleep.

There were no windows in the room and they had
taken my cell as well as my watch and my brand-new Walther PPK. So it was impossible to tell how much time had
passed. I awoke from sleep and knew I was hungry, but
it could have been nine at night, four in the morning or
nine AM the next day.

I spent about an hour working out and training,
then lay doing Sudoku puzzles in my mind until I fell
asleep again. I was eventually awoken by the door opening. I sat up. There was a woman in a dark gray suit with
a white blouse and a string of pearls around her neck.
She was blonde, probably fake, with intelligent eyes and a
hard mouth. She was holding an attaché case and watching me with her hand on the handle.

I said, "Do I get to see a lawyer, or are you holding
me under the Patriot Act?"

She didn't answer. She closed the door and went

and sat behind the large, polished wood desk, in the large, shiny black leather chair. I watched her from the black leather couch.

She said, "You just killed eleven men. A few nights ago you killed six men and facilitated the murder of a seventh. That's eighteen men in a week. You're like a one-man genocide. How do you sleep at night?"

I shrugged. "The ones that keep me awake are not the ones I killed. Anyway, you talk. It means nothing. Aren't you supposed to show me your badge and tell me who you are?"

She shook her head. "No."

"So you're not a Fed."

She opened her attaché case and pulled out a file. She opened that carefully on her desk, as though she was scared the contents might spill out and cause a genocide.

"Harry Bauer," she said. "You were named by the orphanage where you were left. You were never adopted. Above-average IQ but found it impossible to take discipline or instruction. After you left the orphanage you bummed around for a couple of years and finally went to Europe, where you joined the Special Air Service, a British special forces unit. It was not surprising they wound up asking you to leave, but it is surprising that it took eight years."

"Am I supposed to be impressed that the Federal Bureau of Investigation has people who know how to carry out research?"

She ignored the question, cupped one fist in the other and leaned her chin on them.

"When somebody leaves a unit like the SAS the way you did, no honorable discharge, no court martial, just a quiet departure immediately after a mission in Afghanistan, or some similar location, we take an interest."

"Why? Your jurisdiction is domestic."

She raised her eyebrows. "If you're talking about the Bureau, I'd have to say that you're a little out of date. The Bureau's jurisdiction is spreading exponentially with the threat of terrorism. In this cyber age, where weapons of all descriptions have global reach, the terms 'international' and 'domestic' are losing their meaning. But even if you were right, Mr. Bauer, I thought we had established that I am not a Special Agent of the FBI."

"So who are you?"

She made a face, gave her head a quick shake and shrugged her shoulders. "I don't have to tell you. I don't have to tell you anything or explain anything or abide by any rules or protocols. I don't exist. I am not even here, and never was."

I leaned back on the sofa and felt my chin. I had stubble and absently made a rough calculation of how long I'd been there.

"So if you're not law enforcement, you're from the Firm. Why is the CIA interested in me?"

"As far as I am aware, they're not, especially."

I stifled a yawn. It was only partially an act.

"OK, so you want to quit the theatrics and cut to the chase?"

"How much did you get away with?"

I didn't even try to stifle the yawn this time. "I have no idea what you're talking about. I would like to go home."

She lifted a super-slim laptop out of her attaché case, opened it and spun it so I could see the screen. It showed the parking lot where I had taken the cash. The Mercedes was there, and so were my VW, the RV and the

BMW. The Audi was visible outside the gate.

And so was I. I watched myself get busy, wiping them all out, one by one. It wasn't nice to watch. She waited till I was finished, then spun the laptop back and punched the pause button.

"Satellites," she said. "You can't always rely on them. But we had plenty of advance warning in your case, Mr. Bauer, because we've been watching you since you got back from Afghanistan. That, incidentally, was a very impressive performance. Very clean and efficient, and devastating."

"Why? Why have you been watching me?"

"That's not relevant. The fact is we have everything you did this morning on film, from several angles, and we have audio too."

"Audio of what?"

She smiled—it was more a mild, ill-concealed gloat —and pressed a couple of keys.

The sound quality was good. It was crackly, but clear and the voices were easily distinguished.

"*You take long time to come back. Where is Dima and Fjodor?*"

The sound of the rucksack dropping on the sofa, footsteps.

"*They're downstairs. Did you ever see three and three-quarters of a million bucks before, in cash?*"

"*Yes, and much more. Why downstairs?*"

More footsteps. "*They said they needed a drink. I could use one myself. Look, I want to show you something...*"

A thud, the rattle of wheels, a muffled gasp.

She pressed pause again. "Do I need to go on?

I shook my head. "Who are you, and what do you want?"

"Is that how much you got away with? Three and three-quarters of a million?"

"I guess that's something you don't know. Who are you and what do you want?"

She shook her head, like I'd asked a "yes-no" question.

"I told you, I am nobody. I don't exist. The question is, do you realize how thoroughly sunk you are?"

I thought about it and decided there was nothing to be gained by bullshitting.

"Yeah, probably. So now what?"

"So now I can file all this data away in a vault and forget about it, or I can hand it over to the DA. There will be a sensational trial, and you will no doubt become a public hero, write your autobiography and sell the film rights to Hollywood, so that when you come out of jail, in three hundred years, you'll be rich."

I studied the ceiling for a while, then sighed noisily. "Are you ever going to tell me what you want?"

"I want you to come and meet somebody."

"And then?"

"Let's take it one step at a time. I figure meeting somebody is a better option than prison right now. I want to be sure that you understand you are as screwed as a two-dollar whore during shore leave."

"Colorful."

"Accurate. There is no way out for you. Do you understand that?"

"I understand."

She pressed a button on the desk and spoke.

"Bob, bring Mr. Bauer's belongings, please." Then she released the button. "How much did you get away with, Mr. Bauer?"

"You mean you really don't know?"

"I want to hear you say it. It's in a sports bag in the bottom of your wardrobe, in your quaint little bedroom in your quaint little house on Shore Drive."

"I haven't counted it yet, but it's around three and a half or three and three quarters."

The door opened and a young guy in a suit came in. He had a Macy's bag which he handed to me and left. Inside I found my PPK, my cell and my watch. The woman said, "What were you planning to do with it? Spend it at a rate of five hundred dollars a week?"

"No. I planned to take it to Belize."

She stood. "We are going to go downstairs now, to a car. Then we'll take a drive. We'll be watched all the way, by satellite and by helicopter." She pointed to the bag in my hands. "You can see I am trusting you. Do something —anything—stupid, and the entire federal system will come down on you like a ton of bricks. You won't stand a chance." She gave something like a smile. "Not even you."

I nodded. "I understand."

I stood and she held out her hand. "Colonel Jane Harris, JSOC."

I took her hand, studying her face. "Joint Special Operations Command?"

"Let's go."

We rode the elevator down to the basement garage in silence. As we stepped out of the elevator and into the parking area, a black Grand Cherokee SRT pulled up and two guys in suits with wires in their ears got out. One covered me with a piece in his hand while the other opened the door for us to climb in the back.

I sat on her left. The doors slammed and locked, and a couple of seconds later we were climbing the ramp at speed, heading for the road.

"You've been looking for a job," she said, and glanced at me.

"And you're going to offer me one; one where I do the government's dirty work with full deniability, and in exchange you don't put me in a supermax for the next three hundred years. I'm way ahead of you, Colonel."

She smiled. It was a nicer smile this time, but she offered it to the window instead of me, as we made for the FDR Drive.

"Is that what we're going to do?"

"Isn't it?" I raised an eyebrow at her, but she kept her eyes on the road outside.

"The first thing I am going to do is introduce you to a colleague, and then the three of us will have a dialogue..."

"Meaning that you will tell me what you want me to do, and I will agree because I have no choice."

She turned a smile that had become icy on me.

"Quit whining, soldier. You're alive and you've got your PPK. It could be worse. Incidentally, shouldn't you be using a man's gun?"

We drove fast, weaving through the traffic, but after the Robert F. Kennedy Bridge we took a circuitous route, turning back on ourselves several times through the city. We finally crossed the Harlem on the Henry Hudson Parkway, and after that we took the toll road and headed north, past Yonkers for a little more than half an hour, until we came to Pleasantville, in Westchester. We drove through the town and then, weaving through quiet, leafy streets, took the Bedford Road and after five minutes turned into Apple Hill Lane. A couple of minutes after that we rolled through a large, iron gate into sweeping parkland and apple orchards, along a winding gravel path that took us finally to what looked like a genuine Jacobean manor house, gables, tall chimneys and all.

The chauffeur and his pal got out first, scanned the area and opened the doors for us. Then they escorted us to the gabled portico over the front door: a massive oak affair that looked like it would probably withstand a direct rocket strike. She slipped an incongruously small Yale key into the lock, opened it and went inside. The door closed behind us.

We were in a stone-flagged hallway, about ten foot square. The walls were stone too, and directly in front of us there was another, massive wooden door. This one had no lock, but there was a steel box beside it. Colonel Harris opened it to reveal a screen and a keypad. She punched in a code. An electronic voice said, "Please stand closer for face and eye recognition."

She took a step closer and six green lasers scanned her face and her eyes. Then the voice said, "Please state your name."

"Colonel Jane Harris."

There was a metallic clunk and the door swung smoothly inward.

I followed her through into a large lobby with high ceilings supported on wooden rafters, a checkerboard floor and an elegant staircase sweeping up to the next story. To right and left there were closed doors which I imagined led to drawing rooms, libraries and a study that smelled of pipe tobacco.

Colonel Harris spoke over her shoulder as she crossed the lobby toward the farther door on our right. Her voice and her steps echoed among the shadowy rafters above our heads.

"You should know, those two doors we just went through are made of two-inch steel plates, sandwiched between oak. Get trapped in there, and you're dead meat."

"Good to know."

She didn't pause. She reached the door and pushed through into a study that smelled richly, as I had imagined, of pipe tobacco. Two gabled, leaded windows and a set of French doors in the far wall overlooked sweeping lawns, a pond and woodland. A large fireplace on the right gave warmth to a nest of burgundy chesterfields. The floors were polished boards, strewn with Persian carpets in oxblood red and a deep, rich blue. The walls were paneled in dark oak, and floor-to-ceiling bookcases occupied every available space. On the far left there was a sizeable oak desk, and behind it a man in his early sixties. He looked youthful and vigorous. He was slim, handsome, tough and wiry, with eyes that were sharp and ruthless.

I knew him. I knew him well.

"Brigadier Alexander 'Buddy' Byrd."

He stood and smiled at me, and held out his hand. His voice, when he spoke, was what the Brits call cut glass.

"Bauer," he said, like he was welcoming me to a dinner party, "Good to see you again. Good of you to come. Please, sit."

He gestured me to a black leather chair across from his own and the colonel and I sat. My mind was racing, trying to make sense of what was happening. Before I could say anything, the brigadier had started talking again.

"You're probably surprised to see me here, Bauer. Our last meeting in Afghanistan was more like a farewell."

I nodded. "Yes sir. I was arrested in New York by the FBI, handed over to a colonel, in plain clothes, from an unnamed unit and have been brought before a British brigadier, whom I last saw when he ejected me from the Regiment. I'd say I'm a little surprised, sir."

He nodded, like he agreed with me, but offered no explanation. Instead he said, "Shame you had to leave the Regiment. I always considered you an asset. Remind me, what was it, exactly, that happened?"

"Sir?" I frowned.

"In Helmand, in the caves. I never really got your version of the events. What happened?" I hesitated and he smiled. "We only ever heard Captain Hartmann's version. According to him they rescued Ben-Amini from you, because you were about to assassinate him." He gave a small shrug. "We always assumed it was an American ruse to get hold of Amini."

"I told you when you gave me the option to resign..."

"Only briefly. Remind me."

I sighed. "We, the troop, had witnessed what Ben-Amini had done in Al-Landy just over a week earlier. You get used to seeing atrocities, but this was something special. It went beyond anything any of us had ever seen before. He raped, tortured and murdered an entire village, because the coffee shop owner had encouraged them to club together to buy a TV. Children, little girls of four or five, begging for mercy for their parents..." I shook my head. "I don't want to remember that. But they come back to me in the night. Every night. The images, the memories, the dead. And worse than the dead are the dying, and those watching them die."

The room was very silent, very still for a moment.

Outside I could see the tops of the trees swaying slightly, silently under the pale sky.

"We moved into the cave, neutralized his men, and he was lying on the floor, curled into the fetal position, weeping. I knew we were supposed to take him alive if we could. We were all mad that he was going to be given some kind of amnesty in exchange for cooperating and providing intel. We thought he should be punished. There was no plan or conspiracy, we all intended to do our jobs, but when I saw him..."

He waited a moment, watching me. "What happened?"

I told the Sarge..."

"Bradley?"

"Yeah, Bradley. I told him to go take a leak, I'd keep an eye on Mohammed. I told Skinner and Jones to do the same."

He smiled and shook his head. "No, you didn't. They were with you. It was Jones who told him to piss off. Don't lie to me, Harry."

"I don't remember it that way, sir. Either way, Captain Hartmann turned up, said he had instructions to take the prisoner, and said he would report me for attempted murder."

"Would you have killed Ben-Amini, if Hartmann had not turned up?"

"If Sergeant Bradley had gone to take a leak, sir, yes, I would have."

"Good."

"What's this about, sir? I was invited to leave. If I left, I would not face a court martial. And, with all due respect, you have no jurisdiction here."

"Don't worry, Bauer. You are not on trial. And, as it

happens, it was my intervention that scuppered the court martial. I told them to give you the option of resigning."

My frown deepened. "Why?"

He stood, glanced at the colonel beside me. "Jane, drink?"

"G and T, please, Michael."

"Bauer? Scotch, wasn't it, neat?"

I nodded with narrowed eyes and an arched eyebrow. Brigadier Byrd laughed and opened a cabinet, from which he extracted glasses and bottles and fixed three drinks. He handed the colonel her G and T and gave me a whisky, keeping another for himself.

He sat.

"You know what happens when politicians get involved in war."

"I thought politicians were always involved in wars."

"Politicians cause wars, Bauer, but sometimes—increasingly—they also get involved in running the war. And when that happens, nobody ever wins. Everything results in compromise and shared profit. And people like Mohammed Ben-Amini go free and are actually rewarded, instead of, as you say, being punished for what they have done."

He spread his hands, then laced them over his belly as he leaned back.

"And it's not just the compromises they make. There is also the question of jurisdiction.

"When you were about to execute Ben-Amini, you were under the jurisdiction of the British Army, but whose jurisdiction was he under? And Captain Hartmann, whose jurisdiction was *he* under? And how about the cave? It gets awfully complicated. And in the end, all too often, the bad guy gets away scot-free."

He held my eye for a long moment. Finally I said, "Why am I here, sir?"

"Because," he said, "we want to offer you a job."

SEVEN

I took a pull on my whisky, savored it and sighed.

"Yeah, I'd got that far, sir. But it sounds like you want me to assassinate somebody."

He shook his head. "That's only partly true, Bauer. Let me explain." He thought for a moment, chewing his lip, then reached for his glass and took a sip.

"In the 1980s and '90s the world changed, a lot. Thanks to the Thatcher-Reagan alliance, Socialism around the world began to implode, the Soviet Union collapsed and the Cold War became more of a tepid dislike. But, ironically, as the polarization of world power fell apart, so our enemies around the world began to multiply. Instead of being 'over there'"—he gestured east —"they were suddenly everywhere."

"Our? Who's 'us'?"

He stared at me for a long moment, then shifted his gaze to his glass and frowned.

"That's harder to explain. For now, let's say it's a loose alliance of Western democracies, the USA, Canada, the UK, Australia and New Zealand."

"The Five Eyes."

"Yes, an associated project. These five nations— and we are not talking about the acting governments at any given time—found that we have certain common shared interests that are based on a common view of democracy, free trade, rule of law..." He made an "and so on" gesture with his hand. "Values that are not always shared by other Western democracies. So, after the collapse of the Soviet Union, and the proliferation of hostile nations and organizations that followed, these five Anglophone nations, with common roots and values, came together to form Cobra."

"Cobra?"

"It was actually the brainchild of Russell Bertrand. He is still the director. Exactly how he got the governments of these five nations to agree is something of a mystery. Some theorize that he had damaging information on most of them and threatened to use it. Whether that's true or not, he managed to swing it, and Cobra was founded."

"What is Cobra?" I asked.

"Cobra, to borrow an Americanism, takes out the trash. We are not officially recognized, but we sit uneasily within the gray area of national security, where the executives of the member nations have special powers. We identify targets that we feel should be eliminated, we propose them and, usually, we eliminate them. Sometimes member governments come to us and ask us to take out a particular target. Our criteria for elimination is that the target in question should be truly and unambiguously evil beyond any doubt, they should be a significant threat to other human beings, and must have committed a crime, or be, demonstrably, about to commit a crime, that is truly and unambiguously evil."

I snorted. "You're insane. Who decides what is truly and unambiguously evil?"

He gestured at me with an open, upturned palm. "You, for one, in the caves in the Sulaiman Mountains."

"I am not an organization funded by five states. I was a man acting in hot blood."

He gave a small laugh. "I fail to see how that makes it more justifiable. We have a growing body of literature, from academics and judges, who define for us what 'truly and unambiguously evil' means. You are welcome to read it. Mohammed Ben-Amini would fit very comfortably into that definition. Pol Pot, Slobodan Milosevic, Saddam Hussein, countless more I could list for you that, under any rational view, would benefit the world by not being in it."

I was shaking my head. "That is what Delta Force, the Seals, the SAS and the SBS are for. They operate within the law and they are accountable to..."

He interrupted me. "Are you saying that you were wrong to want to kill Ben-Amini?"

I hesitated. "It was illegal and the Regiment was right to sanction me."

"I am not talking about laws and rules, Bauer. I am talking about morality. Would a person, any person, knowing what Mohammed Ben-Amini had done to the village of Al-Landy, be morally wrong to kill him?"

I sighed, closed my eyes, searched for words and reasoning that evaded me. Finally I shook my head. "No, they would not."

"You have the training, the skill and the experience to do it. And we will pay you very handsomely. Also..."

He smiled at the colonel and she turned to me. "You get to keep what you took from Rusanov and Marku. We'll even launder it for you. We figure you earned it. As a rule of thumb, if there are spoils from a job, you're entitled to them, but we don't sanction out-and-out theft."

I rubbed my face with my hands and muttered, "Jesus! You want to hire me as a professional assassin."

"Yes. But the difference between us and the CIA, for example, is that for us it is not enough that somebody is the enemy of a member state. They have to be truly and unambiguously evil for us to act."

"I feel like I just stumbled into *Alice in Wonderland* meets *James Bond* by way of *Star Wars*."

He chuckled. "The world is a stranger place than we might think, Bauer. Especially in the halls of power. What those chaps get up to..." He shook his head. "They are truly a law unto themselves."

The colonel spoke suddenly.

"Don't make a decision now. Spend a couple of days here, rest, enjoy the facilities. Ask us any questions you need to ask..."

"I only have one question."

"What's that?"

"Can I pick my first target?"

They exchanged a glance. She answered.

"That depends to some extent on who that target is."

"Mohammed Ben-Amini."

Byrd smiled. "He was the target anyway, Bauer. He is part of the reason we wanted to recruit you." He sighed again and studied his drink, tipping it this way and that. "But it's delicate..."

I interrupted him. "Yeah, he's the US's baby. They won't be happy if you take it upon yourself to eliminate him."

The colonel stood and walked over to the leaded windows. She was a dark silhouette against the brilliant green light from the lawn. "Correction. He's the CIA's baby. There were plenty in the administration and the defense community who wanted him eliminated. Al-Landy was not the first of his atrocities, and believe it or not, there are actually people in government who still care about things like that. But the CIA were persuasive that the information he had on the jihadist movements and targets was worth keeping him alive for."

She turned to face us. "What they were less convincing about was why, having debriefed him, he should not go on trial for war crimes and crimes against humanity."

I nodded a few times, thinking.

"So where is he?"

Again they glanced at each other. Again the colonel answered.

"We don't know for sure. It's not easy to get information out of the Firm, and when you can, you can't be sure the intel you have is reliable."

I looked at the brigadier. "That's not a hell of a lot of use, then."

"We've narrowed it down to two probabilities. He's either in Paris or in Los Angeles."

"You've got to be kidding me."

When the colonel spoke there was ill-concealed tension in her voice.

"Do you have some technique for getting viable information out of the Central Intelligence Agency, Mr. Bauer? If you have we would be very interested to hear it."

I sighed. "Fine, point taken, Colonel Harris, but it's tactics one-oh-one that you do not mount an operation on unreliable intel; and 'either Paris or LA' is what I would call pretty unreliable intel. Which is it, Paris or LA? And the street address would be pretty useful too, as well as the plans to his house."

"You're right." It was Byrd and he was nodding. "Of course you are. But that is going to have to be part of your mission. We have people in LA who are looking for him. We think he is more likely to be in Paris..."

"Why?"

"Because he was on the news in the UK and in the States after you captured him, and they would want him to be as anonymous as possible. In continental Europe he was practically unheard of. The chances of his being recognized there are far fewer."

I grunted. My experience of the Firm was that they didn't give a damn about that kind of consideration. "You're thinking like a soldier," I said. He looked mildly startled. I figured he wasn't used to being spoken to like that. "The Firm will change your face if they have to. They don't worry about that kind of thing, and with their budget they don't need to. They'll want him close at hand and easily accessible for debriefing, interrogation and consultation. And they'll want him happy, too. He's in LA, living large, believe me."

The colonel sighed audibly. "Our analysts believe he is most likely in Paris, so if you accept the assignment..."

"I already told you I would."

"Then you'll be going to Paris, and the first part of your mission will be to track him down and brief us on his whereabouts. Then we'll proceed to stage two, which will be the execution."

"Keep going with that clunky military thinking, and the CIA is going to outthink you at every turn." She looked mad but I shook my head. "You need to be a lot more fluid and hands off. I'll go to Paris. If he's there I'll find him. And then I'll kill him. After that I'll tell you how I did it."

Her cheeks flushed. "You will obey orders, soldier!"

I planted a lopsided smile on my face and showed it to Byrd, then I showed it to Colonel Harris.

"I am not a soldier, Jane. I got kicked out of the Regiment for wanting to assassinate this guy, remember? We tracked him across Helmand, across the desert and then up into the Sulaiman Mountains, to a single cave, where I was about to kill him. Isn't what I did then, exactly what you want me to do now?

"We had near zero communication with base and we took instructions from no one. We had our target and we did our job. And that's the way we are going to do it now. Take it or leave it."

Brigadier Byrd knew what I was about. He had commanded the Special Air Service and he knew what worked. He smiled at the colonel and gave a small shrug.

"It's how they operate," he said. "And it works. Old dogs, new tricks." He turned back to me. "But I want regular updates. I want to know where you are and what you're doing."

I gave a single nod. "Agreed."

"Now, take a couple of days, relax, enjoy the amenities while we sort out a few details. You have a pool, tennis court, gym… You'll be operative in three days tops. Meantime, relax."

I spent the next couple of days living in relative luxury. The food and the wine were good, and the amenities were superb. There were no people, other than a few anonymous staff, including maids and a butler, who were immune to any attempts to engage them in conversation. So I trained a lot, swam a lot and worked out a lot. In the evenings I read in the library or watched a movie. I saw nothing of the colonel or the brigadier.

On the third day they were there for breakfast on the terrace, sitting at a wrought-iron table that had been set with a white linen cloth and napkins, a jug of orange juice, a pot of coffee and another of tea for the brigadier; sausages, eggs (scrambled and fried), bacon, mushrooms, fried tomatoes and abundant toast. The brigadier also had a large manila envelope beside his plate.

He watched me step out and sit down, smiling but without speaking. The colonel asked, "Sleep well? Good morning, by the way. Are you rested?"

I nodded and started helping myself to bacon, eggs and toast, and black coffee.

"Restless more than rested. I feel I'm wasting time." I glanced at her with a raised eyebrow and asked, ambiguously, "How about you?"

Her eyebrow arched in response to mine. "I'm neither restless nor wasting time. But you can relax, you'll be flying out today."

I set the plate in front of me and started buttering toast.

"For Paris?"

"For Paris."

"I told you that's a mistake."

"We have a panel of analysts who say you're wrong."

"Does your panel of analysts work for the CIA?"

Brigadier Byrd cleared his throat.

"Either way, Bauer, right or wrong, you are flying to Paris this afternoon."

He picked up the manila envelope and dropped it beside my plate.

"You have a false passport which is indistinguishable from a real one because...," he shrugged and smiled, "it is essentially a real one. You also have a driving license cleared to drive in Europe, a credit card and three thousand euros in cash. You have a cell phone with a series of numbers on it which all link back here. This is standard procedure. Obviously any call to those numbers will get you one of our operators. They are briefed to confirm your backstory. So if you're questioned by anyone, for God's sake keep it brief and simple."

I opened the envelope and poured out the contents. In addition to what he had said there was a ticket, business class, to Paris. Byrd kept talking.

"You are Tex Miller, of Phoenix, Arizona. You have a cattle ranch and you are traveling to Paris for pleasure. You are a widower. You have no children. Your other details—address, social security number and so on—are all there, along with pictures of your house. Before you go you'll have an hour's briefing with your operators to get your story straight."

I nodded while I examined the documents. They were all genuine.

"That's good. Do I get a pen that fires a laser, and an Aston Martin with cannons?"

He didn't smile. "You can buy one of those with the money you took from Rusanov. You fly American from JFK to Charles de Gaulle, departing this evening at five twenty-five PM. You arrive five thirty-five AM. You will stay at the Four Seasons on Avenue George V." He pronounced it the French way, "Avenoo George Canz," with a soft "G," like he was drooling. "At noon you will walk north up the Avenue to the Champs-Élysées." He said it, "Shonz Ely-say." "Do you know Paris?"

I shook my head. "Not really."

"Step out of your hotel and turn left. Keep going till you come to a large avenue. You'll see..."

"I've been to the Champs-Élysées. I know what it looks like."

"Good. Diagonally left across from the Avenue George V, you will see the George V Café. Sit outside. You'll have a copy of the *New York Times*. Read it conspicuously."

"How do you read a paper conspicuously?"

He sighed and smiled at the same time. "Don't fold it. It's a broadsheet. Make sure the name, *'New York Times'* is visible."

"What if there's some other American there reading the *New York Times*? Shouldn't I wear a carnation in my lapel too?"

"You're being facetious."

I shook my head. "I'm sorry. It sounds like a lot of Cold War bullshit to me."

"Tried and tested. Live with it. There are lives at stake. Your copy of the *Times* will be three days out of date. Not four, not two, three. Somebody will approach you. At that time of day the terrace is always crowded. They will ask if they can share your table. They will give you your instructions from there."

I had been eating while he was talking. Now I mopped the egg from my plate with a piece of toast and pressed it into my mouth and spoke around it.

"I'll need a weapon. At least one."

"Your contact will provide you with a Glock 19."

"I want the Sig Sauer P226."

The colonel snorted. "The SEALs are phasing them out. The Glock is a superior weapon."

I drained my coffee, looked at her and took a deep

breath. I'm not a male chauvinist, but she was getting on my nerves.

"Yeah, it's a nice gun. Small and light, like the Walther PPK, suitable for a girl. Like a lot of men, I have big hands, so I like the fatter butt of the Sig. For you, being a girl, I'd recommend the Glock 19. Me, being a man, I want the Sig Sauer P226, full-sized TacOps, please."

The brigadier remained expressionless. When I'd finished he said, "Then that's what you'll have. Your contact will provide them."

"Thanks. And a Maxim 9. I'll need a Maxim 9, too."

I stood. The colonel watched me and said, "Are you a misogynist, Mr. Bauer?"

I shook my head. "No. I hate men and women equally. But I am not going to put myself and the lives of those I work with at risk just to kowtow to politically correct pseudo ideologies."

Her mouth dropped and her eyes went wide. "*Pseudo ideologies?*"

I nodded. "I'm not going to discuss politics—or pseudo politics—with you, Colonel. But I will tell you what a pseudo ideology is. A pseudo ideology is a petulant, infantile demand that you should have the right to put my life at risk because of your gender. Dwarfs don't make good netball players; six-foot-six guys who weigh eighteen stone are not good for dancing the part of Princess Odette in *Swan Lake*. They also make crap jockeys. So maybe the lifelong dream of the dwarf was to be a netball player, and maybe the muscle-bound giant always wanted to be a ballet dancer, or a jockey. That's tough shit. It's life. It doesn't make society anti-dwarf or anti-giant, and a campaign to force netball teams to accept a percentage of dwarfs, and ballet companies to accept a percentage of giant men to dance women's roles, would be stupid. That would be a pseudo ideology."

Her cheeks were flaming and her eyes were bright. "You're saying I should look after the kids and stay in the kitchen, like a good..."

"No. I think you're probably a terrible cook and would be a negligent mother. What you do with your life is your business. But what you do with mine is my business. I have seen too many people die and get maimed in the name of equality. War is not about equality. It's about inequality. The toughest, the strongest and the meanest win. The weakest die."

By now her face was crimson. I ignored it and turned to the brigadier, who was stirring sugar into his coffee, suppressing a smile.

"Is there anything else, sir?"

"No!" he said quickly. "I think that is quite enough for one morning."

"Then I'll go and prepare for Paris."

I left, wondering what the hell had got into me. I thought it was stupid to use women in the field in law enforcement and combat, but it wasn't something I felt strongly about. Yet there was something about the colonel that made me want to rumple her uniform, and mess up her hair. I went down to the gym, smiling to myself.

EIGHT

The Four Seasons on George V Avenue was a luxury hotel that was very aware that it was art deco and within the Golden Triangle of Paris. It tried hard, too hard, to live up to those standards. Staying in that hotel was like being smothered to death by an exquisitely beautiful Parisian woman wearing the most expensive perfume in the world: you knew you should be enjoying it, but you were panicking all the same.

I checked in at the front desk at six thirty AM. Outside the sun was already rising and the dawn chorus was in full voice along the avenue. The concierge gave me my key and the buttons showed me to my elaborately luxurious room, by way of an antique elevator. Once he'd opened up the room and pulled back the drapes, I gave him twenty euros to bring me a bottle of single malt. In France it was almost time for breakfast, but my body clock was arguing it was time for a nightcap. My body clock won the argument.

He delivered a bottle of The Macallan after I had hung up my clothes and, after a second nightcap, I had a shower and a shave and lay down to sleep for four hours. At eleven AM I rose, had a second shower and dressed appropriately for an American in Paris.

Paris is supposed to be the most beautiful city in the world. Maybe I'm a philistine—I probably am—but I prefer New York. I prefer San Francisco, too, and in Europe there are also cities I prefer: Prague, Cordoba, Copenhagen, Oslo, even Rome. But there is no denying that George V Avenue is easy on the eye and that that part of Paris has a unique, nostalgic charm evocative of an age which, from this point in history, seems saner and more human.

I strolled among the 19th-century buildings, under the shade of the plane trees, and even thought about buying a pack of Gauloise cigarettes.

At the north end of George V Avenue is the Champs-Élysées, the Elysian Fields which, as names go, is pretty overblown for what is little more than a pretty avenue. They say the Americans go in for overstatement, but even Austin, Texas settled for the somewhat more sedate Congress Avenue and East and West 15th Street rather than the Elysian Fields or Pathway to Paradise.

I crossed the avenue at the lights opposite the George V Café and found a table outside. There I sat, ordered a double espresso and two croissants, and unfolded the copy of the *New York Times* Colonel Jane Harris had given me before I'd departed for the airport. They hadn't been wrong. The place was packed, mainly with tourists, Brits and Americans in khaki Bermuda shorts and baseball caps. Their dull faces said they knew vaguely they should be ordering croissants and coffee, though they weren't exactly sure why. They knew it had something to do with *La Belle Epoque,* which might have been a cabaret where poets and painters got stoned with loose women, it didn't really matter, because while they were drinking their coffee and eating their croissants, they could look it all up on Google on their iPhones.

Hell, they didn't even need to learn about it or re-member it. They could store it all on a cloud.

Welcome to the 21st century, *La Moche Epoque.*

I was tearing open my second croissant when a shadow blocked out my sunlight. I looked up and saw a pretty woman in a light summer dress in cream and vio-let. She had on large sunglasses and a straw hat with a violet band. She smiled and showed me expensively nice teeth.

"Excuse me," she said, "it's very crowded. Do you mind if I share your table?"
I noted absently that her accent was educated West Coast. I shook my head. "Not at all, but I'm expecting someone."

She frowned. "I notice your *New York Times* is out of date. Three days, no less!" Then she raised an eyebrow. "A lot can happen in three days. Perhaps you're waiting for me."

I felt momentarily stupid and put down the paper. "Who knows, perhaps I've been waiting all my life."

She sat and leaned across the table. Her smile was naughty and infectious. "Tell the truth. You were expect-ing a man, weren't you?"

"Is that bad?"

"Unforgivable," but she didn't sound like she meant it. "Please, don't let me interrupt your reading. Let's at least try to pretend we didn't mean to meet."

I picked up the paper and smiled at it instead of her. "I figure you're attractive enough to distract a man from his reading. Will you have a coffee? I was about to order some calamari and a white wine."

"You shouldn't drink and flirt. You never know where it might end up. Look what happened to Kourtney

Kardashian."

"You shouldn't believe everything you see on *Star Trek*. And besides, who says I'm flirting?"

She arched an eyebrow. "I think I'll join you in that white wine."

She signaled the garçon and when he came over she ordered in flawless French. When he went away again I reached my hand across the table and said, "Tex Miller, of Arizona. How do you do?"

She stared into my face for a moment like I'd just told her I was a flat Earther, gave a small laugh and said, "Mary Brown, how do *you* do?"

"I'm not big on the whole John le Carré, Cold War thing. So forgive me if I don't play along. I'm not a spook and I doubt anybody on this terrace is, or, for that matter, knew that I was coming here. I'm pretty sure if we watch the buzzwords, we can discuss whatever business we have freely right here. Would you agree?"

She gave another small laugh and shook her head. "No. What is your background, Tex? You're a soldier, right?"

"So what?"

"My background is different."

"You came from the Firm?"

She nodded. "Mm-hm. Recruited out of Harvard."

"Do I need to be impressed?"

"No, you don't need to be so damned touchy and defensive, either. I'm just telling you, that was ten years ago. I am experienced and I am good at my job. So we talk about this and that, and then we go somewhere else and we talk about the other."

The waiter brought our calamari and an ice bucket with a bottle of cold Chablis in it. He poured and went away.

I said, "You could tell me what part of the city you think I should explore. I am new to Paris. You, I gather from your lack of accent, are not. Where should I visit? Please don't say the Eiffel Tower or the Louvre. They are a given."

She sipped her wine and studied me over the rim.

"I'm beginning to realize you are a pain in the ass."

"I figured Jane had already told you that."

She nodded as she speared a ring of battered squid. "She did. I thought maybe she was exaggerating. If you are genuinely curious about Paris, and want to get to know it the way the French know it, then I would recommend taking a stroll around the areas where you don't get a lot of foreigners or tourists."

"Such as…"

She took a deep breath and sighed. "Oh, so many places. The *Place de l'Europe* is fun, for example, because the entire square is a bridge over the railway lines. Nearby, on the *Rue de Madrid* you have the European Library, countless gardens and of course every street is an architectural gem."

I chewed and spoke around a squid ring. "Any street in particular? How about bars or restaurants I should visit, that are off the tourist routes?"

"Well, there is *Le Coin*, on *Rue Larribe*, which is reliable and very French. But if you felt like taking a girl out for dinner and drinks, then there is the naughty but interesting *Au Bois d'Acacia*."

"What's naughty about it?"

"The food is rather exotic and it stays open late. I like it."

"Where is it?"

"On the corner of *Rue de Constantinople* and *Rue de Naples*." She fixed me with dead eyes and said, flatly, "I can't remember the number."

"Guess I'll have to take you, so you can show me."

"Guess you will, cowboy. By the way, shouldn't you call me ma'am every now and then?"

"I thought I was a pain in the ass, ma'am?"

She stuck out her bottom lip and shrugged.

"That's OK. I don't mind being taken out to dinner by a pain in the ass." She screwed up her nose at me and managed to look cute doing it. "Besides, you might have redeeming features."

"I was thinking the same about you. Like, you might be able to get me some of those things I miss so much from back home."

"Back home in Arizona?"

"Yeah, Arizona, Texas, Wyoming..."

"I get the idea. You're not talking about bison steak, are you?"

I shook my head. "No. I have a buddy back in the States..."

"A buddy?"

"Yeah, buddy, don't labor it, you're the one recruited from Harvard, remember? He said he'd see to it I had the things I needed."

She smiled and winked. "Stay cool, Tex, you're getting sloppy. I read you loud and clear. Hershey Bars, peanut butter and green Tabasco sauce comin' right up."

We looked at each other for a while. I couldn't decide whether I liked her or if she was getting on my nerves. Finally I said, "Can we do that now?"

"What, get your Hershey Bars?"

"Yeah. Get my Hershey Bars."

She sighed loudly and signaled the waiter. He came over and she asked for the check. I gave him forty euros, told him to keep the change and stood. She stood too. She was having trouble concealing the fact that she didn't like my way of doing things, and she was getting mad. We stepped out from under the parasols onto the crowded sidewalk. I said, "Where to?"

"I'm parked around the corner, *Rue Balzac.* We'll take my car." We started walking. She walked slow and kept stopping to look in windows. As we rounded the corner into the narrow shade of *Balzac* she said, "I should talk to Buddy and Jane about you. You're about as subtle as a rhinoceros, and if you don't control your impatience, you're going to get us both killed."

I didn't answer and we made our way to a cream SEAT Ibiza parked at a meter outside a hotel that was also called Balzac. Balzac was obviously the thing here. The lights bleeped on the car and she climbed in behind the wheel. I got in the other side and we took off, negotiating the narrow, one-way systems around the center of the city, heading ever east. After a moment she glanced at me.

"The car has been scanned for bugs. We can talk freely here."

I studied her a moment. She'd lost the smile and the flirty voice. I said:

"What makes you think Ben-Amini is in Paris?"

She sighed. "Are you serious?"

I suppressed a hot flush of irritation. "Yeah, I'm serious. What is the precise intel you have that makes you think he's here?"

"Bill Hartmann took him into custody a month ago."

"Give or take."

"Try not to interrupt, Tex. We know for a fact that he was taken first to Bagram, where he was held in solitary confinement for his own protection."

"*How* do you know that?"

"Because it's a matter of official record." I grunted and she went on. "From Bagram airbase he was flown on a USAAF plane, in the custody of the Central Intelligence Agency, to Langley AFB and then, allegedly, driven to CIA HQ. But the fact is that after he arrived at Bagram airbase, nobody besides Bill Hartmann's team set eyes on him. And after his alleged arrival in Virginia, there is no trace of him in the States."

I shrugged. "Isn't that to be expected?"

"No. Up to a point, but the intelligence community is always buzzing with rumors. Some of them deliberately planted, some leaked, some are just speculation based on extrapolation and deduction. The trick is to be able to tell one from the other. Bottom line is, if something is going down in Washington, Quantico or Langley, somebody will know about it and talk about it to somebody else. That is the nature of intelligence. The fact that there was absolutely *nothing* being said, either in DC or Virginia, was of itself odd."

She fell silent while she navigated the *Arc de Triomphe* and turned north up the *Avenue de Wagram*.

"Now," she said, as she settled into the flow of the traffic, "what you probably don't know is that Paris is the Firm's second largest operational base."

My face told her I was surprised. "Why Paris?"

"Because Paris, not Brussels or Berlin, is the heart of Europe. Germany is volatile and unpredictable, and it hangs there between the East and the West. Culturally they are unstable. Hell, look at their recent history, the

Kaiser, the third Reich, then the Soviet Union, the wall. But France has always been the big prize, and its great virtues are that it is politically very stable, and culturally very..." She hesitated while she thought. "...*accommodating*. Look at the way they just walked out of Paris and left it to the Germans rather than have the place bombed. Look at how they will always negotiate with terrorists. They make a lot of noise and bluster, but when the chips are down, they will always accommodate you. So, in exchange for certain favors, Paris allows the CIA to run its European operational base from here."

"I assumed that would be London."

She shook her head. "That would be duplicating the work. We share with MI6 and MI5."

"We?"

She glanced at me. "I still consult for the Agency."

"Do they know you work for Cobra?"

"That's none of your beeswax, Tex. Anyway, the point is, Cobra's operatives in Paris began to pick up chatter that the Firm had a guest here in Paris. Buddy sent me over with a small team a couple of weeks ago and we spotted a couple of Bill Hartmann's men and a few of Ben-Amini's boys too, who went missing from Afghanistan after he was taken by Hartmann."

I was quiet for a while, watching the graceful avenue slip by, with its rows of trees and elegant buildings. We were now on the *Boulevard de Courcelles,* passing the *Parc Monceau* on our right. Eventually I said:

"But you haven't actually seen him."

"No. We haven't seen him in person. But I wouldn't expect to, and the word is he's here. And his men and Hartmann's men are here."

I stared out of the side window, wondering why I

was so sure he wasn't. We came to the *Place de la Bataille de Stalingrad* and turned south. I sighed and shook my head.

"He's in LA."

She rolled her eyes and sighed. "OK, let me turn your question back on you. What makes *you* think Al-Amini is in Los Angeles?"

"Because the Firm wants you to believe he's in Paris. What use is he to them in Paris? They don't want to share whatever intel they get from him with Europe. France isn't a target for the Taliban. London is, but getting into the UK is so easy they don't need a base in France. They can make a base in the UK itself. Hell, they catch them over there and then they let them out on parole. If you told me Hartmann had Ben-Amini in London I might buy it. But Paris makes no sense. They want him in the States, to hand, where they can debrief him a stone's throw from Virginia and prime him for whatever they want. He's in LA."

She shook her head. "You used a lot of words, Tex, but you didn't say anything. The smoke is where the fire is. Hartmann's men are here, Ben-Amini's men are here. Mohammed Ben-Amini is here."

"I guess we'll find out when I kill him."

We didn't speak again till we came to the *Porte de Vincennes* roundabout. She followed it to the left down the *Avenue de Paris* and after a little over half a mile she turned right down *Rue des Vignerons* and left into Franklin Roosevelt Avenue.

"Franklin Roosevelt? Seriously?"

"What can I tell you?" She pulled up outside an apartment block with wooden doors that had glass panels and a number "20" over the top. The block was six stories plus what Europeans call the ground floor. It was painted white and had small balconies with balustrades. She killed the engine and looked at me. "They like to think of themselves as international. They also have a Winston Churchill Avenue."

She opened the car door and stuck her left leg out.

"Come on, Tex, let me give you your Hershey Bar."

NINE

Her apartment was on the sixth floor with views to the south of rooftops and forested parkland beyond, and to the east, the massive presence of the Chateau Vincennes. The apartment wasn't big, just one bedroom, but the living room was spacious and light, with comfortable, minimalist furnishings, parquet floors and leather couches. She pointed me to an oak sideboard and said, "You want to fix a couple of drinks while I get your toys?"

I made two martinis dry and she came in with a large sports bag in her hands. I handed her her drink and she gave me the bag. I sat with it on my lap and unzipped it. Inside were two small cases. I took them out and snapped the catches. Inside one was the Sig Sauer P226 TacOps, with two extended magazines and two boxes of 9mm rounds. It was clean, new and in good working order.

The other contained the Maxim 9, the integrally suppressed handgun. It was chunky, but easier to holster and carry than a handgun with a screw-on suppressor. I checked it over and set about loading the magazines for both guns. She sat and watched me.

"I'll take you to the *Au Bois D'Acacia* tonight. It's…," she shook her head and made a face, "I don't know, fifty yards tops from the safe house where we believe Amini is being held."

"OK, we'll drive past it on the way, looking for somewhere to park. Let me get a look at it." I sipped the martini. "How many people does he have with him at any one time?"

"His two boys from Afghanistan, and during the day a couple of agents from the Firm."

"Do you have a floor plan of the apartment?"

"No."

"You have a team watching them now?"

"Of course. Twenty-four seven."

"OK, tell them to inform you the moment the CIA agents leave the apartment tonight."

"Just like that?"

I smiled. "What? You want me to connect with my inner ninja first?"

"Don't be an asshole all the time, Tex. You need to recon the place, make a plan, run it by Control, clear it with the colonel..."

"And start formulating a new plan because by the time HQ are through following procedure Ben-Amini will be back in Kabul, or Islamabad, or Hawaii, drinking Copacabanas! Forget it. Do you have any intel on his movements, their movements or the apartment itself that you haven't given me?"

"No."

"Then you tell me what more reconnoitering I can do than finding out when the CIA have left. If you can't provide me with the floor plan of the apartment, I may as well go in tonight. Correct me where I am wrong."

"Geez, you're a pain in the ass!"

"You told me they leave in the evening. You told me

his two boys stay with him. Am I wrong?"

"No."

"What am I going to learn by watching the apartment another week when you've already been watching it for two weeks?"

"Nothing! But the colonel wants plans submitted before we take action!"

"*We* are not going to take action. I am."

"Tonight..."

"Maybe. We go have dinner. Your team lets us know when the agents leave. If we're sure it's just him and his boys there, I'll go take a look."

"You'll need backup."

"Yeah, I could use backup. But what I don't need is to be carrying someone who's going to need looking after and will probably get me shot. I'd rather do it alone."

"You are one disagreeable son of a bitch."

"I'm sorry. I promise to be nicer after the job is done. Maybe you can take me to the Louvre and explain Fauvism to me."

"Go screw yourself."

I smiled. "Pick me up at eight? We'll have a cocktail before dinner."

"Was there anything else, Tex?"

I drained my drink and stood. "Yeah, stop calling me Tex."

"What should I call you?" She gave a small laugh. "How about Dick?"

"Funny."

She was still laughing as I closed the door and made my way down in the elevator.

I took a stroll to the *Avenue de Paris* and hailed a cab. I told him to take me to the *Au Bois D'Acacia*, on the

Rue de Constantinople. I had to tell him three times because he pretended he couldn't understand my American accent. I wrote it down for him and then he understood.

When we got there it was gone two PM. I sat outside and ordered a steak and fries and a glass of house red. From where I sat I had a reasonably good view of number twelve, where the safe house was located. I took my time over the steak and fries, had a second glass of wine with a cheeseboard and then a coffee and a cognac. It took about two hours, and by the end of it there was no sign of any activity at the apartment.

At four PM I paid my bill and left. I strolled down slowly, toward number twelve, making like I was checking the messages on my phone. When I was twenty yards away, a dark Audi turned into the street and double parked with his hazards on in front of the entrance to the block. I stopped, staring at the screen of my cell. A guy got out of the passenger side. He was tall, olive skinned, with balding hair and a black mustache. He was wearing an expensive, single-breasted charcoal gray suit with a tie. He walked around the hood and went inside the building. The Audi took off.

I called Mary and walked very slowly toward number twelve. The phone rang twice and she answered.

"Be very brief."

I laughed. "Hey, sugar. Listen, I was thinking, maybe you should talk to your friends about that photograph."

"What are you talking about?"

"Exactly. I think it would look gorgeous on our wall. I'd say call them right away and see who's been in. You might be surprised."

"Where are you? Did you go to *Rue de Naples*?"

"You just know that has to be a great big yes, sweet cheeks."

"That was *very* unwise. You are a damned liability!"

"I love you very much too, darling, but try to stay focused. Will you call them for me? See if they have the photo and get back to me?"

A loud sigh. "Are you telling me somebody unexpected entered the building?"

"How do you manage to be right *all* the time?"

"I'll get back to you."

"I adore you too, sweetie-pie."

She hung up.

After an agonizingly slow walk I got to the intersection with the *Rue de Rocher* and spent a long time staring in the window of a shop that sold beds and sofas. I didn't pay much attention to the beds or the sofas, I was looking at the reflection of the street behind me in the glass. After about ten minutes, which is a very long time to be staring in a shop window, the shop assistant came out and stood in the doorway, staring at me. I smiled at him and walked slowly back up Naples, toward the Hotel Napoli on the corner, looking at my phone again. It rang and I stopped to answer it.

"Hey pumpkin."

"He's new. They got photographs. They haven't seen him before. They've sent them back to HQ for facial recognition."

"Oh that is good news. Because you know the origin is simply not the same."

"What are you talking about?"

"Remind me, where was the item from?"

"Afghanistan?"

"Exactly! You *are* a wonder! But, sweetheart, this

one is *not!*"

"How can you be sure?"

"Trust me. I know. And right now I really wish you were here, darling, to see all the wonderful things that Paris has to offer…"

As I said it, I was watching the same guy I'd seen earlier step out of the building. He was talking on the phone, looking up and down the street. I strolled slowly closer, speaking like I was totally involved in my conversation, but listening carefully to what he was saying.

I said, "I haven't seen the Eiffel Tower yet, but that is next on my list. And, the more I hear of what people are saying, the more convinced I am of what I told you just now. Anyhow, honey-bunny, you should go talk to your friends again. I can't wait for dinner."

I hung up. What I had heard from the guy in the gray suit had got my mind spinning. But now the Audi was back and the guy in the suit was putting his phone away. The back passenger doors opened and two men got out. One was Arabic. I could tell from his look and from his speech, which I was overhearing as I sent an email to myself with the registration number of the car on it. He was clean-shaven and wore a dark blue suit.

The other guy was blond, tanned and well dressed, but he was speaking in Spanish to the guy in the blue suit. And the guy in the blue suit was translating to the man with the mustache. They all shook hands and got back in the car, which took off toward the Golden Triangle. I searched for a cab, planning to follow the Audi, but there wasn't one to be seen anywhere.

I thought for a moment of going up and kicking the door down, but all I would achieve with that would be either to get shot, arrested or both. So I headed back toward my hotel and on the way I called the brigadier.

"Bauer, how are you getting on?"

"I'll tell you tonight, sir. Meantime, I need a Paris license plate run. Can you do that?"

"It'll take a while, but yes, we can do that."

I read him the number. There was silence on the other end. I said, "What is it?"

"That number, I don't need to run it. The letters CD tell you it's a diplomatic plate. It belongs to the Mexican Embassy."

I stopped dead, then sighed and ran my fingers through my hair. "*Mexico?*" I sighed again. "There were two guys. One of them was speaking Spanish. The second guy was translating into Arabic for a third who I believe had been up at the apartment with Amini. But sir?"

"What is it?"

"The Arabs. They were not speaking Dari or Pashto. They were not Afghan. They were speaking a very formal, stilted form of Arabic. I'd swear it was Yemeni."

"Yemeni?"

"I'm no expert, but I know enough Arabic to know that it wasn't Afghan and it wasn't Iraqi. I'm pretty sure they were from Yemen. Mexicans, Yemeni and Afghans... The Firm is playing a very deep game here, sir."

"Yes, what are your plans?"

"Off the record?"

He gave a quiet laugh. "Off the record."

"I'm going to wait till the agents have gone tonight. Then I'm going to go in and do my job."

"I'm sorry, Bauer. The connection failed there for a moment and I didn't hear you. Still, I mustn't keep you. Keep me posted."

"He's not here, sir. He's in LA."

"Call me later. Let me know how you get on."

I hung up and made my way back to the hotel. It was a forty-five-minute walk and I used the time to try and think. I had come here expecting to find an Afghan Arab. Instead I had found two extremely well-dressed Yemeni Arabs and a Mexican, in an Audi belonging to the Mexican Embassy.

It had long been accepted in the defense community that any kind of alliance between Islamic jihadists and Mexican cartels was unlikely in the extreme. I had studied the possibility at one time, when it had emerged as a nightmare scenario among war games experts at the Pentagon. But it was eventually laid to rest and the general view was summed up in a report commissioned by the JCS:

"An analysis and comparison of the organizational structures and overall strategies employed toward the United States and the West in general, plus an analysis of group identity, ideology and structural authority and decision-making systems, shows stark differences between these two groups—not least that jihadists are, by definition, Islamic and the Mexican cartels are overwhelmingly Catholic. With these differences in mind, and placed in the context of what makes cooperative relationships work in the private sector, cooperation between these two groups emerges as profoundly unlikely."

It had struck me as complacent at the time, and right now, in retrospect, it struck me as dangerously complacent. The PLO and the IRA in the '70s had also been an unlikely alliance between Catholics and Islamic jihadists, but it had been a very effective one. The imperative needs of the moment have a way of overcoming ideologies.

As to structural authority and decision-making, any decent administrator can adapt those to the needs of the moment. And both the Mexican cartels and the many jihadist groups had proved themselves to be nothing if not good administrators.

And now they were talking, right here in Paris. The billion-dollar question was, what the hell were they talking about?

There were other questions, too: were these meetings connected with Mohammed Ben-Amini? Or had the activity been spotted purely because Cobra had been on the lookout, watching the movements of the CIA?

And that brought me to what might, after all, be the most important question of all. Why were the Mexicans and the Yemenis meeting outside a CIA safe house?

And then again, if they were meeting outside the safe house, who was on the inside?

For a brief moment I had a flash of Sergeant Bradley just before we concluded an operation in Colombia. He'd looked at me and snarled, "Sometimes the simplest solution is to just shoot everybody."

He'd been right that time. I wondered if that same philosophy would work this time, here in Paris.

I arrived at the hotel no wiser. I went up to my room and had a long, hot-cold-hot shower and changed my clothes. Then I went down to the bar and ordered a martini, dry. While the Australian in the burgundy waistcoat was shaking it, I called Mary. She answered on the first ring.

"Good evening, Tex."

"We need to talk."

"For once we agree on something."

"Meet me at my hotel, in the bar. Come now."

She might have protested at my tone. I didn't know. I'd hung up. I had a bad smell in my nostrils. It was the putrid smell of corruption that spooks and politicians carry around with them.

She showed up a little more than half an hour later, when I was on my second martini. She was in a short black dress with a single string of pearls around her neck. I sat at the bar and watched her approach. If she knew how good she looked, she didn't show it. She looked mad instead.

I said, "What'll you have?"

She ignored me and spoke to the barman.

"Manhattan, bourbon."

While he was mixing it she turned to me and stood very close. She pressed her index finger on my chest and smiled. It should have been a pleasant sight, but it wasn't.

"Don't presume to give me orders, Tex. And don't ever hang up on me again. It is disrespectful, arrogant and vulgar."

I offered her a sweet smile in return.

"Yeah, see, the problem is, I am disrespectful, arrogant and vulgar."

She gave her head a small shake and narrowed her eyes. "Don't explain. Just don't do it."

The barman placed her drink on the bar and I jerked my head toward a table in the corner.

"Let's sit."

She carried her drink over and I followed her. When we were sitting I sipped my drink and asked her:

"Ten years as an analyst or in the field?"

"Both. Why?"

"And now, working for Jane and Buddy, are you logistical support or...," I labored the word, "...*executive?*"

She arched an eyebrow. "Logistical support. It takes a special kind of person to execute operations."

"Does the Firm know you work for Buddy?"

"You already asked me that, and you're getting on my nerves. What is this about?"

"How about you tell me?"

"How about you cut the crap, cowboy? I am this close," she held up her forefinger and thumb to show me how close, "to walking out of here and calling in an abort code."

I nodded, wondering if that wasn't the right course of action anyway. "You want to explain to me what a Mexican diplomatic car was doing picking up a Yemeni from a CIA safe house? A safe house where our target was supposed to be?"

She went a pasty shade of pale. "What are you talking about?"

"I figure you spoke to your team who are watching the apartment, right?" She nodded. "Where are they, in the hotel at the end of the road?" She didn't say anything, but her eyes told me that was where they were. "They told you a well-dressed guy with a mustache got out of a dark Audi and went in." She nodded. "Then they told you he came out, talking on his cell, and a moment later the same car came back, two guys got out, one looked European, the other was an Arab. They spoke for a moment, shook hands, got in the car and drove away. Correct?"

"Yes."

"Well the two Arabs were not Afghan, but probably Yemeni, and the third guy was not European but Mexican. And what your sharp-eyed observers failed to see was that the car was from the Mexican Embassy. Now that scenario might fit into the nightmares of any member of the national security forces. Where it doesn't fit is in a safe house run by the Central Intelligence Agency. So, as that is an agency you are in bed with, perhaps you'd like to explain."

Her face flushed. "I am not '*in bed*' with them! I consult for them!"

I leaned forward, feeling the anger building in my belly.

"Don't bother to explain the difference. Just tell me, what is going on?"

Her eyes were bright and her cheeks red. "I-don't-*know!*"

My gut told me she was telling the truth. My brain told me my gut was a schmuck. I told them both to agree to a truce until she was wearing something less distracting.

"Opinion?"

She took a deep breath and flopped back in her chair.

"My opinion? My opinion is that teams need to co-operate. And if you want this team to be successful, you are going to need to rethink your approach. As far as I am concerned this operation is compromised, partly because of the new evidence that has emerged, and partly because of your rhinoceros approach to everything. You have been hostile and on the attack since we met today and frankly, walking down the *Rue de Naples* like that today, talking on the phone, was just plain stupid. I'm sorry. I don't like working with you, and I will not work with you if you continue to work this way."

I studied her face while she spoke, and after she'd gone silent I kept observing her, looking for a tell, any small sign that she was acting or lying. I didn't see one, but that didn't mean it wasn't there.

I said, "I'm sorry."

"What?"

"I apologize, unreservedly. I guess I'm used to working with soldiers, under very different conditions. Men who kill other men for a job tend not to be very sensitive."

She took a deep breath, went to say something but took a sip of her Manhattan instead. When she'd swallowed and licked her lips with the tip of a very pink tongue, she spoke, looking at her glass instead of me.

"People tend to think of the Firm as a bunch of evil, ruthless, unprincipled gangsters. It was like that once." Now she looked up at me. "And I don't doubt it still has its fair share of power-hungry Machiavellis. But most of us are just fairly normal people with a high IQ, who want to serve our country."

"Noted. I am…" I paused for emphasis. "I am *very* reluctant to walk away from this job. I am more convinced than ever that Ben-Amini is not here. But I am also very keen to know who *is* here, in that apartment. I want to know what the Firm's game is, and above all I want to know what these Yemeni guys in three thousand-dollar suits are talking about with Mexican diplomats."

She nodded. "Agreed, as long as you stop busting my…" She paused and smiled. "…ovaries."

I smiled. It wasn't entirely false. I figured it was even odds that she was telling the truth.

"OK, Mary Brown, what do you say we go and have a nice meal?"

She dropped her left eyelid and winked, which made me feel odd, and said, "All right, Tex Miller, I know a cozy little place on the *Rue de Naples*. How does that sound?"

I arched an eyebrow at her. "It sounds almost as good as you look."

Her face told me that, for now at least, the mission was saved.

TEN

The waitress left with our orders. Mary Brown, by candlelight, sipped her second Manhattan of the evening. I made an effort to ignore how good she looked doing it and said:

"So, opinions?"

She picked the cherry out of her drink and chewed it. I noticed her nails were very red, and matched her lips.

"Al-Qaeda is far from finished. They have thrived during years of lawless anarchy in Yemen and made a stronghold there. And with the virtual collapse of ISIS and the death of Abu Bakr al-Baghdadi, they and their affiliated groups are capitalizing on the power vacuum that's been left behind—in Syria *and* Iraq. Since Bin Laden's death...," she paused, gazing out the window, shaking her head, "far from collapsing, al-Qaeda has been reinventing itself. They have actually gained ground in most of the Muslim world, in parts of Africa, Syria and, like I said, in Yemen."

"You think these Yemenis might be al-Qaeda?"

"We have very little to go on, but I've had my eye on al-Qaeda for a long time. They have survived for more than three decades, largely because of their ability to innovate and refine their tactical techniques and procedures. They are *very* focused, and they *learn* as an organization." She shrugged. "At first glance it looks like what we are seeing here is some innovative thinking."

I frowned. "Like what?"

She stuck out her bottom lip, like that made it easier to think. "Let's come back to that in a minute. Let's look for a moment at the bigger picture. We are pulling virtually all our troops out of Afghanistan, and what we leave behind there is yet another huge power vacuum…"

"Ready for al-Qaeda to exploit."

"Exactly. Now, what al-Qaeda has over all the other jihadist organizations is that it is largely backed and funded by powerful members of the Saudi elite. That means they don't just have lots of money, they also have almost a hundred years of experience learning to play political power games with the West and manipulate our governments and our politicians. This is an important point that should not be underestimated—the brains in the shadows behind al-Qaeda have been to Oxford and Cambridge, Yale and Harvard, and most important of all, to Sandhurst and West Point. They know how we think, and they have powerful friends in high places."

I nodded, staring at the growing darkness outside the window.

"So, if ideologically and structurally, ISIS would be incapable of forming an alliance of convenience with Sinaloa, al-Qaeda would have no such problems." I frowned again. "But for what purpose?" Yet, even as I uttered the words, I knew the answer.

She gave a small shrug. "I'm talking off the top of my head here, but Afghanistan is famous for two things, right…?"

"The Taliban and white poppies. Opium."

"It seems to me that right there al-Qaeda and Sinaloa have an interest in common, if not necessarily a common interest."

"So what are we saying, that Sinaloa and al-Qaeda are negotiating some kind of deal involving Afghan poppies?"

She stared at me for a long time, then gave her head a small shake.

"No. I'm saying that that is one, more or less obvious interpretation of what we saw today. Another is that it was the Mexican guy's birthday and they happen to be friends."

"Sure, but that still leaves unanswered what the hell they were doing at the apartment."

"We don't know that he was at the apartment. We only know he was at the apartment block. This is Paris. He might have a mistress there. Hell, he might live there."

I shook my head. "Not with that suit he doesn't."

The waitress brought us some smoked salmon and little bits of toast, and a bottle of white wine in an ice bucket. When she'd left I asked Mary, "When can we expect an ID on these guys?"

"Maybe tonight," she said and stuffed a piece of toast and salmon in her mouth. "Maybe never."

My scowl told her to explain.

"If they're not in the system, they can't be recognized, Tex."

"Stop calling me that."

"Why?" She laughed and stuffed another piece of salmon and toast into her mouth. "It's your name, isn't it?"

"Is Mary Brown yours?"

"Sure."

"Well Tex Miller isn't mine. I spent almost ten years of my adult life in special forces and tracked Mohammed Ben-Amini right across southern Afghanistan, all without having to lie about my name..."

She became serious. "This is a very different game."

"Is it?" I smiled on one side of my face, where it looked ironic, and quoted: "Fearlessness is better than a faint heart for any man who puts his nose out of doors. The length of my life and the day of my death were fated long ago."

"That's cheerful. What is it?"

"An early form of Existentialism. It's from *Skirnir's Journey*, an early Viking poem. I think it is cheerful. If the day of your death is already fated, what's the point in worrying? My name is Harry, Harry Bauer."

Her eyes went wide. "You shouldn't tell me that. Bower, like a tree?"

I shook my head. "The name is all I know of my father. It's English, probably originally Saxon, related to the word 'neighbor.'"

She chewed her last piece of toast and salmon and sipped her wine while watching me. "My goodness," she said at last. "It is human."

The waitress took away our plates and while she was bringing my steak and Mary's swordfish, Mary's phone pinged.

She read it without expression and when the waitress had gone she glanced at me.

"The agents have gone. This team has been watching twenty-four seven for the last two weeks. They are certain the only people in there right now are two Afghans and, we assume, Ben-Amini."

I nodded once and signaled the waitress. She scuttled over, smiling.

"Give me a glass of the house red, will you?"

She went away to get it and Mary, who'd been watching me and frowning, said, "Did you hear me?"

"Sure."

"So what are you going to do?"

"First I'm going to finish my steak." I leaned back and let the smiling, scuttling waitress place a glass of red wine in front of me. When she'd gone I went on. "Then I'm going to go up to the apartment while you wait for me. If Ben-Amini is there I will kill all three of them. If he isn't, I'll kill one of the bodyguards in such a way it will convince the other to tell me where he is. When he does that, I'll kill him too."

She kept staring while I ate my steak. Sometimes I stared back while I chewed. Eventually she said, "My God, what are you?"

"What did you expect? It's my job. I get paid to do this. And you...," I pointed at her with my steak knife, "you get paid to provide the logistical support. My hands are as clean as yours, Mary Brown. How clean are your hands?"

I turned my attention back to my steak and spoke to the plate.

"You should talk. Keep staring at me like that and you'll start drawing attention to us."

"I..." She looked away at the window, at the ghosts of the streetlamps and the fleeting shapes of passersby. "I never met anybody who was... Who was like that."

I glanced at her, a little surprised. Then smiled down at the last piece of steak as I cut it in half.

"You are a brilliant analyst, am I right? Buddy recruited you straight from your desk. This is your first venture into the field."

"Yes."

"In at the deep end. Eat your swordfish." I signaled the waitress. I'd already checked on the door that afternoon, so I knew the answer before I asked. "Do you accept American Express?"

Like many places in Europe they didn't. She looked apologetic. "Visa, Mastercard…"

I smiled. "No problem. ATM?" I made a gesture like I was sticking a card in a wall. She burbled in French, pointing down the road. I nodded and glanced laughing at Mary, who had gone the color of old wax. I said, "Translate, darling."

She blinked a few times. "Down the road, on the right, a hundred meters, yards, *Crédit Agricole*."

"Thanks." I stood and paused, smiling at the waitress, and faltered in French, "*Comme Schwarzenegger, je reviendrai!*" She giggled nervously and I grinned at Mary. "Like Schwarzenegger, I'll be back."

She goggled at me like she'd slipped into *Alice in Wonderland* meets Elm Street, and I left while the going was good.

I hunched into my shoulders and walked quickly down the street toward number twelve. When I got there I took my Swiss Army knife from my pocket and rammed it hard into the lock, then turned and let myself in.

The lobby was dark. There was no porter and no desk, just a bank of mailboxes on the wall highlighted by the diffused streetlight. The floor was tiled and at the far end there was an old, concertina-style elevator. On the left was an elegant staircase with a wooden bannister. I took the stairs and sprinted up them three at a time. The safe house was on the sixth floor and by the time I got there I was breathing hard, struggling to do it quietly.

There were two apartments. The one I wanted was apartment A. The nearest. I took a moment to catch my breath, then stepped silently to the door and listened carefully. I could just make out the rise and fall of the TV. People never read anymore. If people read more, fewer of them would get shot.

I pulled the Maxim 9 from my waistband and blew out the lock, then pushed the door open and stepped inside.

The light in the hall was out. I could make out a corridor on my right with a couple of black oblongs that were half-closed doors. Ahead was a blank wall and on the left was another door. This one had a luminous rim and from it came the sound of Arabic TV, and two voices talking over the television.

I closed the front door silently and held it in place with my foot, aiming the Maxim at the upper-middle of the living room door. It opened suddenly and there was a startled man staring at me. He was unmistakably Afghan, with a long robe, a hat and a straggly beard. I adjusted slightly to the right and shot him through the throat, dead center. There was a spray of gore out the back of his neck, but he remained motionless. I moved up fast, pushed him aside and stepped into the living room.

It was large, spacious and practically bare. The floors were carpeted in cheap synthetic fabric. There was an IKEA sofa, a couple of chairs and a freestanding TV. There was not much else besides, except another Afghan getting to his feet with wide eyes and flapping hands.

I didn't stop moving. I reached him in two strides and, holding the gun in my left hand, I smashed a right hook into his jaw that sent him groaning to the floor.

There I knelt on his right arm, which must have been painful, and stuck the big, ugly Maxim in his groin, which must have been alarming. He was whimpering, confused and very frightened. I said:

"Mohammed Ben-Amini, *'ayn?*" Which means, "where"?'

He shook his head feverishly, trying to brush the gun away from his groin, repeating, "*Ana la 'aerif! Ana la 'aerif! Uqsim biallah! Uqsim biallah! Ashfaq! Ana la 'aerif, uqsim. Arhamni ealaa Allah!*"

All of which meant pretty much, "I don't know, I swear by Allah, please have pity on me."

I took his hat, stuffed it in his mouth and put a 9mm round through his knee. He screamed hard. His neck welled up and he turned very dark red. I wanted to feel compassion, but all I could think of was the children these bastards had raped and murdered in front of their parents; and the dazed, exhausted horror of the children's eyes as they watched their parents butchered. The nightmares that did not let me sleep, now robbed me of my compassion. I leaned down into his face and repeated my question:

"Mohammed Ben-Amini, *'ayn?*"

He gibbered and shook his head. I took the hat out of his mouth and he sobbed.

"*Ana la 'aerif! Ana la 'aerif! Arhamni ealaa Allah!*"

He wanted me to have pity. Pity came, in the end, in the form of a 9mm slug between his eyes. Then his suffering stopped. I wondered for a moment, thinking about the horror those villagers endured, how much suffering has murder stopped? Theirs had ended with their deaths, but I carried their suffering with me, into every dark hour of the night.

I crossed the room quickly, back into the hall, wiped away my prints, pulled the door closed and slipped down the stairs and back out into the street. I was aware I was sweating and the air felt suddenly chill. I walked slowly, keeping out of the light of the streetlamps, with my hands in my pockets, and entered the *Au Bois D'Acacia* smiling like a man who has achieved something.

Mary had finished her swordfish but looked queasy. I offered her a big, cheerful smile, which she accepted only half-heartedly. I called over the waitress and told her we'd have two espressos and two cognacs. Mary looked like she needed one, and I knew for damn sure that I did.

"What happened?"

"You'd better get a grip, sister. You look like you just saw the ghost of my great-aunt Augusta."

"Your who?"

"My great-aunt Augusta," I said. "She was a bit like Obi-Wan Kenobi. Terrifying in life, but even worse after death."

"That's not funny."

"Even so, you need to get a grip. Now smile and tell me you love me."

She closed her eyes and after a moment opened them and sighed loudly. "Darling," she said. "I love you far less than you might hope, but far more than you deserve, and I dearly hope I never have to set eyes on you again."

The waitress delivered our coffee and cognac and I took a hefty pull on the spirit and smacked my lips.

"That is in fact the nicest thing anyone has said to me all day. He wasn't there. There were two Afghans. They are no longer with us, and they were not able to provide any useful information. Did you hear from your people?"

She shook her head and drained half her drink. "I don't think I can keep this charade up much longer. Can we leave, please?"

I leaned back in my chair, smiling like she'd said something cute.

"Of course, sweetheart, but I am going to give you one final warning. Get a grip. If anyone notices the state you're in, fifty yards from where those guys are going to be discovered tomorrow, and they put two and two together, they will make four. So you'd better reframe, sister, and do whatever it takes to look normal. Start laughing and get some color in your cheeks, or I am going to have to give you a spanking."

It did the trick. Her cheeks flushed and her eyes got bright.

"You are a *Neanderthal!*"

"Whatever it takes, honey. Now start laughing and we can leave here arm in arm, like a normal couple."

It was hard, I could see she was struggling, but she leaned across the table smiling and put her index finger on my nose. "When are you leaving, dumpling?"

"I don't know, sugarplum. I have to talk to Buddy."

"I sure hope it's soon."

"Me? I'll miss you and all the nice things you say. Let's go."

I paid the bill and we left, arm in arm like a loving couple. As we made our way toward her car I said, "Give me the keys."

"What? Why?"

"Because you're in shock and any minute now you'll get very cold, start shivering and you'll want to go to sleep."

"I'm not in shock! I didn't even see what you did. I just feel queasy, that's all."

"Keys."

She must have secretly been grateful, because she opened her bag and put them in my hand. Then she squeezed my arm.

"Where are we going?"

"To my hotel room."

"Why?"

"To talk to Buddy. Why else?"

"I don't know," she said, and sounded suddenly drunk. "You're such a bad man, I thought maybe you wanted to have your evil way with me."

"I do," I said, and opened the car. "But I want you to be conscious when I do it."

We climbed in and slammed the doors. "God I hate you," she said. But she didn't sound like she meant it.

ELEVEN

The concierge carefully studied his screen as I walked Mary through the lobby to the elevators. Once the doors had hissed closed on us she draped her arms around me and rested her head on my shoulder. Her breath was warm and slightly moist on my neck and my ear as she muttered, "What the hell is wrong with me?"

I didn't tell her I was about to ask Brigadier Buddy Byrd the same damn question. The elevator doors hissed open and I half carried her to my door, slipped the key in the lock and bundled her inside. I transferred the key from the door to the housing on the wall that made the lights work, let the door clunk closed and picked her up bodily. I carried her to the bed, took off her shoes and slid her under the covers. She turned over and began to snore softly.

I pulled out the cell they had given me at Cobra and called the brigadier. He answered on the first ring.

"Yes, Bauer, report."

"Before I do that, I need to ask you about Mary Brown."

He was quiet for a minute, then, "What about her?"

"She's passed out in my bed."

"Have you had intercourse?"

"No. She freaked out when I went to do the job. I think she's in shock. There is no way this girl is fit for field work..."

"She is a brilliant analyst. She is not supposed to do field work. Why was she with you?"

"She was showing me where the house was."

"Couldn't she do that on a map?"

"Sir, I expect that if I have a contact on a mission they will be professional."

"She is, highly professional. But she is not intended to do field work. Has she compromised the mission?"

I thought about it, looking out over the rooftops of Paris toward the Seine, and sighed. "No, but it came damn close."

"Did you do the job?"

"No. And we have a problem."

"Explain."

"Mohammed Ben-Amini was not there. Two of his boys were. I killed both of them, but I had a talk with one of them first. I was persuasive, but he swore he had no idea where Ben-Amini was. Meantime, the Firm has been having some interesting visitors to the safe house, including two Yemeni businessmen in very expensive suits, and a Mexican..."

"The incident in the diplomatic car."

"One thing Mary Brown did point out before she went to pieces, this could be al-Qaeda moving into a growing power vacuum. They have a strong base in Yemen, and as we move out of Afghanistan, we're leaving a power vacuum there, too, which they may be aiming to fill. And like she pointed out, one thing Mexico and Afghanistan have in common is poppies."

"All right, but that's not your job, Bauer."

"Whose is it," I snarled, "the CIA's? They are the guys providing a venue for these meetings."

"We don't know that."

"But we do know that there were agents in the apartment when this guy showed up."

"Do we know he went to the apartment?"

I hesitated. "No. But we don't know he didn't either. Mary sent the photographs off for facial recognition, but we haven't had a reply yet."

"I know, Bauer," he said dryly. "I am in the loop." He was quiet for a moment. Then said, "All right, I want you to stay on task. If we haven't had an ID by tomorrow morning I want you on the next flight to LA. Meantime I'll have a talk with Gina and see what's going on with that apartment."

"Gina?"

"The director."

"Right. And sir, Mary…"

"You made your point, Harry."

"Good. If I haven't heard from you by nine AM, I'll book a flight."

"Good." He chuckled then. "Enjoy your night on the sofa."

He hung up and I leaned my ass on the windowsill while I watched Mary sleeping comfortably in the middle of the bed.

Then her phone pinged.

I went to her bag and pulled it out. It was an iPhone 11. I showed it her face and it unlocked. It was an e-mail from somebody called Pete. It just said:

"Mustache, Hussein Saleh, board of directors Consolidated Yemeni Oil; clean shaven, Captain Jaden Abdullah of the Yemeni Air Force; non-Arab, Bernardo Muller, Mexican Embassy attaché, known to have connections with 'El Mayo,' Ismael Zambada, head of the Sinaloa Cartel."

That was the extent of the e-mail. I closed it, marked it unread, wiped my prints and slipped it back in her bag.

I grunted and made my way to the bathroom where I had a cold-hot-cold shower, dried myself off and pulled on my shorts before returning to the bed. There I shoved Mary over to one side, muttering, "Make room," at her. Finally I pulled the covers over me and switched off the light.

After a couple of minutes I heard a comfortable sigh and Mary Brown turned, grabbed me and put her head on my shoulder.

"You're a son of a bitch," she muttered.

"I'm not sure this is a good idea."

"It's OK, I sobered up." It was a statement that should have been comforting, but wasn't. She squeezed tighter and whispered in the dark. "I think you were right. It was mild shock combined with alcohol. But I feel a lot better now." With that she gave me a kiss on the neck and said, "I can't sleep dressed."

Then she was sitting up and pulling off her small black dress, and underneath it there was just the soft luminescence of her pale skin.

* * *

In the morning she smiled at me from the bed as I stepped out of the bathroom, toweling myself dry.

"Good morning, you son of a bitch."

"This is why Freud called you the Dark Continent."

"Yeah, but what the hell did he know?"

I sat on the bed and started pulling on my socks. "You got a ping last night."

She sat up and draped herself over my back with her arms around my neck.

"I got more than that, as I recall."

I kissed her and stood to pull on my pants. "On your phone. It might be a response to the facial recognition request."

She regarded me with baleful, hooded eyes and reached for her bag.

"Wham bam, thank you ma'am, huh?"

I gave my head a small shake and pulled on my shirt. "I spoke to Buddy last night while you were sleeping. He said if we had no response by nine AM I should get the next flight to LA."

"Oh..." She watched me in silence for a moment, then unlocked her phone and opened the e-mail.

"What does it say?"

"You were right. They're Yemeni, big shots too. The guy with the mustache is Hussein Saleh. I know the name. His full name is Hussein bin Saleh Al-Saud. He's related to the Saudi royal family. He's also on the board of directors of Consolidated Yemeni Oil. The other guy is Captain Jaden Abdullah, he's Yemeni Air Force. The third guy is Bernardo Muller. Shit! I thought I recognized his face. He's a recent Mexican Embassy attaché, known to have connections with Ismael Zambada, 'El Mayo,' the new head of the Sinaloa Cartel. He's the liaison between Zambada and the national government. He rarely leaves Mexico. Now suddenly he's here in Paris."

She swung her legs out of bed and stared at me. For a moment it was hard to focus on Zambada. I picked up her dress and threw it at her.

"Get dressed. Let's have breakfast."

"What the hell are they doing?"

"A deal. Drugs for arms. It has to be something like that."

"Yemen has no drugs production capability, and it has barely enough arms for its own conflict." She stood, apparently unaware that she was stark naked. "Which brings us to Afghanistan, but then why was Mohammed Ben-Amini not there?"

"I don't know. Get dressed, will you?"

"What's the hurry? We got our IDs." She went to the bathroom and stopped in the doorway, turned back and pointed at me. "I'll tell you why Ben-Amini wasn't there. Because the CIA were speaking on his behalf."

"*What?* That's insane..."

"Is it? Does the name Oliver North ring any bells?"

She closed the door and a moment later I heard the water hissing. I went to the window and stood looking down, unseeing, at the street below. The CIA speaking on behalf of Mohammed Ben-Amini in a deal with al-Qaeda and Sinaloa. It made no sense. What benefit did the Agency get from such a deal? It was hard enough to see the gain to either al-Qaeda or Sinaloa, but it was impossible to see the benefit to the CIA.

Unless I was missing something.

She came out of the bathroom ten minutes later, still naked and toweling her hair. I turned back to the window and spoke to the rooftops.

"What am I missing?"

"Why won't you look at me? Was last night such a big mistake?"

"I'm trying to focus. I haven't much time and this looks like a big deal. No, it wasn't a mistake. But this isn't the time."

She didn't answer, but I could hear the rustle of clothes. Finally she said, "On the face of it, al-Qaeda needs weapons, but not drugs. Sinaloa has a lot of drugs and a lot of weapons. So there is no immediate marriage of supply and demand there. It's true that if they joined forces, they could cause a lot of damage to the USA, and the rest of the Western world, but where is the benefit to Sinaloa? Sinaloa needs a rich, prosperous USA to buy its drugs, right? I would need time to think this through."

I turned to face her. She was dressed and was combing her hair. She was no less distracting.

"Are we talking about weaponizing drugs?"

She shrugged. "It's possible. The Russians contemplated it during the Cold War. But it's not as easy as it sounds. Apart from a handful of drugs like heroin, most substances are not that addictive, unless you have an addictive personality. Also, it's a slow, pervasive attack on the fabric of society, rather than the big, dramatic kind of violence that al-Qaeda likes to go for. I don't think this is about weaponizing drugs, and I don't think it's exactly a drugs for weapons deal. Obviously drugs and weapons are going to play a part, but that is not what this is about."

"What is it about, then?"

"I don't know. I need to talk to somebody..."

"Who?"

She took lipstick from her bag and started painting her lips. "Need to know, cowboy."

She was mad at me and hiding it badly. "You can't talk to the Agency about this, Mary. We don't know who's involved, or how."

She put away her makeup and came over to stand in front of me, real close. "You do your job, Harry, and I'll do mine. If you have to leave, give me a call before you go. Otherwise, we'll meet this evening. I think we could both use some distraction."

She kissed me on the cheek and walked out, closing the door behind her and leaving the smell of her perfume and a very empty space.

I checked my watch. It was nine thirty. I'd had no word from the brigadier. He must know by now that I had the information about the people at the CIA's safe house. So why wasn't he giving me instructions? Did he want me to go after Hussein Saleh, Captain Jaden Abdullah and/or Bernardo Muller? Did we have a change of target? Or was he leaving it up to me?

I felt a sudden flush of anger. It was unprofessional. And lack of professionalism led to people getting hurt and killed.

I picked up the phone and called the brigadier again.

"Yes. Don't do this too often."

"I need instructions. Are we changing targets? Should I go to LA? This feels sloppy."

"Do nothing. I'm making inquiries. You'll get instructions."

"When?"

"Today. Take the day off. Relax. Enjoy Paris. Take Mary to lunch."

"She's making inquiries. She still consults with the Firm. I don't like this situation, sir. It's a mess."

"No. Tell her not to do that. Call her. Tell her to stand down and do nothing. Get out of Paris for the day. Go to the beach or something."

He hung up and I called Mary. It rang twice and she answered.

"I am driving. It's not safe and it's against the law. What do you want?"

"Buddy says you're to stand down, don't make inquiries..."

"Too late. I made some discreet inquiries. They're going to get back to me with more relevant intel. It's OK, I made it sound innocuous, like I was just researching background."

"Well the boss says don't. We have to kill time. He said we should go to the beach."

"The beach?"

"Or something."

"I prefer something. Are you going to continue to be an asshole today? You were fun last night."

"I'll be fun. I promise. I'm going to hire a car at the desk and come over and pick you up. You choose where you want to go."

"OK, cowboy." She blew me a noisy kiss and hung up.

I called down and told reception I wanted to rent an F-Type Jaguar convertible for the day. He said that was no problem at all. So I packed my bags, put the P226 in my belt and the Maxim 9 in the safe in the wardrobe, and went down to sign for the car and collect it.

It took twenty minutes for the paperwork to be done and for the car to arrive. I punched Mary's address into the GPS and let it take me at a leisurely pace through the streets of Paris, feeling the sun on my face and trying to relax while I let my unconscious mind work out what purpose was drawing al-Qaeda and Sinaloa together. Not drugs for weapons, she had said. What then? What purpose did they each have if not drugs and guns?

Sinaloa was driven by lust for money and power.

Al-Qaeda was driven by ideological fanaticism and hatred. Their aim was to establish the empire of Allah on Earth: all *kafirs* must be either killed or enslaved.

Much as I turned it around and around in my head, it was like a Chinese puzzle: everything you tried cancelled out everything else you tried. Al-Qaeda was not buying drugs. If they wanted them they could grow as much as they liked in Afghanistan. And if they wanted weapons, they could buy them from suppliers a lot more easily than having to go all the way to Mexico. On the other hand, Mexico had all the drugs and weapons it needed, right there in their own country.

So what? What the hell were they talking about in that apartment, with the CIA?

By the time I got to Franklin Roosevelt Avenue I was none the wiser. I parked outside her block, killed the engine and climbed out of the car, deciding to take Buddy's advice and enjoy a day of rest, with a beautiful, intelligent woman. There was fuck all else to do.

TWELVE

W hen I got to her front door it was open a couple of inches. I stood a moment and listened, but I couldn't hear anything. I looked at the lock. There were no obvious signs it had been picked, no scratches or scuffs. I eased the door a little farther with my toe. It didn't creak, so I pushed another couple of inches and stepped inside. I could smell coffee, toast, and fresh air from an open window. But there were still no sounds.

I took the P226 from my belt and followed the long passage to the living room door. It too was a couple of inches open, and here the smell of fresh air was stronger. I eased the door open a little wider and saw the big oblongs of luminescence lying across the wooden floor, at the end of leaning dusty beams. The calico sofa was also bathed in light. Her shoes, the ones I had taken off that night, were on the floor beside it. Her bag was lying in the nook of the arm and the back, on a cushion. It was open and I could see her phone.

I turned and made my way back along the corridor to the kitchen. There was an open carton of milk on the surface beside the sink. Next to it was a cup, and next to that was a saucepan. There was milk in the saucepan ready to be heated. A coffee percolator sat in the middle space between the electric rings. It was still warm, but not hot. The coffee had come up, but the rings were cold. I wondered how long it would have taken for them to cool.

My mind was making a movie: she'd come in feeling tired from the night before. She went to the living room, kicked off her shoes, dropped her bag on the sofa and opened the windows. Then she went to the kitchen to make coffee and toast to nurse her hangover. The coffee had come up and she was about to heat the milk. That was twenty minutes ago, half an hour tops.

It wouldn't have taken her that long to get to her apartment. So she had been somewhere before she came home. Where? I skipped it and went on with the movie in my head.

Something had drawn her away from her coffee. Did somebody ring at the bell? Did she think it was me? No, she would have known I couldn't make it that fast. So she went to the door, opened it, and for some reason never closed it.

I stepped out into the corridor again and moved to the john. There was nothing unusual in there except the lid was up and it hadn't been flushed. So I moved on, past the open front door, to the bedroom.

That was the only door in the apartment that was closed. Had she forgotten the coffee and gone to sleep? I listened at the door. There was no sound of breathing or snoring. Using a handkerchief I turned the handle and pushed the door gently open.

For a moment I wanted to laugh. She was lying on the bed. She still had her little black dress on. In a split second I saw the movie complete itself. She had come in, needing to pee. She'd gone to the living room, forgetting to close the front door, dropped her shoes and bag, opened the windows, run to the bathroom, peed, forgotten to flush, started to make coffee, come to the bedroom to change her clothes and fallen asleep.

All that took a fraction of a second. Then the smile faded from my face because I saw that her eyes, which had looked closed in the dimness of the room, were in fact slightly open.

A wave of nausea washed over me. My belly burned hot and I could feel my heart pounding high in my chest. Her face was turned to my left, toward the window. I stepped to my right and walked around the bed, so I was looking at the back of her head. Her hair was matted, caked in blood, as were the sheets just beneath the inch-wide gash at the base of her skull.

The grief was intense and bitter, but I suppressed it fast. There would be time for that later. Now I moved quickly to the living room, took her bag and dumped the contents on the floor. I sorted through everything but found nothing of interest except her phone. I took that to her bedroom, showed her face to the screen and it opened. I checked her WhatsApp and her text messages, but there was nothing there of any interest so I had a look at her recent calls.

There was one she'd made about fifteen minutes after she left me at the hotel. The next one in the register was when I called her. I sent the number to Buddy with the message, *Last number she called. Trace it.*

Then I checked her maps and GPS for the last location she'd used it for. It was one of those rare hunches that pays off: *Rue Condorcet 18*, that morning at ten thirty. She had saved the location as "George."

I slipped out of the front door and closed it behind me. Then I ran down the stairs, climbed into the Jaguar, punched *Rue Condorcet 18* into the satnav and took off at a nice, sedate pace.

As I pulled onto the *Avenue de Paris* I called Buddy. He answered straight away.

"This is becoming a habit, Bauer. It isn't advisable. What's going on?"

"Mary has been murdered in her apartment."

"Jesus!"

"Who did she go and see this morning before she went home?"

"No one that I'm aware of. What makes you think she went to see anybody? I told you to tell her..."

"She told me she'd made some discreet inquiries and they were going to get back to her. Two gets you twenty she spoke to somebody in the Agency. They shut her up."

"Don't jump to conclusions, Harry. There are *a lot* of interests at work here."

"Yeah. Do you know what's going on?"

"I have an idea, but I'm not sure. You need to get out of France right now. Charter an air taxi. Go to London and get the next available flight to the USA. I'll have somebody pick you up."

"Sure. OK. I'll keep you posted."

The GPS took me north and east, and the farther we went in that direction, the more rough and seedy the surroundings became. This was not the elegant Paris of the Golden Triangle; this was the ugly underbelly of a failed empire trying to sweep its abandoned policies of multiculturalism and euro-federalism under an ever-dirtier carpet.

I turned off the *Avenue du President Wilson*, onto *Avenue Gabriel Peri*, and then left and north onto *Rue Con-*

dorcet. There I cruised slowly past dirty old houses and peeling, whitewashed walls with faded graffiti, over an intersection and past a vast, ugly school that looked more like a prison than a place of learning. All the while I was watching the numbers drop until I came to a big, pink, double-fronted house that had the number twenty over the door. Beside it was an alleyway that had been sealed off with cinder blocks and a steel door. Beside that was a dirty, unpainted house with bare concrete walls. That door had the number eighteen. Out front there was a white Citroen van. I felt the hood. It was hot. So I went and hammered on the door.

It was opened after a moment by a big, black guy. He was six four and built like a brick shithouse. His shoulders were massive and so were his thighs. He considered my face with hostile eyes and said, *"Oui?"*

"I'm looking for George."

"Who are you?"

He was American. I smiled at him. "I'm the guy who's looking for George. Are you George? I think you're George."

"Yeah? Maybe I am, dude. What's your problem? Did I screw your wife? Either tell me who you are or get the fuck out of my face!"

I gave a small laugh and raised my hands as I looked down at his shoes.

"I apologize. I meant no disrespect." Then I looked into his eyes and smashed my right instep into his balls. His eyes went wide and he doubled up. I didn't hit him again. I didn't need to. I made a fist and gripped his nose between my index and middle finger, and twisted savagely. I pushed him back as I did so. He screamed a little and stumbled back, trying to get away from me. I followed and kicked the door closed behind me.

His living room was the first door on the right and I shoved him in there, then kicked his feet out from under him so he fell on his back on the floor. I stepped over him and pulled the drapes half closed, then drew the P226 and shoved it in his groin.

"You're a big, tough, dangerous guy, George. You know, there's a chance you could still overpower me and kill me. But if I were you, with your testicles hurting the way they are right now, I wouldn't risk it. After all, you might just get out of this alive anyway, if you're smart, you cooperate and tell me everything I need to know."

His voice was a thin, feeble rasp.

"Who the fuck are you?"

"Now that's a bad start, George. What you should have said is, 'What do you want to know?' Then I would have known that you were keen to cooperate. Now, let's get something clear. I ask you questions and you answer without hesitation and without lying. Break those rules once, and I will blow your left kneecap off. Do I need to prove that I am serious?"

He shook his head. "No. What do you need to know?"

"Why did Mary come here earlier? You may know her by a different name. She's cute, attractive, little black dress."

He swallowed hard. "She, oh man, she needed to ask me something..." I shifted the muzzle of the Sig to his left knee. His hands flew up, panic in his eyes. "No! No! Wait, she wanted to know if my employers were doing business with Afghan terrorists."

"Who are your employers?"

"I can't tell you that..."

I pulled the trigger and the 9mm slug hammered through his knee at point-blank range. He screamed, went pasty, sweaty gray and passed out. He was sweating profusely, like he had a fever. I went to the kitchen, found a bucket and filled it with cold water. Then I returned to the living room and poured it over him. He came to, gasping and groaning.

I knelt beside his right knee and put the muzzle on his kneecap.

"You can still save the leg if you're quick. But if I have to blow your other kneecap off, and then I leave you here without calling the ambulance, you'll probably die of gangrene infection. If I do the same to your shoulders, it won't be worth surviving, pal. Life just won't be worth living. My advice to you, George, is stop this process before it gets completely out of hand. Now, again, who are your employers?"

He was weeping like a child, his wet lower lip curling and trembling. "The Central Intelligence Agency..."

"And *are* they doing business with Afghan terrorists, or with al-Qaeda?"

He shook his head. "No. No, that's crazy."

"OK, good. See? We're doing well now. So I have just one more question and then I'll call an ambulance for you. Where is Mary now?"

"I..."

"Think, very carefully, before you answer. I need the truth. Lie to me, and what is left of your life will be hell. Remember, you don't know how much I know. And if you lie I might well catch you out. So your best policy, your *only* policy right now, is the truth."

He swallowed three times before he said, "She's dead."

"Who killed her?"

"I was ordered to…"

"By whom?"

"My unit chief…"

"Name?" He swallowed again, three times. "Don't make me do it."

"Samy, Samy Arain."

"And he is in charge of the deal with the Afghans and al-Qaeda?"

"I don't know anything about that. Honest…"

"What's your full name?"

"George Santos."

I nodded. "That beautiful young woman you killed today? She was a CIA consulting analyst. And she was my friend."

I shot him between the eyes and went out to my car. I stood a moment on the narrow sidewalk, looking up at the pale blue sky. It didn't feel any better having killed George, but still I knew it was something that had to be done. Her death could not go unpunished, or unavenged. Like all those other victims, the dead who came in the night, who tormented my dreams. They had to be avenged, and maybe, one day, their souls could rest.

I climbed in the Jag and drove sedately back to the Four Seasons. There I phoned for an air taxi to take me to London. I packed my bags, wiped my prints off the Maxim 9 and the P226, had the hotel store them in a safe deposit box and charged it to my credit card.

Then I drove the Jag to Paris, Charles de Gaulle Airport. I handed over the keys at the rental office, found the AirTaxi office and was fast-tracked through security. Twenty minutes later I boarded a Gulfstream 550 and, twenty minutes after that, I was sipping a martini dry, looking down over the receding countryside of northern France.

I remembered Mary Brown saying to me that this was a very different game than what I had been used to. She had been right. Soldiering was black and white. The objectives were clear. You didn't get involved in the politics, or the espionage. You did your job, and you went home.

But this, this was hard to grasp. A CIA cell in Paris, commanded by one Samy Arain, charged with doing a deal with the Mujahidin and al-Qaeda, and Sinaloa, a deal so sensitive, so important, that they were prepared to kill their own consulting analyst in order to keep it quiet. Here, in this *Alice in Wonderland* no-man's land, there was no way of telling who was your enemy and who was your friend. Here, there could be no friends. Everyone was an enemy.

Did I want this? Was this something I wanted? Now that I was in, could I ever leave?

I asked the hostess for another martini and closed my eyes. I didn't sleep, I spent the next half hour deciding what I was going to do, and in what order. My first priority would be to give peace and rest to those souls, the slaughtered villagers of Al-Landy. So, my first order of business would be to find Mohammed Ben-Amini, wherever the hell he was, and execute him. After that, when I was done with him, I would go after Hussein Saleh, of Consolidated Yemeni Oil, his colleague, Captain Jaden Abdullah of the Yemeni Air Force and, last but not least, Bernardo Muller of the Mexican Embassy in Paris, close pal of Ismael Zambada, "El Mayo." And when I was done with them, I would decide whether I wanted to resign and buy a ranch in Wyoming.

Or whether I wanted to keep on taking out the trash.

THIRTEEN

In the end I flew to Boston. I was met at Logan International Airport by a man whose neck was wider than his head. He was wearing an expensive Italian suit that made him look like his name was Tony and he took care of business. He was holding a photograph and methodically checking the faces of passengers emerging from arrivals. When he saw me he stepped over and spoke in a surprisingly agreeable voice.

"Mr. Bauer?" I told him I was and he said, "Lieutenant Bernstein. The brigadier sends his regards. I have a car waiting, may I take your bag?"

The waiting car was a black Chevy Tahoe. The lieutenant opened the rear door for me and closed it as I climbed in. I wasn't surprised to see Brigadier Alexander "Buddy" Byrd sitting on the black leather seat, waiting for me.

"You made it," he said, like I'd crossed the Atlantic swimming. "Well done. Sorry about the change of venue. Going straight to Los Angeles struck me as a little on the nose. Have you seen the French news?"

I settled in my seat and Lt. Bernstein got behind the wheel and fired up four-hundred-brake horsepower of whispering engine. I said, "I just got off the plane, sir."

He ignored me and went on as we cruised toward the spaghetti junction at Jeffries Point.

"The *Police Nationale* are scratching their heads over the murder of two Afghan nationals in an apartment on the *Rue de Naples* the day before yesterday. One of the two men appeared to have been tortured before he was killed. They are attributing it to internal conflicts among rival Muslim factions, as it seems the two men had links to the Mujahidin." He examined his black leather gloves a moment. "There was also an, apparently, unrelated murder in one of the poorer districts of Paris, an American, shot in the knee and then in the head. They put that one down to drug trafficking for some reason."

I shrugged. We took the turn for the Sumner Tunnel. "I am not impressed with your organization, Brigadier. Mary Brown should not have died. She should not have been in the field at all. She was murdered by one George Santos, a CIA officer."

"This would be the chap near the *Parc des Beaumonts*, *Rue Condorcet*."

"Yeah. He was acting on the orders of his unit chief, Samy Arain. She'd gone to George after leaving me that morning, to ask him if the CIA were cutting some kind of deal with al-Qaeda."

I turned to look at him as we plunged into the tunnel under Boston Harbor. Amber light slipped across his face in a slow, steady rhythm in the sudden darkness. He was expressionless, looking out at the grim walls of the tunnel. I said:

"That was naïve. It was a naïve thing to do. She might have been a brilliant analyst, sir, but she was still green. George Santos was a killer. When she went to talk to him, she signed her own death warrant. She should never have been put in the field."

After a while he nodded. "I agree."

I snarled, "Then why was she?"

He turned to look at me out of the shadows, revealed momentarily by a lurid, dirty orange glow that faded, sinking him into shadows again. He said, "Don't question me, Bauer. You've briefed me, I understand and I agree, but don't question me."

We drove on in silence until we emerged into bright sunlight at North Washington Street. Then the lieutenant started a process of weaving in and out of roads, doubling back on himself and checking his mirror a lot.

"Where are we going?"

Byrd gave his head a brief shake. "Nowhere, just yet. Listen, Harry, you need to understand something. We are not a law enforcement agency. We are not, in fact, any kind of official agency. We are a private enterprise; we do not even officially exist. We are tolerated by the powers that be by the grace of an inspired mixture of self-interest and blackmail. It is not for us to investigate or monitor the activities of US federal agencies. If the CIA think it behooves them to make a deal with al-Qaeda, then that is a decision for them."

"It stinks," I snarled. "Is it also a decision for them if they decide it *behooves* them to murder our operatives?"

"No. And I agree, it stinks. Did you kill George Santos?"

"Yeah."

"Good. They'll think twice before going against our operatives in future."

"So what now?"

He raised an eyebrow at me. "Are you still on-board?"

"Of course I am."

"Then you go to Los Angeles."

"Do we know he's there? Or is this another wild goose chase?" Before he could answer I went on. "How much does the Central Intelligence Agency know about you? Because it seems to me they are playing you like a fiddle. How much did George Santos pump out of Mary Brown before he killed her? And while we're at it, how many naïve college kids have you recruited? Because if you have a lot of girls like Mary Brown on your payroll, you're probably leaking like a damned sieve."

I saw the lieutenant glance in his mirror. The brigadier watched me without expression for a while, then said, "Are you done?"

"I don't know."

"First let's get something clear. You are employed by Cobra; that does not entitle you to demand access to every piece of intelligence you think you need. How much the CIA knows about us can be summed up as, they know we exist, and that's it. They knew Mary Brown worked for us, now they don't even know that. But they know that her death did not go unpunished.

"The size and nature of our personnel is none of your concern. And finding out whether we are leaking or not, is not part of your brief. But I can assure you, we are not. Now, let me ask you a question."

"What?"

"Are you going to be a problem?"

I thought about it, then gave my head a single shake. "No, not for you, sir." Then I added, not hiding the bitterness in my voice, "But I do recommend you review your recruiting and deployment criteria."

"For reasons already stated."

In other words, I'd already said that, move on. I nodded.

"Yes, sir."

"Good. Now, no, we do not know, one hundred percent, that Ben-Amini is in LA. But, from our own analysis of the intel we have, and from friends we have in the Bureau who are also keeping an eye out for him, we are fairly certain he's there."

"What about the CIA?"

"Not surprisingly they are keeping very quiet. Beyond stating that they arrested him and have him in custody at a secure location, they are saying nothing. Our intelligence suggests that that secure location is south of LA, at Salton Sea."

"Is that San Diego? Some kind of eco-disaster in the 1920s?"

"It's a lake, thirty miles north of Mexicali. It's pretty remote. It was a holiday resort in the early 20th century, but things went wrong. Now it is desolate, largely desert. The I-10 passes about ten miles to the north. It forms the end of the Coachella Valley, where Palm Springs is, but Palm Springs is thirty-five miles to the northwest of the lake. As I said, it's remote, and it is mainly desert."

I nodded. "Remote, but relatively easy access to roads and air transport if you need it."

"Mm-hm, and an hour's drive from Calexico and the Mexican border. A comparatively simple, fifteen-hour drive to Culiacan, in Sinaloa, and a mere hour and a half by private plane. All of which is consistent with your findings in Paris."

I glanced at him and said, dryly, "I thought we were not law enforcement investigators, just executioners."

He didn't answer me and after a moment I noticed we hadn't taken any turns for a while. We seemed suddenly to have a direction. I glanced out of the window and saw we were moving toward the I-90.

"Obviously," he said, "your primary objective will be to eliminate the target. But it would do no harm at all if, as a secondary objective, you could gather intelligence on the CIA's purpose in holding Ben-Amini, his connection with Hussein Saleh and Jaden Abdullah, and above all what they are discussing with Mexico."

I gave him something approximating a smile. "I had that pretty much penciled in, sir. I also want to know a little more about Samy Arain. I want to know if his agenda is personal or sanctioned by the Agency."

"Good." He pulled a large manila envelope from his coat and handed it to me. "I'll need your old passport and credit card. This is your new identity. There will be no liaison. You are on your own. You are Oliver Frost, an electronics technician from New York, on holiday in Los Angeles. You have a driver's license and credit card and a thousand dollars in cash. There is also an American Airlines ticket and papers to collect a rental car. I thought you'd appreciate a Wrangler. You may need it. You're booked in at the Hotel California, downtown LA."

"Great, I can check out but I can never leave."

"So, we can drop you at JFK if you like, though you still have a few hours before your flight is due." He handed me a cell phone. "This is a burner with my number pre-inserted. Call me when you arrive and keep me posted, but do try not to call too often."

I took the phone and put it in my pocket. "Still no laser pen, huh?"

"We're working on it. You'll be the first to test it in

the field, I promise."

I examined his face. I couldn't tell if he was joking. "Drop me at my place, if it's all the same to you. I left the P226 and the Maxim in a safe deposit box at the hotel, back in Paris, if you want to send somebody to retrieve them. I want to collect my own weapons from my house." I saw the question on Byrd's face and smiled. "DHL to the hotel."

"Your Sig Sauer."

"And the Fairbairn and Sykes, sir. I missed it in Paris."

They dropped me at my house on Shore Drive. I watched the Chevy disappear down the road and make a right on Lafayette. Then I let myself into the blue clapboard cottage, dropped my bag by the door and went into the kitchen, where I stood leaning on the sink, looking out at the unkempt, overgrown lawn in my backyard.

When you're dealing with life and death, when you are in an immediate conflict where life is at stake, you cannot afford to get mad, much less allow grief to affect your thoughts or your actions.

In my mind I could see Mary Brown lying motionless on her bed, in the half-light. I remembered the momentary feeling of relief and amusement, when I thought she had succumbed to her hangover, and her lack of sleep. And then there were the vivid images of her eyes, open in the gloom, and the wound at the base of her skull; the knowledge, the implacable, unalterable knowledge, that she was dead.

The knowledge lay there, in her blood, in the simple but irreversible gash in the back of her neck. It cried out for rage, for revenge, for tears. It demanded some kind of outpouring of human emotion. But none came.

It was not that the emotions were not there. I knew they were. But they refused to show themselves. All there was, was a voice in my head that said, "Not yet...not yet..."

I had known her less than twenty-four hours. I had liked her. She had been smart and funny. And innocent. Given time...

I reached in my cupboard and pulled out a bottle of Cardhu. I poured myself a generous measure and pulled off half of it. What the hell! Given time, what? We might have become friends? Lovers? That wasn't the point. It wasn't what I had lost. Just as I had lost nothing in Al-Landy. It was what they had lost, what she had lost. It made no sense.

And pain never hurts so much as when it doesn't make sense.

I went up to the bedroom and opened the trunk at the foot of my bed. Under the bedding and the winter clothes I found the small, gray Samsonite case. I pulled it out and opened it on the bed. I'd had the molded interior made especially. There was the Sig Sauer P226 TacOps in the center, with two boxes of 9mm rounds nestled beside it. Beneath the gun, parallel to it, was the Fairbairn and Sykes fighting knife, sitting razor sharp in its sheath. And packed in the lid were the two holsters: one for battle, to be strapped to the thigh, the other, made of waxed leather to fit under the arm, a concealed carry.

I called the carrier company and told them I wanted a parcel delivered to the Hotel California in Los Angeles, by breakfast the next day. They said they'd send a car to collect it. While I waited I unpacked the case I'd taken to Paris, and packed a new one for California. This one included binoculars, night-vision goggles and things of that sort.

The DHL van came and went, and soon it was time for me to go too. But before I went down to the waiting taxi, I paused for a moment in the bedroom door and looked at the dirty clothes strewn across my bed. They'd still be like that when I returned. I had nobody to deal with that kind of thing, nobody to wait for me to come home.

If I came home.

I wondered briefly what the hell I'd be coming home for, but killed that thought and went down to the cab.

The trip to Los Angeles was uneventful. I played a game in the taxi, in the airport and on the plane, to see if I could spot anyone following me. I couldn't. And when I thought about it, it seemed unlikely they would anyway. The only people who had seen me in Paris were the two Afghans in the apartment on *Rue de Naples*, and George Santos, and all three of them were dead.

But I reminded myself not to be too confident. I knew next to nothing about Cobra, except that so far they had struck me as sloppy and unprofessional. Buddy Byrd liked to portray them as slick and well connected with the higher echelons of the CIA and the Bureau, and maybe that was true; but all it meant was that if Cobra was leaking, it was leaking at a very high level. And if that was the case, then the place I needed to start looking out for a tail was in Los Angeles, not New York.

I touched down at eight thirty-five PM California time, collected my bag from baggage reclaim and went to get my car. It was a nondescript kind of muddy beige that the kid at Avis told me was called Gobi. It wasn't pretty, but I figured it would be just the thing at the Salton Sea.

The sky was turning from dusk to evening as I cruised north along the Harbor Freeway and came off onto West 4th Street, then turned left onto South Olive street. By the time I'd handed the Jeep over to the parking valet, it was gone nine thirty and my belly was telling me it was time for a martini, dry, and a sirloin steak.

I gave the buttons twenty bucks and told him to take my stuff up to the room and leave it on the bed, then I went to find a table on a terrace at one of the two hotel restaurants. The maître d' sat me next to a table of noisy, overdressed beautiful people: the kind who leave their plastic surgeon's designer label hanging out of the tucks behind their ears. I'd picked up an issue of the *LA Times* at the airport and was trying to read it while sipping my drink, but there was an insistence to their yammering that kept drawing me away from the article.

They were in films and they wanted everybody to know about it. I glanced at them and logged them in my mind: two guys and two girls, gender-fluid and not necessarily two couples. One of the guys was older, with a goatee and long floppy hair under a fedora. He was carefully eccentric, a wannabe Orson Welles crossed with Jack Sparrow. He was wearing sunglasses at night, hinting he was a drug user. He was the loudest.

The girls looked like they were aspiring to be in B movies. They were overdressed in too few clothes, with deep-cut necks exposing silicone breasts and bizarrely overdeveloped small muscles. They were trying to laugh through faces paralyzed by Botox, and it was hard to tell them apart, except that one was blonde and the other was a redhead. The fourth character at the table was conspicuously dressed in Armani jeans and a grandfather shirt that was longer than his dark blue blazer. He had long, carefully unkempt hair and a baseball cap. They were not a remarkable crowd for Los Angeles. They were standard-issue rebel bad boys and the girls, though probably not what the Beach Boys had in mind, were standard-issue California girls.

But it was what the wannabe eccentric was saying that had caught my attention.

"...my dear fellow, do you know how difficult it is to get cocaine these days? Or *so I am told!*" They all laughed. He went on. "I am quite serious! They shut down the Caribbean. The poor *Mejicanos* were actually making submarines to try and smuggle it in! But it became quite impossible to get any *kind* of volume past our astute law enforcement boys. So they had to shift their attention to the desert, all the way from the Gulf of Mexico to Baja California, and for a long time it was nigh impossible for border control to stop the flow. It was coming through in trucks, cars, campers, tunnels and hikers—you name it! Blow and crack were just flowing in over the border and law enforcement in California, Arizona, New Mexico and Texas were just overwhelmed."

Baseball Cap stroked his chin with mock thought and asked, "How do you know so much, Brad?"

More laughter, but not from Brad. "I had several Mexican friends who told me all about it. From the late eighties, for three decades, successive administrations were powerless before the deluge of illegal immigrants and cocaine: crack and blow, and eventually heroin too. And obviously, the more Mexican immigrants they had here, the bigger their distribution networks. And we, the rich glitterati, or should I say *you* the rich glitterati, could indulge your passion for snorting to the full, with ever declining prices to boot!"

I was listening to what he was saying, and my mind was beginning to race ahead. It was true that in the '80s, between them, Florida and Texas had managed largely to shut down the Colombian drug cartels' access to the States via the Caribbean. It had been partly that which had allowed the Mexicans to take over the traffic, and Sinaloa to rise to its present dominance. First they had seized control of distribution across the border, and then manufacturing itself. They had simply shifted their focus, as Brad was saying, from sea and air across the Caribbean, to land distribution through, over and under the Mexican border.

Brad was going on. "But now, thanks to Mr. Strange-Hair Trump, Mexican immigration is down by somewhere between fifty and sixty percent! It's outrageous! And with it the supply of blow and crack has dropped through the floor, and, naturally, the prices have started creeping up. I tell you, partying just *ain't* fun no more."

The blonde squealed, "My God! We'll all have to go back to champagne again!"

"My *darling!*" Brad gasped. "I never *left* it, it is the perfect accompaniment to a good old snort!"

"*Allegedly!*" cried Baseball Cap, and received a chorus of approval, like he'd said something witty:

"*Allegedly!*"

"*Allegedly!*"

"Oh, absolutely! *Allegedly!*"

And they all fell about.

The waiter brought me a salad of avocado and prawns and a glass of ice-cold Chablis. I sipped and stared up at the blind, starless sky. So that was what they were doing, then. The borders were closed, so they were resurrecting the spirit of Miguel Angel Felix Gallardo, *El Padrino.*

Now. Now it all made sense.

FOURTEEN

My case arrived, as promised, before breakfast the next morning. I checked it was all there, present and correct, strapped the P226 under my arm in the leather holster, and strapped the Fairbairn and Sykes to my right calf, with the sheath inside my boot. For now I was on recon, and the Sig Sauer and the knife would do just fine. Later, when I moved to execute the plan, if I needed more firepower, Ehrenberg, in Arizona, was little more than two hundred miles away on the I-10.

And the I-10 was what I took after a quick breakfast of espresso and croissants. Named here the Christopher Columbus Transcontinental Highway, it cut through Los Angeles as far as Beaumont, then continued through the Coachella Valley, past Palm Springs and through Thousand Palms to Indio, where it turned east through the desert, toward the Colorado River, Ehrenberg, and Phoenix.

It was a hundred-and-thirty-mile drive to Indio, and I took it easy, enjoying the California weather. I arrived shortly before eleven AM and took Highway 111 south and east through Thermal and Mecca, into ever more wild, apocalyptic desert landscapes: gray dust and sand, peppered with palms and what looked like acacias, struggling to survive in a dry, semi-toxic environment where the only water came from a lake that should never have existed, and was every day more poisonous.

I followed the road on, through a landscape of desolate, ruined and crumbling marinas and holiday resorts, stark and corroded under the Sonoran, Colorado Desert sun.

Eventually I came to a fork in the road, where an expanse of dry, yellow grass stretched down to the water, and far across the lake I could see the misty forms of the Santa Rosa Mountains. I stopped at the intersection and observed a couple of peeling, eroded signs that advertised new homes for sale. It didn't look like many people had taken up the offer—aside from the Central Intelligence Agency, that was.

There was a green sign that said the road was called Mecca Avenue. I drove down it for a couple of minutes, slow, looking around me, studying the surrounding area. The road was flanked by damaged and dying acacias, occasional oaks, and, scattered here and there across the dust and the dry grass, the ubiquitous palms. There was, despite the desert nature of the area, plenty of cover, especial for a nocturnal assault.

Soon, as I approached the water's edge, one and two-story houses began to appear. They were rundown, dilapidated, overgrown with untended trees and shrubs. They all looked uninhabited. The power lines were supported on old wooden pylons, and on many the cables had snapped and dangled, lifeless down the poles.

After a quarter of a mile the road turned sharp left, and here, on the corner, was a large house of recent construction, with a high perimeter wall. On the inside of the wall, tall palms grew and looked well-kept. I estimated the size of the entire place, including the surrounding gardens, at about a hundred yards by seventy-five. At a quick mental estimate that put it at about twenty-two thousand five hundred square feet.

The walls were too high to see over and the big, steel gates in the south wall were solid, and offered no view of the interior. What was clear was that there was an abundance of trees on the inside, but whether they were all palms, or whether there was foliage closer to the ground, was impossible to tell.

I drove around for a while: Damascus Avenue, Tripoli, Algeria... Perhaps they had wanted to evoke *A Thousand and One Nights*, but with the desolation and the inescapable feeling of a post-apocalyptic desert waste-land, all those names managed to suggest was the devastation of the Middle East, right here in California.

I made my way back to Highway 111 and drove slowly back to Mecca, where the fondness for Middle Eastern names continued. But unlike what I had seen of that other Mecca, where Kaaba was, here the streets were wide and well-kept, clean and orderly—with very few people on them.

I drove about for a bit until finally, on the corner of Date Palm Street and Seventh Street, I found Mecca Palms Realtors, pulled over and killed the engine. I stepped into the growing heat and the sunshine, crossed the broad sidewalk and pushed through the plate-glass doors.

There were two people sitting at wooden desks, a man in back in a blue suit with the kind of heavy-rimmed glasses nobody wears anymore, and an attractive, middle-aged woman with a white lace blouse and a blue suit, and the kind of reading glasses that make a lady look like a librarian with interesting secrets. They both looked up as I came in, and the woman smiled.

"Good morning, how may I help you?"

I jabbed my thumb in the direction of the lake. "I was just looking around Salton Sea. Biggest lake in California. Cryin' shame state it's in. Land down there must be dirt cheap. What you got for sale on the waterfront?"

She made an expression that wanted to be a smile but was more like a wince.

"We don't actually have a lot. What did you have in mind?"

I snorted. "I'd buy the whole darned thing if it was available. I only saw one house that showed signs of habitation. Down the bottom of Abu Dabi Drive or some shit, don't mind my language, miss."

She fixed her smile and blinked a few times. "Mecca," she said. "Mecca Avenue."

"Who owns that?"

"Well, I am not absolutely sure. The land was sold privately. The buyer had a lot of money but refused to go through an agent. We thought it was a developer, didn't we, Phil?"

She didn't look at him, but he nodded and smiled. "Uh-huh."

"Then they just tore down the old building and built that vast *palace* in a matter of six months. *We* thought it would be the first of many, didn't we, Phil?"

"Uh-huh."

"But it wasn't. There has been no movement since. Except that the owner seems to have moved in."

"The owner, huh? What kind of a guy is he? You think he might sell?

The man in back made a doubtful face and looked at the back of the woman's head, to see what she might say. She examined her pencil from various angles and made the same kind of doubtful face, like it had seeped through from the back of her head to her face.

"He is, curiously enough, an Arab. He has actually only been seen a couple of times, by the boy delivering the groceries, the satellite TV engineer, and who else, Phil?"

"Glen, when he went to fix their router."

She nodded. "And Glen. He is reclusive, for sure."

"A reclusive Ay-rab, huh? Find all kinds in your backyard these days, and that's for sure!"

She leaned forward, her eyes wide and her eyebrows knit. She spoke quietly with elaborate lips, like she was mouthing the words instead of speaking them. "They say," she said, "that he has armed guards!"

"No! For cryin' out loud...!"

"Well *what* is he guarding that is *that* valuable, is what *I'd* like to know!"

"You have a point," I said. "Perhaps it's hisself? How many guys has he got there? What about dogs?"

"Mrs. Vanderveldt, that's Bobby's mom, the boy who delivers the groceries? She says that *he* says there are *a dozen* men there. They do two shifts, he says, twenty-four hours night and day."

"Holy cow!" I said, "You don't say! And I guess they have dogs and everything!"

"Dogs, really nasty ones, those Rottweilers? At least two of them, patrolling the grounds."

"Not a very friendly guy, and like you say, what has he got that is so valuable? You don't like to cast aspersions just because a man happens to be an Ay-rab, but all the same..." I didn't want to ask her about alarms because it might look too obvious, but I was hoping she'd go there herself. Instead all she said was, "Exactly!"

"These people, I have nothing against foreigners, mind," I said, holding up both hands, "We are all, after all, the children of immigrants..." They both made doubtful faces and I pressed on. "Though they were immigrants who built this country, not *destroyed* it! These people come here and they think it's like it was back home, where you can do as you please. But this is America. Here, you can shoot a man in self-defense, fair enough, but we don't take the law into our own hands. We install an alarm system, and we let the cops do their job, am I right?"

She sat up straight, wide-eyed. "Oh, but that's the thing, *they haven't!*"

I frowned. "Haven't what?"

"Installed an alarm system!"

Phil sat back in his chair, nodding knowingly. I muttered something about her kidding me and he waved a pencil at me.

"You know why, don't you?"

She ignored him and added, "My brother-in-law was on the construction team. Absolutely no alarm systems were installed."

I knew exactly why they hadn't, but I jerked my head at him and asked, "Why you reckon?"

"Because," he said, and pushed his glasses up his nose, "if they have an intruder, they want to deal with him their own way, and dump the body in the lake, no questions asked."

"Absolutely no alarm system," she repeated as though he hadn't spoken. "Video surveillance cameras, oh yes, plenty of them, but no alarm system."

I sighed and shook my head. "And then they call *us* lawless. But you say you don't have any properties on your books that I can look at right now?"

"Not actually *on* the lake..."

"And how did he get it, if you don't mind me asking?"

"Seems he approached the owner direct. Must have known him personally..."

Or accessed the land register, I thought.

"Well," I said. "I'll drop in again before I leave town. Meantime, let's just hope that ain't a darned bomb factory they're buildin' down there!"

They both watched me leave with alarmed faces and I made my way back to the Jeep. Phil had been right on the money about why they had no alarm system, but the woman had also been right that they had twenty-four-hour video surveillance. I had spotted the cameras mounted on the walls. Any attempt to break into that compound was going to be difficult, and met with extreme force.

And I still didn't know for sure that it was him in the house.

I crossed the sunny street. The midday temperatures were rising in the glare of the sun. I put on my shades and climbed into the cab of the Jeep. As I pulled away, south down Date Palm Avenue, toward the 111, I called Brigadier Alexander, "Buddy" Byrd.

"Yes."

"I've had a look at the place. It's a fortress. All you can see from the road is the walls and the outer perimeter cameras. I need a couple of flyovers and aerial photographs."

"OK, I'll arrange the flyover and email you the pictures. What about intel on what's inside?"

I shrugged as I crossed the Hammond Road roundabout and turned north onto the highway.

"So far the only people who have had access to the interior of the house are the delivery boy from the grocery store, the satellite TV engineer and the IT engineer, to fix their router. I don't see myself delivering groceries, so can we interfere with their electronics and have me drop in as an engineer?"

"You're talking about EMP weapons. Let me get back to you on that. We may be able to arrange something. The only other alternative would be to enlist the aid of the electric company, and that's not going to happen. The FBI and the CIA can do that, but we can't."

"You have access to an EMP generator?"

If I sounded incredulous it was because I was. That technology was little short of science fiction.

"Maybe. We have a range of weapons under development, and one of them is an EMP generator. It hasn't been tested in the field yet..."

"How big is the damned thing, sir? Last thing I heard they were being flown around in jumbo jets."

He laughed. "They've been shrinking. We can fit one with a modest range into the back of a Dodge RAM."

"What's a modest range?"

"About half a mile."

"Jesus! Are you serious?"

"Of course I'm serious, Bauer."

Of course he was. He was always serious.

"When will you know if we can use it?"

"I'll have to talk to a couple of people and get back to you tonight."

"If we have access to this thing, maybe I won't need to recon the inside. I might move straight to the execution phase."

"Hmm..." He sounded doubtful. "We'll talk about

it. Anything else?"

"No, just get me the flyover pictures ASAP."

"You'll have them this evening."

I hung up and cruised the valley, toward Indio, where I would join the I-10, west and north bound. EMPs were among those weapons, like lasers or microwave rays, that you always associated with science fiction. You heard that there were boys at the Skunk Works, or at White Sands, who were working on them and developing them, though you never really believed it would come to anything. But, I reminded myself, that was also true of stealth technology not so long ago. Now it was a part of the standard arsenal.

An EMP that could be loaded into the back of a RAM, and had a range of half a mile, would be one hell of a weapon. I just wondered what the power source would be. One thing was for sure: You wouldn't be plugging it into your car battery. I figured they'd be pre-charged cells, or batteries, good for a single discharge.

I'd have to wait and see.

I got back to the Hotel California after lunch, so I went to the bar, climbed on a stool and asked the Australian kid in the burgundy waistcoat if he could wrangle me a steak sandwich and a dry martini. He said he could and fixed the martini before disappearing to find the steak.

I had taken my first sip and bobbed the olive a couple of times when I felt a presence next to me. I looked up and saw a woman who was on the wow side of good-looking. She was leaning with her elbows on the bar and smiling at me.

"Did you scare away the waiter?"

"Yeah. I sent him to get me a steak sandwich. He promised to come back, though."

She nodded at my drink. "That looks like exactly what I need."

"I'd let you have mine, but I already bobbed the olive. Have a peanut." I slid the bowl of peanuts over and smiled at her for the first time. "Hard day at the office?"

"Something like that. I'm in real estate, and the market is just going crazy at the moment. I had some clients I was supposed to meet today. We're talking big, big numbers. And they just never showed up. No call, no message, nada."

"That sucks." I jerked my head at the returning barman, who was carrying my steak sandwich. "But here comes the cavalry. Thanks..." The last was directed at Bruce, the boy from Oz, and I added, "And fix the lady a vodka martini, shaken, not stirred."

She had the good grace to giggle and held out her hand. "Miriam Grant."

I took her hand. She had a good, firm grip. "Oliver Frost."

I bit into my sandwich, wondering if I was going to invite her to dinner.

FIFTEEN

She was funny, beautiful and great company, and for those reasons I decided I could not invite her to dinner, or indeed see her again. At least not until the job was done.

While I finished my sandwich, she asked me what I was doing in LA. I told her I was on holiday, and, to deflect the conversation, I asked her about real estate in Southern California. Then I sat and listened with half an ear, while I thought about the EMP and tried to devise a plan B if I wasn't able to knock out the villa's electronics.

But all the while I couldn't quite silence that other part of my brain that was thinking that Miriam was witty, intelligent and engaging, and I was enjoying being with her. She wasn't babbling. She kept drawing me back from my thoughts because she said things that were perceptive and worth listening to. And that was when I made my decision not to see her again. The last thing I needed was that kind of distraction.

I wiped my mouth and fingers on a paper napkin and drained my drink. When I looked at her I could see she had read the gesture and was disappointed.

"Gotta go," I said.

"Yeah." She shrugged. "Me too, I guess. Thanks for

the drink." She slid gracefully off her stool and hesitated. "How long are you in town?"

"Couple of days…"

She made a rueful face. "But I guess you're real busy, being on holiday." There was an edge of irony to her voice and for a moment I wasn't sure what to say, but she laid a hand on my arm and laughed. "Don't sweat it. I'm just pulling your leg. I need to get my head down and find some new buyers anyway. Imperial County is a hard sell."

Something clicked in my head and I frowned.

"Imperial County? That's on the border, right? Calexico…?"

"That's the one, nestled snug between Arizona and Mexicali. Exactly where nobody wants to live." She didn't hide the sarcasm in her voice. "That's why these buyers were such a godsend…" She patted my arm. "Anyway, look, I have bored you more than enough with my silly problems. Thanks for the drink, and you have a real swell holiday…"

We had been making our faltering way toward the lobby as we spoke. Now we stood outside the elevators and I stopped her as she made to leave.

"Hang on, Miriam, you haven't bored me at all. Look, are you free tonight?"

She smiled but made a show of checking her schedule on her cell. "Well, I am, as a matter of fact, from seven thirty onward. Why, what did you have in mind?"

"Dinner. You know a nice restaurant? Maybe you can convince me to buy Imperial County."

She laughed and agreed to pick me up in a taxi at seven thirty.

I watched her walk across the lobby with a swing of her hips that most women don't remember how to do anymore. She became a black silhouette against the bright glare of the plate-glass doors, and then she was gone.

I rode the elevator to my floor, thinking about Imperial County, tucked snug between Arizona and Mexicali. The main town down there was El Centro, which was, as the name suggested, roughly at the center of a broad expanse of farmland and ranches that extended all the way down to Calexico and the Mexican border. It was a no-brainer that farmland and ranches would have large barns appropriate for storing bulky produce and keeping it dry and safe from the elements. So, reaching a little, it might make sense for anyone running any kind of contraband from Mexico into California to want to buy real estate in that area.

But that was the kind of long-standing, old-school thinking that belonged in the last three decades of the last century. In the last twenty years things had changed a lot. Cocaine and then heroin had become the main products to cross the border, pushing the cartels' turnover up into the hundreds of millions, even billions of dollars every year. And they were developing ever more innovative and creative ways of importing and storing their goods.

The safe house by the lake, the Yemeni guys in Paris, the CIA... They were all parts of a puzzle that did not fit into the old model. Something else was going on. Something completely different.

Maybe I was way off track with Miriam. Maybe I was just giving myself an excuse to take out a beautiful woman. God knew I had had a lack of that kind of thing in recent years. But still, I thought, her buyers had made me curious. She might provide useful information. I had nothing to lose by talking to her.

That was what I told myself.

I spent a couple of hours in the hotel gym then went up and showered cold-hot-cold, and when I stepped out, toweling myself dry, my cell was ringing.

"Yeah, Frost."

There was a short laugh at the other end. It was the brigadier.

"We'll make a Cold War operative of you yet, Mr. Frost."

"Funny."

"Check your emails. I've sent you satellite and fly-over pictures of the house and compound."

"Cool, what about the other thing?"

"I can get one to you by tomorrow. We have to bring it down from Canada."

"Canada? Why?"

"That's where they're developing it, Frost. It is still experimental, but I am told the results so far have been very good. This is a chance to try it in the field. Your observations will be very useful."

"Oh." I nodded, then shook my head, like he could see the expression on my face. "That's great."

"Now pay attention. About half a mile southeast of you is East 2nd Street Parking. You walk north on South Olive for about two hundred and twenty yards. Then turn right onto West 2nd street. Proceed for another half a mile until you reach the intersection with South San Pedro Street. There you will see, directly in front of you, a multi-story car park."

"Or parking lot."

"Precisely. Because you Americans like to be confusing wherever possible, East 2nd Street Parking in fact has its entrance on South San Pedro Street. Enter, take the lift—the elevator to you…"

"I lived eight years in England, sir. I know what a lift is, and a rubber and Durex."

"Splendid, all useful stuff. So you take the lift to the seventh floor, that is the penultimate floor, one from the last."

"I get it, the penultimate floor, number seven."

"There you will find a Dodge RAM 3500. In the rear there will be a large metal case, bolted to the truck."

"And that will be the business."

"Yes. Tomorrow morning you will receive a special delivery, an envelope with the keys to the truck and the operating instructions for the machine. Any questions?"

"No, none at all."

"Good. I'll leave you to it. Enjoy your evening." I was about to hang up when he stopped me.

"Just one thing, before you go. Our Yemeni friends seem to have disappeared off the radar, along with Muller. It is just possible they will turn up there. But if they don't, it could be handy…"

"If I tried to find out where they are. Yeah, I planned to do that anyway."

"Good man. Let me know how you get on."

I hung up thinking to myself that however long I worked with Brits, I would never get used to how they talked about war, killing and torture like they were making arrangements for the vicar's tea party: "Just dropped a couple of ten megaton nuclear devices on Moscow, old chap." "Super, did you happen to notice if there were any survivors?" "Not a one, old bean." "Topping. Cup of tea?" "Love one!"

With that surreal dialogue playing in my head, I

got dressed and made my way down to meet Miriam. She was already in the lobby when I got there, and stood on tiptoes to give me a kiss on the cheek.

"I don't know what kind of thing you like…"

She said it as she linked her arm through mine. I didn't let her finish.

"Everything," I said, "However big, however small, I'll eat it."

Her eyes went wide and her cheeks turned pink. "My goodness! Well in that case we'll go to the Perch. It's not far, it's on a rooftop and they have live music. You'll love it. They have big and small things to eat."

As it turned out it was a ten-minute walk, fifteen if you were strolling on a pleasant summer evening with a beautiful woman on your arm. We cut through the Angel's Knoll gardens, down the steps beside the weird old tram, and it was on the corner of South Hill Street and West 5th.

It was not like any restaurant I'd been in before: a weird but engaging mixture of Rick's Bar in Casablanca, a Parisian café and a palace from a distant planet in *Star Wars*. I liked it.

We sat on the terrace, overlooking downtown Los Angeles and drinking very good martini cocktails. She had the baked brie with fennel, apple and pecan slaw to start with, I had the *moules* in saffron sauce and we shared a bottle of Brut Cava from Penedes. For the main course she had pan-roasted salmon with eggplant purée, and I had the *filet mignon au poivre* with asparagus and mushrooms. You can't drink sparkling Cava with peppered steak, so I ordered a big, beefy Barolo.

Right then, under the Californian night sky, sipping ice-cold Cava and eating saffron mussels, while looking at Miriam in the wavering light of the small firepit beside us, every one of my senses was acutely alive, and enjoying itself.

Miriam sipped her wine and studied me, smiling, over the rim of her glass.

"So, what do you do for a living, Mr. Frost?"

I tipped a mussel into my mouth from its shell and raised an eyebrow at her.

"I'm a hired assassin." Her eyes went wide and she laughed. "I work for a secret organization. We take out the very worst of society: men who wear man-buns, kids who wear their pants below their buttocks, women who dress up as vaginas in public and then talk about it in monologues, and all vegans, irrespective of whether they are beautiful people or not."

Her eyes went even wider and her jaw went slack. Her glass, halfway to her mouth, stayed there.

"My God!" she said. "You are primeval!"

"Probably. I'm hoping the pan-roasted salmon will keep you here long enough to prove that I'm actually a nice guy."

She giggled and her glass finished its journey to her mouth. When she put it down again her voice was a little husky.

"Oh, I have no problem with primeval."

"I'm glad to hear it." I mopped saffron sauce with a hunk of warm bread. "Did your buyers ever show up?"

She shook her head, then frowned. "It was all very odd, Oliver. They claimed to be a consortium of developers. They wanted to buy property along the California-Mexico border to build a couple of holiday resorts. They seemed to believe that relations between Mexico and the US were going to suddenly, magically improve and property values would suddenly rocket. I thought they were out of their minds, but hey! That's for their market researchers to tell them, right? Not me."

I made a face like an intelligent, reasonably well-informed guy might make, who doesn't understand a thing. Then I asked her, "Mexicans?"

She made an expression that was almost a wince. "I don't *think* so. I never actually met them. We exchanged a few emails and talked on the phone a couple of times..."

I gave a small laugh. "I mean, were they called Zambada, or Guzman, Moreno...?"

I saw a tiny twitch of her brows. "No, the one I spoke to was actually called Omar."

"Omar? That's an Arab name."

"Yeah." She laughed. "But sometimes Latin Americans have weird names, don't they? Like Hector, Ovid, Nemesio, and wasn't there some notorious Panamanian called Omar Torres or something?"

I nodded. "Torrijos, General Omar Torrijos, commander of the Panamanian National Guard under Noriega. That's true. So this guy was also called Omar? What was his surname?"

"That wasn't Latino at all. Qasim. Omar Qasim, sounds more Arabic that Latino."

I gave her a lopsided smile. "Yeah, Omar. It means flourishing, long lived, and Qasim means, one who distributes. I think somebody might have been having an erudite joke at your expense."

"Oh, my God, you speak Arabic? Who *are* you?"

We both laughed. "I told you, I'm an international assassin."

The waiter took away our plates and delivered Miriam's salmon and my steak. He let me try my wine, then, when I nodded approval, poured me a glass and left.

"Seriously, though," I went on, "I have worked in Arab countries for a while and I picked up some Arabic along the way. Qasim is a common surname and it means 'he who distributes.' Coming from a guy who wants to buy extensive farming property on the California-Mexico border, sounds to me like nominative determinism."

"Say what now?" She stuck a piece of salmon in her mouth and sighed. "Sooo good!"

"Nominative determinism is a theory that says people gravitate toward jobs that fit their names, like Judge Laws, or a guy called Salmon might become a fish-monger..."

"And He Who Distributes would become a drug trafficker."

"I'm being facetious, but yeah. Especially if he's spinning a yarn that relations between Mexico and the US are about to get better. I don't think the president got that memo."

"So fake name?"

I shrugged. "Who knows? How far did you get in your dealings?"

"I spoke to a few people who had property and lands down near the border, and arranged to meet Mr. Qasim and his associates today, but they never showed and never got back to me."

I concentrated on my steak and my wine for a while. The meat was tender and succulent, and the wine was superb. She was quiet too, focusing on her fish. After a moment she looked up and frowned.

"You seriously think they might have been dealers? You think I should inform the cops, or the FBI?"

I gave my head a little tilt. "Any Arab businessman

investing in the States would be aware of the tensions with Mexico at the moment, especially the issues with the wall. He'd be better off investing almost anywhere else in the country, rather than the Mexican border. The only financial attraction I can think of in that particular area, is the cocaine and heroin routes that run through it. And unless I am very much mistaken, it is going to get a damn sight more difficult to get that stuff through in the next few years."

"Unless you have property on the border..."

"If you have property on this side, with a nice, big barn, and property on that side, you can build a tunnel. They have builders and engineers at their disposal."

"Jesus! How do you know this stuff?" I smiled and she laughed. "I know! I know! You're an international assassin!"

"Yeah, I also read the papers and watch *Narcos*."

"Ah! Fibber! What do you really do for a living, Oliver, seriously?"

"Nothing interesting. I'm an electronics technician."

She drained her glass and held it out to me. I refilled it and she said, "You're a liar."

"I am?"

"Hotel California, those casual clothes you're wearing are expensive, the way you talk... Nope. You are not an electronics technician."

I had been sloppy and overconfident, and now I was going to have to rectify that, and fast. I gave my head a twitch and put an ironic smile on my face.

"OK, you got me. I was in the *Army* for a long time, since I was seventeen. While I was there I studied electronics and became something of an expert. When I left, I set up a small company that makes a small device, which I patented, which allows highly sophisticated nocturnal telescopic sights to gauge distance by using an invisible UVA laser. I supply the Army and I make lots of money."

"Well, I am impressed. It's a lot more exciting than selling real estate."

I snorted. "You may live to regret those words. If Omar gets in touch again, I would think very carefully about how you proceed."

She hesitated. She looked worried but tried to hide it.

"If he does, if he gets in touch, can I call you? I know it's stupid but..." She shrugged. "I haven't really got anyone else I can talk to..."

"Really?"

"That sounds lame and needy, right? Oh God, that is typical me..."

I shook my head. "Not at all. Feel free to call me. Even if Omar doesn't get in touch."

Her cheeks colored. "Shucks, what's a girl to say?"

I refilled my glass and arched an eyebrow at it. "Yes?" I suggested.

She giggled. "OK, yes."

Later that night, even as a couple of miles away, the Von KleinSmid Center carillon rang out the witching hour, I kissed Miriam goodnight and helped her into a taxi. She smiled at me a little resentfully, and said, with an edge to her voice, "You're a real gentleman, for such a primeval guy."

"I want you to respect me in the morning. Can I call you?"

"I'm not sure I will respect you, but yeah. Call me."

And I stood and watched the cab disappear into the

night.

SIXTEEN

I sat at the desk in my room, sipping whisky and scowling. The aerial and satellite photographs showed what was basically a small, military compound loosely disguised as a house. It was an oblong, roughly one hundred yards long and seventy yards across, with a big, steel gate at the southern end, facing the lake.

Within the perimeter wall there was an L-shaped house, with the long upright lying east to west, and the short foot section rising toward the north. And where the upright was just two stories high, the foot of the L formed a tower three stories high. In the nook formed by the right angle of the L there was a patio, with the predictable barbecue, garden table and deck chairs. Beyond it, to the north, was an expanse of lawn, a swimming pool and a tennis court.

At the front of the house, a straight gravel drive led from the gate to two arabesque arches which gave on to a shallow porch and a front door. Clusters of tall palm trees stood at each corner of the house and shaded the eastern extreme of the pool. There was no vegetation close to the perimeter walls, nor abutting the house, so anyone coming over the wall would be immediately visible.

Visible to whom was the worrying part. I counted

a total of eleven men armed with assault rifles. One at each corner of the perimeter wall made four, two at the front door, by the Arab arches, made six, three on the roof made nine, and two more on the tower made it eleven. Plus there were two Rottweilers roaming free, just to make it fun.

The billion-dollar question right then was, were these men CIA, Sinaloa or al-Qaeda?

If they were Sinaloa or al-Qaeda I could take them out without consequences. If they were CIA I, and Cobra, would face serious problems.

In addition I had to assume that there were at least two guards inside the house, plus debriefing agents, negotiators, Sinaloa and al-Qaeda visitors, cooks, cleaners and girls: possibly in excess of twenty people.

Impossible.

Assuming I could knock out their lights, electronic surveillance, telephone and radio, and I could get myself up on the perimeter wall, with night-vision goggles I could take out two, maybe three of the guards, but immediately after that I would be trapped in a firefight with at least ten armed professionals. Professionals I might not be allowed to shoot, even if they tried to shoot me. That was something I was going to have to think about.

Meantime, I figured I had two options—either I went in, or Ben-Amini came out. On the face of it, him coming out was the simpler of the two options, until you thought it through. When you thought it through, two major problems arose: one, actually finding a way to get him to leave, when you had three major organizations committed to keeping him hidden in that house; and two, if you did manage to make him leave, he would have at least as much protection as he had now, and maybe more.

Because right now they believed he was hidden and secure, but if he had to step out, they would be on high alert.

Which left going in.

I stood, took my glass of whisky and carried it to the window. Los Angeles sparkled and gleamed as far as the eye could see, a shimmering matrix of lights, concealing the seething mass of greed and power, and sordid humanity within.

Going in.

In my mind's eye I saw Sergeant Bradley, the Kiwi, lying in the mud of the Colombian rainforest, talking to Lieutenant Walker, hissing at him under his breath. Walker always wanted to complicate things, blow things up and kill everybody. He was good, but he was crazy too. The Sarge was saying to him, "Keep it simple, always go back to basics, feint to the front, strike at the flank..."

We had feinted to the front and struck at the flank, and it had been a success: we had taken the fortified lab, and then Walker had killed everybody and blown up the compound, the arsenal and the half-ton of coke they had stored there.

Feint to the front. So I needed a distraction at the main gate, to draw most of the guards there, immediately after taking out their electronics with the EMP. *Then* go over the wall, either at the side or the back. From the wall take out one or both of the guys on the tower. Then drop to the ground and take cover behind the nearest palm trees. Take out the dogs, go in and take out Mohammed Ben-Amini. Be home in time for martinis and dinner with Miriam.

I smiled. I knew it wouldn't be that simple. I knew I probably wouldn't be coming home at all, let alone for martinis and Miriam. But if I took out Ben-Amini, and gave peace to the ghosts of Al-Landy, that would be enough for me.

I drained my glass and went to bed.

Next morning, I was up at six AM and took the Wrangler for a spin, two and a half hours east of LA to Ehrenberg, just over the Arizona county line, on the banks of the Colorado River. There I had breakfast and spent an hour examining guns and ammunition. I came away with a hefty rucksack, a Heckler and Koch 416, and a Smith and Wesson 500, fifty cal with a box of 500-grain magnum cartridges. I put a couple of other things in my kitbag too, including a suppressor, a telescopic night-sight and a sixty-five-pound takedown bow with twelve aluminum, broadhead hunting arrows. Because there is nothing better for a silent kill in the dark.

When I got back to the hotel, the girl on reception told me I had a package. It was an A4 manila envelope which I took back out to the Jeep and opened. It contained the key to a Dodge RAM, another key to a padlock, and a set of printed instructions, with photographs and diagrams, that showed how to trigger a blast of electromagnetic waves.

I tucked it in my jacket pocket, fired up the Wrangler and set off toward the East 2nd Street Parking, situated, as Buddy Byrd had said, on South San Pedro. I got my ticket at the gate and climbed the ramp to the seventh floor, where I found a space and parked, then stepped out into the concrete gloom. There must have been a hundred or a hundred and fifty cars there, all shrouded in half-light. A lot of them were trucks and SUVs. We like our big cars in this big country.

I took a stroll, pressing the open button on my key, and pretty soon I heard the bleep and saw the flash of lights on a big, bad Dodge RAM 3500, thoughtfully sprayed in dark blue, for minimum visibility at night.

The back contained a large steel box, about four foot square, with a padlock. I returned to the Jeep, collected my morning's purchases and dumped them in the back of the RAM, then climbed in the cab, rolled down the ramp, paid my dues and pulled out onto South San Pedro again. A couple of blocks up North Los Angeles and I merged onto the 101, and the San Bernardino Freeway. I looked at my watch. It was closing on one PM.

I took it easy, with the windows down and the Eagles and Creedence loud on the sound system. At Beaumont I pulled into the Shell gas station, bought a couple of takeout burgers and a bottle of water, and filled four one-gallon cans with gas, which I stowed in the back. A little less than an hour later I pulled into Indio and made my way to the Coachella Farming Supplies store, at the Home Depot Shopping Mall. There I bought two one-hundred-weight sacks of sodium nitrate, loaded it in the back of the RAM and continued on my way.

Ten minutes later I pulled out of Indio and onto the 111. The sun was inching toward mid-afternoon and the desert wind was warm, cruising through those same, familiar fields of dates, grapes and other crops I could not identify, struggling against the dry, gray earth.

I came finally to Mecca Avenue, where Mohammed's safe house was. Or, at least, where we were all assuming it was. But I didn't turn in. I kept going, slow and steady at forty miles an hour, until I came to the end of the complex of chalets and bungalows that had, when the lake was originally created, been the seedlings of a holiday resort. There, well out of view of Mohammed's house, I turned off the road, bounced and jolted across the desert ground for a hundred yards, and wound up on Morraco Avenue, outside a ramshackle collection of barns, sheds and shacks, all built around a large house that was partially in ruins. The whole complex was set back about twenty yards from the road, with a big dusty yard to the side where there were two decomposing boats and an old, rusty Ford truck. None of which looked very functional. It was a place I had spotted last time I was there, and earmarked for future use.

I turned in, going slow to raise as little dust as I could, and pulled up behind the largest of the sheds. Then I climbed down to have a look around. The day was growing hot and I could feel the fine desert dust clinging to the perspiration on my brow. I walked to the big, old sliding door of the barn. It was made of wood attached to a steel frame. Some of the wooden slates had rotted over the years and I was able to peer inside. There were a few old drums, some wooden cubicles that might have been meant for horses, a handful of old tires and not much else.

The door was held closed by a padlock the size of my fist. It was corroded and rusted, and even with a gallon of oil and a set of lock picks, you'd never get it open. But the wood it was screwed to was so rotten a couple of thumps with a rock pulled it free. The door rolled open, I swung back into the cab of the RAM and drove it inside, where it was cool, shaded, and most important of all, out of sight.

I knew from the satellite photographs that Ben-Amini's safe house was a quarter of a mile away, and well within range of the EMP device. I spent the next hour examining that device and digesting the instructions. They weren't complicated. It came with four lithium ion batteries which could be used only once and then had to be recharged. They were three foot in length and weighed about fifteen pounds each. You slotted the battery into its housing, locked it with a clockwise twist, and then flipped the charge switch. You waited five minutes till a green light came on, and then pressed the red button. All electronic equipment in a radius of one mile—half a mile each way—would then instantly be fried. That would include, the instructions stressed, your own cell phone and the transport vehicle, unless they were properly insulated. It would also fry the instruments of any aircraft flying overhead.

Fortunately, a note appended to the instructions confirmed that the RAM's electronic systems were properly insulated, and if I left my cell in the cab, so would that be.

The next hour I spent carefully mixing the two hundred weight of ammonium nitrate with large amounts of gasoline, turning it into a thick, muddy sludge. That I packed tightly into four tough garden refuse sacks, each weighing about fifty-five pounds, and dumped the lot in back in the rear of the RAM. I also put together the bow and slipped six of the arrows through the straps on my rucksack.

That was about all the preparation I could do before dark. So I settled down, ate my burgers and slept for four hours. It was going to be a long night.

I awoke at nine in the pitch dark. I drank some water and pulled my night-vision goggles from my rucksack. I checked my P226, fitted the suppressor and slipped it under my arm. Then I loaded the Smith and Wesson and put it back in the rucksack.

I swung down from the cab, put the rucksack on my back and grabbed the 416. I rammed a magazine in, slung three more from my belt and put another three in the rucksack.

Then I pushed the door open, clambered back in the cab and moved slowly out of the barn. I didn't follow the roads. I left my lights off, stayed in low gear and rolled quietly over the dirt, at the back of the crumbling, empty houses, until I came to Damascus Avenue, which ran parallel to Mecca. Down at the end, Mohammed's safe house occupied the entire area between the two roads. I figured his compound was about eighty yards from where I was right then.

I pressed the gas gently, then went into neutral and let the truck freewheel silently forward till I was about forty yards away, and in the cover of a large acacia tree. There was no moon yet, but I could make out the dark bulk of the perimeter wall. I stopped, killed the engine and swung down from the cab. I climbed into the cargo bed and opened the EMP case, slammed in one of the batteries and set it to charge. I gave it five minutes, and when the green light came on I hit the button.

It was odd. Nothing happened, except that the glow from the safe house vanished. Other than that there was total silence and stillness.

I sprang down from the truck and hauled myself back into the cab, gunned the engine and let the weight of the vehicle carry me to the corner by the main gate of the house. Inside I could hear dogs howling and muffled voices, occasionally raised in shouts. They were Arab voices giving instructions.

In silence I made two running trips back and forth from the truck and stacked the four sacks of high explosive against the gate. Then I turned the truck around and pulled the Smith and Wesson from the rucksack. I took careful aim and hammered a five hundred grain round into the sacks. The detonation was massive. Four pounds of that mixture can blow an SUV apart. This was over two hundred pounds, and at forty feet in almost lifted the RAM off its wheels and tipped it over, but by that time I was already accelerating toward the back of the compound.

With my ears ringing I turned off the road and pulled in tight against the wall, about level with where the tower was, inside the compound. I jumped out, pulled on my night-vision goggles, slung the HK416 over my shoulder, grabbed the bow and clambered onto the roof of the truck. From there I jumped for the wall, pulled myself up and sat astride it, seeking the guards on the roof of the tower. I found one, a black silhouette against a green sky. There was a lot of shouting and screaming, and the guy I'd found kept running back and forth, like he didn't know where to go or what to do. I figured he was maybe sixty feet away. It wasn't an easy shot, but I was good with a bow, this kill had to be silent, and this was the only way.

I knew at some point he'd freeze, so I drew, waited and when he did I loosed the arrow and skewered him through the chest. He went down and I nocked another barb, then waited. I didn't have to wait long. I heard a shout above all the other shouts and his pal came into sight, probably wondering what the hell had happened. I pulled and loosed in one fluid movement, and the shaft thudded home through his sternum. Two down.

I looked into the shadows of the garden, saw everything was as it should be, and dropped.

SEVENTEEN

I made it to the first clump of date palms. The guards couldn't see or hear me, on account of they had no lights and no cameras, but the dogs could smell me. They came thundering across the lawn like two green daemons let loose from hell. I knelt, held the Sig out at arm's length and waited till I could see their eyes. By that time I could practically smell their breath. I squeezed off one round that took off the nearest dog's skull, and by the time I shot the second one he was just three feet away and my heart was hammering in my throat.

By now the guys had sorted through the rubble and had seen that no vehicle had collided with the gate, but a bomb had been deliberately placed there, and they had realized that the loss of light was connected to that event. In fact, it was dawning on them that their security had been breached and they were under serious attack. But they couldn't see their attackers anywhere. So they were now running around like headless chickens and I could hear one of them, probably their CO, bellowing for somebody to get a damned flashlight.

By that time I had dropped the bow, holstered the Sig and stepped out from behind the palms with the HK416 at my shoulder. The pool was a strange, luminous, liquid green surrounded by black lawn. The white walls of the house also shone a luminous green in what little starlight there was, and at either side of the house I saw two men come running. I figured they were returning to their posts at the back of the house.

Above, on the lower roof terrace, I saw another two men, peering into the dark below, searching for an attacker. They couldn't see me yet, and I had to act fast, before they did. The first shot I fired would reveal where I was, and before I did that, I wanted to be out of the line of sight of the guys on the roof. So I pulled the Fairbairn and Sykes from my boot and sprinted for the next clump of palms, almost level with the side of the house. The guy who was running up heard my footfall, stopped and squinted into the blackness. He saw me, but by then I was already on top of him and as he opened his mouth to shout I rammed the blade of the fighting knife through his throat and sliced savagely to the side. He was half decapitated and a fountain of blood sprayed high into the air.

I stepped in close as his knees folded and lowered him softly to the ground. I dropped to one knee, up against the wall of the house, slipped the knife in my boot and rasped, "*Tati! Tati!*" *Come* in Arabic.

The guy who'd been hurrying up the far side of the house appeared, eerie in green and black, running toward me, calling "'*Ayn 'ant?*"

He was asking where I was. He never found out. I put two rounds through his head and blew what brains he had across the paved patio. And the guys upstairs were shouting and screaming so loud, nobody heard the suppressed shots.

The plate-glass patio doors were open. I made for

them, but a sudden thought made me retrace my steps and search in the pockets of the guy I'd just shot. I found his cell phone, then moved back into the house, closed the doors and locked them. I made first for the kitchen and examined the stove. It was gas, as I'd hoped, and that made me smile. I opened all the taps, called myself on his cell, then I left his cell by the stove. I stepped out, closed the kitchen door and sprinted up the stairs with the assault rifle at my shoulder. Upstairs was where I figured Mohammed would be.

Even with night-vision goggles, it was hard to see. There was no moon outside, and no artificial light for miles around. What I could make out, in the black and green nightmare world, was that the stairs made a dogleg and rose to a broad landing. On the left as I came up there was a door which I figured led into the rooms below the tower. Ahead of me there was a long passage into darkness, and on the right, at the far end of the landing, was another door. There was also another staircase, presumably leading up to the tower.

A door crashed open up there, voices shouted to each other and boots tramped. I had killed the two on the roof of the tower, so these must be the three or four men from the roof terrace, who'd gone up and discovered the bodies. I sprinted, my heart pounding hard. I needed to catch them while they were still in the narrow stairwell. They couldn't see me, but they heard me. Muzzles flashed green in the blackness. I dropped to the floor and snaked around the bannisters. The flashes from their automatic weapons made it impossible to see. So I opened up and emptied the magazine, thirty rounds in two and a half seconds into the confined space. If I didn't get them, the ricochets would. Their grunts and cries said I was right.

Mohammed could be in any of a number of rooms, but my gut had told me from the word go that he would be in the lower part of the tower, isolated from and protected by the rest of the house. I didn't have time to confirm the kills in the stairwell, but I was pretty sure they were either dead or dying. I scrambled to my feet and crossed the landing in three long strides, slamming in a new magazine as I went.

One round took care of the lock. I kicked in the door and stood back as a hail of lead tore splinters from the wood and gauged plaster from the walls. I lay flat, eased around the doorjamb and, as the volley of fire paused, I saw two men in suits kneeling with weapons at their shoulders, waiting. They were as blind as everybody else, except me.

Two controlled burst of three rounds took them down. Then I was on my feet and in the room, searching.

It was a sitting room with a table, chairs, a sofa, armchairs and a TV. A window showed me men running outside. It would be moments before they were swarming up the stairs.

I saw another door, figured it was a bedroom, and I kicked it open. There was a man huddled on the floor, whimpering and covering his head. I took a handful of his hair and dragged him to his feet. I snarled in his ear.

"I can do a lot worse than kill you. Cooperate and I won't hurt you."

I ran him out of the room, toward the door to the landing. He was sobbing and burbling, begging me not to hurt him. Voices and running boots told me my escape route was cut off. I had an immediate choice to make: kill the man I had found, assuming him to be Mohammed Ben-Amini, and then try to fight my way out, or try to take him alive and interrogate him, but risk getting killed in the process and failing in the mission. At a rough estimate I figured I had killed nine of them, which left anything from four to eight more.

I spun him to face me and drove my right fist into his solar plexus. He went down and I knew he wasn't going to get up and go anywhere anytime soon. Three strides took me to the top of the stairwell, pulling my cell from my pocket. The voices and the running boots were loud, reaching the bottom of the stairs.

I found my last missed call and dialed the number of the phone that was sitting beside the stove in the kitchen. It rang once.

Explosions, close up, do not roar as they do in movies. It is not a deep rumble, like a volcano. It is a hard, jarring flat smack of air. The house shook, plaster fell from the walls and the ceiling, glass shattered from the windows. I leaned over the bannisters and started picking them off with short, controlled blasts as they reeled and tried to make sense of what was happening. I could see six men in panicking confusion. I took out two, moved down the first few steps and took out another two with short staccato bursts of fire. The last two were falling over each other, scrambling to run. I took one down and the other got away.

I went after him, leapfrogging the bodies that littered the stairs. He was running, a green and black figure panicking in a green and black nightmare. He ran blind toward the glow of the plate-glass doors and the pool outside. He could hear me and turned toward me, stupidly staggering backward. He hit a coffee table and fell. I drew level and stepped on his hand.

"How many left?"

"Just me, please sir, mister, just me, please, I have…"

Wrong answer. I shot him once in the head and ran back up the stairs to find Mohammed.

I found him on his hands and knees, vomiting as he tried to get to his feet. I helped him, with a hand to the scruff of his neck, and ran him across the landing and down the stairs to the front door and the gravel drive to the gate.

The improvised bomb had done a lot of damage. It had blown the gate off its runners, knocked down part of the wall, killed one of the guards, strewn rubble and debris across the lawn and even shattered the glass in the front door. We ran across the scene of devastation and stepped out onto Tripoli Drive. Mohammed was silent, aside from a slight whimpering. I dragged him around the corner and ran him, stumbling, the hundred yards toward where I had left the truck. In the distance I could hear the thud of a chopper. It might have been two.

I wrenched open the passenger door, shoved the 416 in Mohammed's face and growled, "Get in!"

He didn't argue. He clambered in while I rammed another battery into the EMP. Then I slipped in behind the wheel and, keeping the lights off, I rolled slowly away from the devastated compound. Every cell in my body, every neuron in my brain, was screaming at me to floor the pedal and get the hell out of there. But I kept it to no more than fifteen miles an hour, rolling across the dirt with the window open, so I could hear the approaching helicopters.

A flash of light in my mirror and I knew they had arrived at the house and were playing their spots over it. I glanced at Mohammed. He was staring at me in terror, but I could read his face. He was thinking that I was going so slow, he could jump from the cab and the choppers would save him.

Jeet kune do is my preferred fighting style. It is all about non-telegraphic, explosive speed. And your primary target is always the tip of the jaw. Hit that, and the fight is over. He never saw it coming. I smashed my fist into his chin, his eyes rolled up in his head and he slumped back in his seat.

That was when I looked in the mirror again and saw that one of the choppers was peeling away from the house, moving in what was promising to become a grid pattern, searching for whoever had devastated the house. I figured the other was on the radio, calling for ground reinforcements. I slammed on the brake, jumped from the cab and vaulted into the back of the truck. Five minutes had passed and the light was green. I slammed my fist on the red button. The spotlights disappeared and the thud of the choppers stopped.

The next thing was the almighty crash and scream of tortured steel as the two birds dropped out of the sky and hit the ground.

Then I got back in the cab, spun the wheel and made for the road. When I hit the blacktop I turned right for about half a mile or a little more, then turned left into the desert along Parkside Drive. I still had my lights off. I rolled along at five or six miles an hour. I wasn't in a hurry and I didn't want to draw any attention; not that there were many people out there to notice me.

About three quarters of a mile along the drive there was a dirt track I had seen on the satellite pictures. I found it and turned into it. One and a half miles due north, northwest across the open desert, the track led me to the Coachella Canal, or more precisely, to a dirt track that crossed a bridge over that canal. After that there was no road, no dirt track, no path. It was just desert, funneled into a shallow, broad canyon that grew narrower and deeper the farther in you drove.

A moon, in its first waxing, was morphing orange over the horizon on my right. What little light it gave showed the terrain ahead becoming impassable, strewn with boulders and pitted with holes. I stopped and killed the engine, swung down and walked around to the passenger side. There I wrenched open the door, took a handful of Mohammed and dragged him out of the cab. I slapped his face a couple of times to bring him round, then dropped him in the dirt.

I had taken my goggles off, but he still hadn't got a good look at me. Now he squinted at my face in the slowly growing light of the moon.

"Who are you?"

I hunkered down, got up close and let him study my face.

"You don't recognize me, Mohammed? I'm the guy who was going to execute you in the caves in the Sulaiman Mountains, before your pal Captain Hartmann came to your rescue."

His eyes went wide but all he said was, "Oh..."

I said, "Do you remember?"

"I remember you, and those other men. You are like machines. Killing machines."

I shook my head. "Do you remember the people, the children, the women, the mothers and fathers, the old people...? Do you remember all the people from Al-Landy?"

He pulled down the corners of his mouth, hunched

his shoulders and spread his hands. "They were *kafir*. They had heard the word of God, but still they reject him. I had been, personally, to teach and instruct them. Many mullahs had gone. But they turn away and reject the word of Allah."

"You raped children!"

"Allah says a *kafir* woman can be slave for a jihadi!"

"You made them watch as you decapitated their parents, for crying out loud!"

He raised his hands, pawing at my face, terror and tears in his eyes. "To teach! To teach! Maybe they repent in death and their souls can be saved!"

I roared at him, "*You laughed as you did it! You enjoyed it! You didn't need to kill those people! You butchered, raped and murdered innocent people! Old, weak men and women, fucking children!*"

My voice echoed out in the darkness, leaving a terrible silence behind it. I grabbed the scruff of his neck in my fist and dragged him toward me. "*Can't you see that what you did was evil? What is wrong with you?*"

He gave his head a small shake, searching my eyes. "It is the will of Allah…"

"The will of Allah…?"

He nodded. I stood and stamped down hard on his right knee. I heard and felt it snap. He screamed, but now he wasn't going anywhere. I reached in the back of the truck and pulled out a half-full one-gallon can of gasoline that was left from the fertilizer bombs I'd made. I used half of it to dowse his legs up to his hips. He was hysterical, screaming and holding out his hands to try and stop me.

When his robes were sodden I put the cap on the can and tossed it back in the truck.

"Don't sweat it," I said. "It's the will of Allah. You know, the look on your face, in your eyes, it's exactly the same look I saw in the faces of those people you raped, tortured and murdered in Al-Landy. Maybe I am helping you, teaching you something about empathy and compassion. What do you think?"

"Please! Please! No! You right! I was bad, wrong, God is merciful! Forgive me! Please!"

"Shut up! You get a chance to save yourself, you son of a bitch, which is more than you deserve."

"What! What! Anything! I do anything!"

"You get one chance, Mohammed. Lie, cheat, try to be smart and the deal is off. You burn. Understood?"

"Yes, yes, yes! Please, anything!"

I pulled the massive Smith and Wesson fifty cal from the rucksack and thrust it in his face. "One slug from this baby will ignite the gas, and I will leave you here with your legs on fire, to die in the sand the way you deserve. Now listen carefully and listen good. You don't know how much I know. You don't know who I spoke to in Paris or what I saw. There will be trick questions. It is not worth your while to lie. Lie just once, think too long, hesitate, and I will ignite the gas. Just once. Understood?"

He nodded. I stood and stepped away from him.

"What is the deal going down between you, the Yemenis and the Mexicans?"

The terror in his face was indescribable. "They..." He reached up toward me, like he was praying. "Please, they want our help..."

"The Mexicans?" He nodded. I went on. "Because all the routes into the USA are closing down, they can't shift the produce..."

He was nodding. "And the plantations in Colombia and Mexico being destroyed. But we can grow!" He laughed. "We can make big, *big* farms in Afghanistan. You can join! Make very rich! Lots of money!"

"Shut up. So by using you to supplement production, using their experience and expertise, you can smuggle tons of coke and heroin into Europe via a thousand routes from Turkey, Greece and Italy, the Balkans and the Black Sea all the way to southern Russia and the Ukraine. With Mexican money and know-how, the possibilities are infinite. But what's in it for you?"

He swallowed hard. "Weapons. Very hard for us to buy weapons now. But Sinaloa cartel has many contacts who can for us buy weapons..."

I started to ask, "But how...," and the final pieces of the puzzle I had started to understand on my first night in LA, listening to the would-be glitterati at the next table, fell into place. I shook my head.

"Son of a bitch! That's what you need Yemen for. Mexico can provide men like Bernardo Muller, with political contacts as well as Sinaloa ones, to buy on your behalf, and the weapons and cash can be flown to Ta'izz, Dhamar or any of a hundred other airfields in Yemen where al-Qaeda has absolute control, or can gain it. From there the weapons and money can be distributed anywhere across the Arab world, especially with the help of members of the royal family, who are sympathetic to the cause. Meanwhile Sinaloa gets a thousand back doors into European markets and expands their empire beyond anyone's wildest dreams. Hell, they can even get to Canada, and a new route back into the USA."

He nodded. "And provide us with operatives who look European! Do not look like Arabs. It is a cooperation on many levels."

He stared at me for a long moment. We both knew what my next question was going to be, and we were both wondering whether it would cost him his life. I drew breath but he spoke first.

"You must be very careful now. Because we have very powerful friends in America."

"What part does the CIA play in this?"

He simpered, spread his hands, shrugged. "I cooperate, they cooperate. They know I have the contacts, like nobody else: Yemen, Mexico, American friends... So I cooperate, they cooperate..."

"What does that mean?"

"CIA need information, Middle East is complicated..." He laughed. "Islam, Israel, Christians, Americans, Europe... So complicated! And so much money, oil, weapons... CIA must be getting much information to control all sides. Also percentage of trade proceeds, to fund operations..."

"And you provided them with all that, and in exchange they keep you in luxury."

"No, just, make me more powerful, spread my influence. I can do favors for them, and they can do favors for me. This is war."

A slug from a Smith and Wesson 500 will shatter two concrete cinder blocks. You can imagine for yourself what it will do to a terrorist's head. I put a single slug between his eyes and his head exploded like a watermelon. It was too good for him, and too painless. But at least he had been executed, and the guts had been torn out of the operation he was planning.

I left him there for the vultures and drove slowly back to the canal. There I wiped the 416 and the Smith and Wesson clean and dropped them in water. Then I drove sedately back to Los Angeles. I dropped the RAM back in the multistory parking, collected my Wrangler and drove back to the hotel.

It was gone midnight, so I went straight up to my room, had a shower and two large whiskies, and fell into a deep, dreamless sleep.

The dead were finally sleeping too.

EIGHTEEN

I awoke because I heard a noise. I lay very still. The light from the city lay across my sheet in luminous pools from the window, but the room was still and dark. I remained motionless, listening, and the sound came again: a soft scratch and then a click.

I snatched the P226 from under my pillow and rolled silently out of bed, then flattened myself against the wardrobe waiting for whoever was at the door to come in. Nothing happened for a moment. Then a long, distorted oblong of light reached across the floor, framing the shadow of a man. The shadow moved and was joined by another. Then both began to swell as footsteps, I counted three sets, drew whoever it was closer.

Then there were three dark, bulky shadows playing flashlights over the bed. I spoke quietly from the shadows.

"Freeze, put your weapons down and turn your backs to me."

A calm, steady voice answered. "Captain William Hartmann, Central Intelligence Agency..." He turned his flashlight onto his ID card.

I flipped on the light. He winced, holding out his ID for me to see, but I kept my weapon trained on his chest.

Beside him were two big gorillas in suits, like him. One was fair with a shaggy Viking mustache. The other was black and built like a quarterback on steroids. I dropped my piece on the bedside table as Hartmann spoke.

"Harry Bauer," he said facetiously, "we meet again."

"What the hell are you doing here, Hartmann?"

"Looking for you, as it happens. Seems I found you."

"You broke into my room."

"At the management's invitation. It's their property, not yours. You only have a license to stay here. We're covered legally."

"You're an asshole, Hartmann." The Viking mustache chuckled. I ignored him and went on, "What do you want?"

"You've been a bad boy today. Somebody wants to talk to you."

I answered softly.

"Fuck you. A, I am not going anywhere except back to bed. B, what I did or did not do today is none of your goddamn business and C, you have no jurisdiction in this country. If you, or the asshole who sent you, think I broke the law, call the cops or the Bureau. Meanwhile, get the hell out of my room before I kick you down the goddamn stairs."

By the time I'd got through saying it, I was real mad. The guy with the mustache stepped forward. He'd stopped sniggering now and was looking pissed.

"You got a big mouth, trooper. You want to watch how you use it."

His eyes were a pale shade of blue that made them look transparent. My voice was almost a whisper.

"Is that a threat?"

He answered the same way: "What if it is?"

He was close enough for me to reach out and put my palm on his chest. He squared up because he didn't realize I was gauging the distance. I spun on my left foot and raised my right foot, then brought my heel crashing down onto his knee. His eyes bulged and his jaw dropped. I could have broken it with my elbow, but I figured he'd had enough. I sidestepped him as he hobbled toward the bed, ducked under the quarterback's massive fist as he swung it at me, and as I came up again I drove a right hook deep into his solar plexus. He went down retching and I picked up the Sig and pointed it in Hartmann's face. He held up both hands.

"We just want to talk to you, Bauer. Find out what you're doing here, have a friendly chat. That's all. You wanna do it the hard way, we can do that too."

I stepped in close. The quarterback was on his hands and knees, and the mustache was keening softly, holding his knee. I thrust my face into Hartmann's and pressed the muzzle of the Sig up under his chin.

"You want to run that by me again, Captain? You threatening me? You think you're going to make it hard for me? How is that working for you right now?" He blinked once, slowly. I snarled, "Get out of my room before I blow your damned head off. You want to talk to me, make an appointment. And Hartmann, next time you sneak into my room at night, I'll kill you. Get out!"

He didn't move. He let his eyes take a walk over my face, then said, "You're in deep shit, Bauer. We'll be back. And next time, you come with us."

The big quarterback finally made it to his feet, helped the mustache to his one usable foot, and the three of them made an ignominious exit, the way they'd come.

I watched them get in the elevator, closed the door and went to get my burner. Buddy Byrd sounded sleepy.

"Bauer, I've been expecting to hear from you. Any news?"

"Yeah. Everything is wrapped up. We need to talk, in person. I just got a visit from the Firm."

"Oh?"

"Our old friend. The one who took my prize. He said they knew what I'd been up to."

"How could they?"

"I don't know. There's a lot to talk about. More than we can cover on the phone."

"All right. Catch the next flight to New York. I'll pick you up at the airport."

"Listen, if you have any pull in DC, you need to get the Firm to pull their boys off me."

"OK, I'll make a call. Try to get some sleep. I'll see you tomorrow."

Try to get some sleep. Sure.

I lay on the bed for another two and half hours with the P226 on my belly. At six thirty AM I showered, dressed, packed and went down for breakfast at a few minutes after seven. I was just sitting down to bacon and eggs and a pot of coffee when my cell rang. There was no name on the screen, just an LA number.

"Yeah?"

"Is it too early for breakfast?"

"Miriam. No, I'm just sitting down to bacon and eggs. Where are you? You want to join me?"

"I'm in the lobby, actually. I was passing by and I had pegged you as an early riser, so I took a chance."

I watched her enter the dining room with the cell still at her ear, grinning. I stood and gave her a kiss and we both sat. She ordered a cappuccino and two hot croissants from the waiter and watched me a moment while I ate. I spoke with my mouth full, breaking a piece of hot, crusty bread.

"I have to leave."

Her eyebrows shot up, then knitted into a frown.

"Oh... I thought..."

"I got a call this morning. I have to go back to New York."

"New York? I thought it was Arizona..."

I shrugged. "I have to go to New York."

"That's disappointing. There were a couple of things..." She sighed. "I feel really stupid now."

"You don't need to, Miriam. I wanted to spend a couple of days with you too, but this was unexpected." I smiled at her. "What did you have in mind?"

"Well, there was a concert. I don't know if it's your kind of thing, a tribute to Oscar Peterson."

"That's my kind of thing."

"And a late meal afterwards."

"When?"

"Day after tomorrow. And those Mexican Arabs got in touch. They were very apologetic, said something had come up, and could they see the properties tomorrow. I thought it would be fun if you came along, and when we were done, you and I could go to lunch and spend the afternoon together." She shrugged. "But if you have to go..."

She could see me faltering. My gut was telling me there was a connection between Ben-Amini's plans and these guys from Mexico. But what didn't make a lot of sense was their pressing ahead despite what had happened the night before.

The waiter brought her croissants and her coffee, and as she broke into the first one she said, "Look, what time is your flight?"

"Next available. I haven't booked it yet."

Her face lit up. "Then book it for this evening! And we'll drive down to the border this morning. I'll show you around and we'll have lunch at a Mexican restaurant! What do you say?"

I went to answer but she kept on talking. "I had really hoped you could come along tomorrow. I have to say that after our conversation, I feel a little scared. But I wouldn't feel scared if you were there."

I nodded. "OK, I'll make a call and see about booking the flight for tonight, or maybe even tomorrow. Let's go and see those properties and have a hot, jalapeno lunch."

She giggled. "Sounds good to me, cowboy."

I excused myself and stepped out into the lobby to call the brigadier again.

"What is it now, Bauer. You seem to have a telephone addiction."

"Listen, something's come up and I don't really know what to make of it."

I explained the situation and he was very quiet for a while. Finally he said, "I don't see how this ties in with Ben-Amini."

"Neither do I right now. There's a lot you don't understand yet. Let me go with Miriam this morning and tomorrow, see who these guys are. Maybe it's nothing, but I can't help feeling it's too much of a coincidence."

He sighed and sounded unhappy. "Very well, if you're sure. I can't say I'm insane about the idea."

I hesitated. "I'm half expecting Hussein Saleh and

Jaden Abdullah to show up with Bernardo Muller. If they do, I might just finish the job."

He made the "hmmm" noise of thinking, then said, "That isn't actually a job, yet. It might be though. Keep me posted."

When I got back to Miriam she was finishing her last croissant. She looked up as I sat, and smiled.

"So?"

"So let's go and look at these properties. And I couldn't possibly allow you to face the Sinaloa cartel alone and unprotected, so I'm going to delay my flight till tomorrow evening."

Her cheeks flushed and she jumped up from her chair, ran around the table with tiny steps and gave me a huge hug and a kiss. It made me laugh, and a couple of minutes later I followed her out into the lobby as she spoke over her shoulder.

"We'll go in my car. I have it parked out front."

As we passed the reception desk she stopped dead in her tracks and turned to face me, moving in close, staring up into my eyes.

"What?" I asked.

She hesitated, then closed her eyes and said, "No! It was a stupid idea, forget it."

"What was a stupid idea?"

She blushed. "I'm behaving like a sixteen-year-old. I was going to suggest you pay your bill and stay the night at my place. And then I'll take you to the airport tomorrow. But it was stupid. I am coming on much too strong. I feel embarrassed now." I laughed and she looked hurt. "Was it a really stupid idea?"

"No. It was a nice idea. But Miriam, you realize, I live a long way from Los Angeles…"

"I know!" She grabbed my lapels and rested her forehead on my chest. "I don't want to marry you, for God's sake! I just thought it would be nice to make the most of the time we have."

"We'll have to lug my bags around all day."

"That's OK."

So I paid my bill, arranged for the Wrangler to be collected from the hotel and carried my bags out to Miriam's Mercedes convertible. I slung them in the trunk and climbed in the passenger seat. She was waiting behind the wheel, grinned at me and fired up the engine. Then we were away, speeding north again toward the freeway. An ironic voice in my head told me I was stuck in Groundhog Day, but pretty soon we were speeding toward the I-10 with the soft-top down under the clear blue California sky, and the last thing on my mind was Groundhog Day.

It was two hundred and twenty miles. It should have taken three and a half hours to get there, but Miriam drove with the kind of zest that seems to warp space and time, and though I am not a fan of German cars, the Merc could shift, and in a little more than two hours we were cruising down the Imperial Valley Pioneers Expressway, surrounded on all sides by infinite flatness, moving fast toward El Centro. Before we got there she took the Yuma exit onto the I-8, going east, and as we climbed the ramp onto the bridge, she glanced at me and smiled, fingering her wind-whipped hair from her face.

"We're almost there. The landscape's not very entertaining here, but we can eat out in the desert, at the Duner's Diner. You'll like it."

We followed the I-8 for another seven or eight minutes among endless, interminable, featureless flat fields, under a sky that was turning from Californian blue to scorched desert blue-white, until eventually we came to the Bonds Corner Road intersection and she slowed and turned south onto a road that had once been black-top, but was now covered in an encroaching layer of dust and dirt. It went perfectly straight for five miles, and by then I had the feeling I had driven through some kind of portal into a Stephen King movie.

At the end of Bonds Corner she turned left. The land continued to be flat and featureless, but now there were more trees, oaks, eucalyptus and pines in sudden dense clusters. She pointed south, across me. "You can't see it," she said above the battering of the breeze, "but that right there is the All American Canal. It runs parallel to the border with Mexico."

We passed a green sign pointing to Bonesteele Road, and then she was slowing, pulling off the road beside a cluster of tall pines. We were bumped and jostled over dirt and dust, headed toward an open gate in a fence. Beyond the gate the dirt track continued for a couple of hundred yards toward a house and a cluster of large barns and sheds. A sign by the gate said the place was for sale.

"Here we are," she said. "This is the first of the properties they seem to be interested in." She gave her head a twitch. "You got me thinking the other night, with what you said. This is good farmland, but it's only half a mile from the canal, maybe less."

We did a big circle, dragging a cloud of dust behind us, and came to a halt behind a large, oxblood barn that formed the north side of a broad yard. There she killed the engine and the desert air carried the dust away, toward the canal. She watched me a moment as I stared away south.

"What do you think...?"

I climbed out of the car and sat with my ass against the door, wondering what I thought. I said, absently, "Omar Qasim, huh?"

Even if the name was an erudite joke, why Arabic? Why not Latin or Greek? Why make a joke like that in Arabic? And why the sudden return of interest, if Mohammed was dead and the safe house was destroyed? It didn't make a lot of sense.

"What did he sound like?" I said and turned to look at her. She climbed out of the car and came to stand next to me.

"I'm not good at accents. An educated Mexican with an accent sounds pretty much to me like somebody from the Mediterranean or the Middle East."

I smiled. "I guess we'll find out tomorrow."

"I guess…"

A gust of warm air lifted a column of red dust, like a ghost rising from a grave, spun it gently and then spread it softly across the yard, while it rattled the leaves of the eucalyptus trees.

Over on my left there was another barn. That one was painted green and looked like it housed tractors and harvesters. The one on my right was part brick and part wood. In its day it might have been a stable.

"Hell of a risk," I said. "Right under the noses of the border patrol. And a big investment."

"You want to look in the barns?" I looked at her and she winked. "This one has a hayloft."

I smiled. "I never could resist a hayloft."

"You're a bad man, Mr. Frost."

She walked to the vast red door, pulling a bunch of keys from her jacket pocket. There was a hefty padlock and as she fitted the key, for a moment I thought about telling her my name was not Frost. But the key slipped in, the padlock came off and the next moment she was leaning, pushing against the door and rolling it back. I went to help her, but she'd stopped pushing, leaving just enough space for two bodies to fit through.

It was like a huge church inside, with a gabled roof and slim beams of dusty light piercing the wooden walls and the ceiling, casting everything about them into deeper gloom. There was a vast stack of hay against the far wall, under a loft that held more of the golden bales. The smell was strong in my nostrils. It wasn't musty or old, but fresh and clean and sweet.

Against the wall on the far right there was a stack of steel drums. Diesel oil, I figured, and bits and pieces of farming equipment lay strewn here and there. Aside from that, the place was largely empty.

A tunnel, little more than half a mile long, and a giant warehouse. The hay could cover hundreds of kilos of dope, and the existence of a functioning farm would make the coming and going of trucks the most normal thing in the world. God knew the cartels had money enough to buy a dozen farms like this one, and to build the tunnels too.

But the growing difficulty in pulling off exactly this kind of operation was why Muller had approached Ben-Amini in the first place. I shook my head. Omar Qasim? The flourishing distributor...

I turned to face her. She was leaning against the doorjamb with her arms crossed, watching me. The sun was bright behind her and I couldn't see her expression. She said, "What do you make of it?"

I shrugged. "It's a perfect setup for a Sinaloa group to bring dope across, and they certainly have the resources to make the tunnel. But I have to say, the Arab connection is baffling. Omar Qasim? It doesn't make a lot of sense."

"Really?" She said it and laughed. "And there was me thinking you had the whole thing figured out, Harry."

NINETEEN

I can't say it surprised me. I guess there had been a niggling there from the start. I'm not the kind of guy women sit next to and get into conversation with at bars. And she wasn't the kind of woman to do that, even if I had been. Plus, the bits of information she'd fed me were just enough to be enticing, but not quite enough to make sense. But I had liked her, and she played the part of the smart but naïve girl next door well enough to be convincing. I had not wanted to believe it, but the suspicion had been there.

I gave a small laugh. "Who are you with, the Firm?"

"Well, Harry, I'm not Sinaloa and I sure as hell ain't al-Qaeda."

"There is no Omar Qasim, is there? No buyers interested in border real estate."

"No."

"And your name is not Miriam Grant."

"None of it, Harry."

"What *is* your name?"

"What difference does it make?"

"Are you going to kill me?"

She laughed a little, paused a moment watching me, smiling, then laughed a lot. Finally she shook her head and said, "I don't know. You're not easy to kill, are you? But you're in a lot of trouble, Harry. You're drawing a lot of unwelcome attention. I thought you SAS guys were supposed to be like ninjas, moving through the shadows, killing and vanishing into the woodwork. But you, you're like a one-man warzone."

"I have no idea what you're talking about."

"George Santos?"

"Who is that, a Brazilian jazz musician?"

"Funny."

"Yeah, I know, deep down funny, where it's not like funny anymore. What do you want?"

"It's one thing killing bad guys, Harry. Even if it interferes with our work, we can live with it up to a point. But when you start killing our assets and our officers, that's a whole different story."

I sighed. "I still have no idea what you're talking about."

"Really? You want to make this hard, Harry? We can make it hard. You want to start by explaining why a dishonorably discharged SAS trooper, living in New York, is staying at a five-star hotel in Los Angeles under a false name?"

"Not really. I can tell you this, though. It's none of your damned business."

She pushed off the door and walked toward me with her hands in her pockets. She stopped when she was a few inches away. Her eyes flicked over my face.

"Maybe it's not. Maybe it is. Where were you yesterday afternoon and last night?"

I put a wonky smile on the right side of my face. "I'll tell you what, take me to Yemen and ask me that. Over there, you have some jurisdiction. Here, you're nobody, nothing. You're wasting my time."

She made a fist and stuck out her index finger, then used that to poke me in the chest. "You killed twenty men last night, Harry. Two of them were CIA officers. Another was a valuable asset for this country. You also destroyed two CIA helicopters. Do you seriously think that you can do that and walk away, with no consequences?"

I made the face of innocence, shrugged my eyebrows and shook my head. "Have you any evidence at all that I did all those things? Can you prove any of what you're saying?"

"We followed you from Paris, Harry."

"What makes you think I was in Paris?"

"Mary Brown makes me think that. She talked to George Santos, before you killed him..."

"Mary Brown? Doesn't ring a bell. Doesn't sound very French, either. But just for argument's sake, let's say I knew who she was." I took a step closer to her and looked hard into her eyes. "What happened to Mary Brown? What did George Santos do when she, allegedly, told him about me?"

"You know what happened to her."

"No..." I shook my head. "You have me confused with somebody else."

"How do you think this ends, Harry?"

"Well, let's see. You think I am a one-man warzone. So the chances of you confronting me here on your own are, what? Zero? Which means that in this immediate vicinity, within this barn, you have at least two men with automatic rifles trained on me right now, waiting for the order to shoot. You haven't given that order yet, which means one of two things: you are not one hundred percent sure that I *am* your man, or you think I have information that could be useful to you. My money is on the latter."

"Two out of three. I am one hundred percent certain that you are my man. And you are alive right now because I think you have information I need. So let me ask you again, Harry. How do you think this ends?"

I smiled down at my boots, turned and took a few steps away from her. The placing was obvious now. One in the hayloft, the other behind the bales of hay. I turned back to face her.

"OK, how does this end? Let's play that game. According to you, I went to Paris and murdered a CIA asset there, named George Santos. Or was he an officer?"

She didn't answer so I went on. "Did I do anything else while I was there, to qualify as a one-man warzone? Did I break in anywhere and kill any other assets? Let's say I did. And then I came back to the States, flew to Los Angeles, killed twenty men, destroyed two choppers and murdered another valuable CIA asset. How is this going to end? I'd say, on the information available, the CIA ought to think twice about making any threats or getting into a conflict, because this guy you're after sounds dangerous. I think he might just take out your two sharpshooters, and then tan your little tush."

We stared at each other a moment. Then I smiled. "What's this information you think I have? Theoretically we're on the same side. Have you thought, maybe all you need to do is ask?"

A small twitch of her brow told me the question had surprised her.

"Who do you work for?"

"What is that information worth to you?" I walked back, so I was just inches away from her again. "What do

I get if I give you that? Because right now it seems to me that I get half a dozen rounds in my back."

"You tell me who you work for and, depending on who that is, you walk away."

I laughed. "Have your boys come out of the hay, let me see them, then we'll talk."

She nodded and said, "OK."

Behind me I heard the rustle of moving bodies. A moment later two guys in jeans and leather jackets appeared on either side of me. They looked like Marines, with thick necks and powerful shoulders. One looked Latino, the other was Japanese or Korean. They both had assault rifles slung over their shoulders. I jerked my head toward the barn door.

"Go stand where I can see you."

They didn't move till she gave them the nod. Then they backed up to the door and stood watching us. They still had me covered.

"How many more people you got here, Miriam?"

A flicker of her eyes, then she shook her head. "Nobody."

I leered at her. "How about if I kill these bozos and strip you naked? Will I find a wire?"

The color drained from her face. "I wouldn't do that."

"I'll bet you wouldn't. But I would. Now let me explain something to you. When I left you eating your croissants this morning, I made a call. That call has been connected ever since, and is being recorded in DC. Now, I have no wish to harm any federal agents, officers or employees, but if these two," I pointed at the two gunmen, "come at me, I will kill them, and then I will kill you, too." I smiled. "I am allowed, under federal law, to defend myself.

"But here comes the trade. I need to talk to Samy Arain. I am betting he's in the barn across the yard with a pair of phones in his ears. Let me talk to him, and I will arrange a meeting between my boss and your boss. We're on the same side; we don't need to go around killing each other, am I right?"

A shadow morphed against the brilliant slat of light in the doorway and three men came in. There was a guy in his mid-twenties, with long, floppy blond hair, skinny arms and legs. The guy beside him was heavy, had acne and a dirty T-shirt that looked like it had been slept in for a week. He had short, dark, un-brushed hair.

But the guy who'd come in ahead of them was in a sharp, double-breasted Italian suit, with a crisp white shirt and a fat, bright tie. He had a three-hundred-dollar haircut and the kind of eyes Bambi looked at the hunters with, before he blew them away.

He looked at me with those eyes, laughed and shook his head.

"Who the *hell* are you?"

"You Samy Arain?" He didn't say anything. He didn't need to. His face told me he was. I went on: "Where are Hussein Saleh, Jaden Abdullah and Bernardo Muller? Does that project still go ahead, even without Mohammed Ben-Amini?"

His eyes narrowed. "So it was you?"

"You answer mine, I'll answer yours." He didn't say anything. I kept pressing. "Do your superiors know you've been running around engaging in plots to flood Europe with cocaine and heroin, in exchange for weapons from Mexico? I mean, I keep turning it over in my mind, and I don't see it. What benefit does the CIA get? Ben-Amini said it was so you could monitor the activity of al-

Qaeda and Sinaloa." I shook my head. "But that doesn't wash. What is the use of monitoring if you can't control? What the Agency wants is control. This was *your* private enterprise, wasn't it, Samy? You had your own little team, ready to profit, and you played the Agency, making them believe that you were turning Taliban and al-Qaeda assets, when what you were really doing was using them to line your own damn pockets, and probably your Belize bank accounts."

There was a moment of strained silence. Then he snarled, "You're full of shit." He jerked his head at my jacket. "Let me see your cell."

I looked down at Miriam. She was frowning at me. I smiled. "If I am about to die, I'm going to do now what I've been wanting to do since you sat next to me on that barstool at the Hotel California."

I was only a foot from her or less. I cupped the back of her head in my left hand, bent down and kissed her. It was unexpected and she went rigid. I was a difficult target, pressed up against her, and I figured, correctly as it turned out, that Samy and his two gunmen would be momentarily too astonished to react.

Momentarily was all I needed. Because while my left hand was holding her head, my right hand slipped past her bosom and slipped out again with the P226 in its grasp. It took less than a second, and with my mouth still engaged, I plugged the Latino and the Korean in the chest, one after the other.

Samy was not slow to react. He sprang forward, grabbed my arm under his armpit and levered the Sig out of my grasp. Miriam was sandwiched between us, screaming and pushing at me. I grabbed a fistful of her hair and slung her to one side so I could get at Samy before he turned my own gun on me.

The two nerds were transfixed, watching the fight to see which way it would go. Samy spun, with the Sig held in both hands, and for a split second it was trained on my chest. But he was too slow. I snatched the barrel, levered up and kicked savagely at his crotch.

He was fast. He sidestepped and delivered a stinging roundhouse to my thigh. It hurt bad and he followed up with a front kick to my belly. Our hands were still clasped on the Sig, above our heads. The kick to my belly hurt and I knew another would wind me. If that happened he would turn the gun on me and it would be curtains. I lashed out again and caught him on his knee. He gritted his teeth and grunted. It hurt, but he knew he was fighting for his life.

I lashed out again, but in that moment an express train collided with me and I was dragged, winded to the floor. When I opened my eyes, needles of pain were stabbing through my lungs, and the nerd with the dirty T-shirt was straddling me, reaching over to pummel my face with his fists. Past him I could see Samy on his hands and knees, reaching for something on the floor that I couldn't see, but I knew what it was. He was reaching for my Sig, and in a few seconds he was going to shoot me, probably in the groin, while this asshole was sitting on me, punching at my face.

Sometimes, in moments of extreme stress, time can pass very slowly. I was gripping at the nerd's wrists. Past his contorted, slavering face I could see Samy, getting to his feet, turning to look at me. In his hand was the P226. He smiled and stepped toward me.

I bucked and drew up my knees, pounding them into the nerd's back. He laughed, leaning forward, trying to get through my guard with his fists. I let go my right hand and his left fist smacked my face. I tasted the blood in my mouth, expecting at any second the tearing, burning pain of a slug entering my belly. I thrashed and twisted savagely, reaching down to my right foot with my right hand. The hard metal handle of the Fairbairn and Sykes was in my fingers. I pulled and rammed the blade into the nerd's ribcage.

He gave a small gasp of surprise. I pushed and rolled. He thudded to the floor with me on top. I kept rolling as the air exploded with flat, hard detonations. My left arm burned and gore sprayed in my face as the nerd's head and face jerked, penetrated by two 9mm slugs that had been meant for me. The knife was still in my hand. Samy was snarling and screaming, following me with the Sig held out in front of him in both hands. He squeezed and a round smashed into the dirt beside me as I sat up and hurled the knife. It hammered home into his gut. But a second before it did his head whiplashed and a plume of blood and gore erupted from his temple. His knees folded and he fell, almost gracefully, to the floor.

She was standing, Miriam, with a Walther PPK in her hand. A small trail of smoke wound up from the barrel, illuminated by a leaning shaft of dusty light. For a moment there was utter stillness. Then the blond kid suddenly scrambled and ran, ricocheting through the barn door, vanishing into the midday glare.

I got to my feet and felt the warm ooze of blood down my left arm. It didn't hurt. The pain would come later. I went and picked up my Sig, slipped it under my arm and turned to face her. She still had the PPK held out in front of her, trained on me now.

"You just saved my life. You going to ruin it all by

shooting me now? Point that somewhere else, will you?"

She lowered it slowly, then slipped it into a small holster under her jacket. She didn't say anything. I stepped up close to her.

"That's a hell of a debriefing you have coming up this afternoon, sister. I wouldn't want to be in your shoes."

She stared up into my face. "Who do you work for?"

I smiled. "The good guys."

"Are you going to kill me?"

"No. That would be rude, after you saved my life."

"You know I'll probably have to come after you."

I nodded. "That's something to look forward to." I hesitated a moment. "You didn't know what Samy was about...?"

"Would you believe me if I said I didn't?"

"Yeah. I would."

"What about Hartmann? Was he involved in this?"

She thought about it. "In retrospect, probably." She handed me her keys. "You'd better go. Take my Mercedes. They'll come and get me."

Outside, I heard the roar of an engine. The blond nerd escaping. I took the keys.

"Where is Hussein Saleh?"

"They were supposed to arrive today, and Muller. But Samy postponed the meeting. Hartmann spoke to him, they told me to get you, to bring you here. I thought he was going to question you. I didn't know..." She paused. "I suppose he would have killed me after he'd killed you."

I walked to the door, then turned and looked back. "It's an ugly game. Don't forget who you are."

She held my eye, and there was an urgency in hers

that seemed to fade as quickly as it flared. She nodded. "Hazel," she said. "I'm Hazel."

I walked to her Mercedes and slid behind the wheel. The engine roared and I rolled out onto the blacktop, then turned west. As I accelerated toward Calexico I called the brigadier.

"Bauer, what's happening?"

"I'm done."

Silence, then, "What do you mean, you're done?"

"Mohammed is dead. Samy Arain is dead, and his conspiracy is busted. This part of the job is done. I'll brief you when I get to New York. But sir?"

"Yes."

"Hussein Saleh, Jaden Abdullah and Bernardo Muller, and Captain Bill Hartmann, they are still at large, and I plan to take them down."

"Ah," he said. "Good. Welcome aboard, Bauer. Welcome aboard."

WHAT'D YOU THINK?

Nothing is more annoying than someone asking for a review, but unfortunately they "matter" or something. I don't know why, but the vast majority of readers won't buy something unless they see that other's already have and had a good experience.

Therefore, if *you* happened to have a good experience at any point during this read, then I would be exceptionally grateful if you would consider taking a moment to leave behind a quick review. Honestly, it can be super short (or super long...if that's your thing), but even a couple words and a good star rating can go *miles* for a self-published author like myself.

Without you all, I wouldn't be able to do this. I'd have to go out and work in the real world...and that's simply not as fun. I much prefer killing people, err—I mean *writing* about killing people...

Anyways, if leaving a review is something you'd be willing to do, that'd be incredible. But even if you don't, I want you to know just how thankful I am that you even gave my work a chance and made it this far. Seriously, you are the bomb!

BOOK 2 EXCERPT

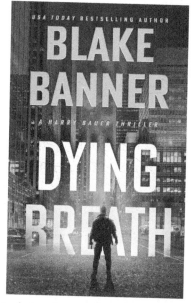

When your only training is as a first class killer, it can be hard to find a job on Main Street. Unless you work for Cobra, the secret agency that takes out the worst of the world's trash. So when Harry Bauer left the Regiment, the toughest special ops outfit on the planet, Cobra offered him a job, taking out the trash.

Bauer had grown up fighting for survival on the streets of the Bronx. He knew everything there was to know about hard reality, and he didn't buy into fantasies or conspiracy theories. Until, that is, one came knocking on his door...

There was nothing unreal about the job: a simple hit at Manhattan's

Mandarin Oriental Hotel, on two of China's highest ranking bio-chemists, and two of the world's most evil men.

But when Cobra High Command asks Bauer to find out why Zhao Li and Yang Dizhou are in New York in the first place, things turn dark. In a mission that will take him from New York to Casablanca, Algeria and Bangkok, Bauer will realize the hard way that some-times conspiracy theories are real...

ONE

I hadn't eaten for thirty-six hours. It's one of the conditions I impose on myself if I go hunting. I eat what I kill, and if I don't kill I don't eat. Some people might think that's a hollow gesture, or a pretentious one. I can't say I care much, but I get mad at hunters who talk about being in nature, a predator pitched against his prey in a primal wilderness, when they're carrying a camouflage tent, thermal sleeping bags, propane camping stoves and sniper's rifles with telescopic sights.

I sleep in the open with a couple of woolen blankets, I cook—if I cook—over an open fire, and I hunt with a sixty-five-pound Osage orange bow from James Easter up in Iowa. I also hunt with my six senses, and I listen: I listen to the hundreds of sounds that are woven into the breeze.

If you use a telescopic sight, you stop listening. The mountains and the forests are full of sounds that talk to you about the constant cycle of life and death in the woodlands: the animals that come and go on silent feet, that hunt in the shadows, that drink and fish in the creeks, streams and rivers which wind through the land. They tell you everything, from the twig that snaps under a deer's hoof, to the murderous flapping of the falcon's wing.

I listen and I look, not through a telescope, but with my eyes; and I look not for prey, but for movement. A bull elk at fifty yards, standing among trees, five feet inside the shade of a woodland, might be all but invisible to a man with a sniper's rifle and a telescopic sight. Because that man will be looking for a bull elk, and at that distance, among tree trunks, a bull elk looks like part of the forest. So if you want to see it, you don't look for it; you relax your gaze and you wait for movement.

You use all your senses. You listen, you smell the air, you taste the air, and you sense how the forest feels. You can't do that if you insulate yourself in a tent, with your TV and your propane cooker. You can only do it if you're in the forest, part of the forest. If you hide from the cold, moist night air, cushion yourself from the hard ground and the stones when you sleep, shut out the snuffling, howling and crying of the night, and rise only after the sun has burned away the chill dew of dawn, then you will be deaf to the whispering of the forest. Better stay at home and get your meat from the butcher.

So, I hadn't eaten for thirty-six hours, and that kind of hunger sharpens your senses. I was lying beside a spruce at the edge of the sparse woodlands to the south of Big Red Hill and to the west of Greenhorn Mountain, in Eagle County, Colorado. I was watching the large clearing spread out before me. It was about half a mile to the nearest trees, over on my right. But a hundred yards away a bull elk stood alone, smelling the morning air.

I'm a good archer, but a hundred yards was a hell of a shot, and would depend as much on luck as on any skill I had. That's OK in target practice, but when you are hunting a living, breathing animal, a bad shot can cause a lot of pain and unnecessary suffering. The animal can get away and it can take days to die. That is something you don't want to happen.

So I waited, chose my moment, and moved forward on my belly, a yard at a time.

After ten minutes he had turned his back on me, grazing at the late summer grass and shrubs, and was moving a step at a time, toward the sparse woods that covered the foothills of the Greenhorn. I was downwind, and though I could hear and smell him, he could not hear or smell me. So I closed the gap with a couple of short, silent runs.

I had closed the distance to fifty yards and dropped to my belly beside a young cypress. He still had his rump to me, but I had moved slightly to my left, hoping to get an angle on his heart. Luck, as luck so often does, played into my hand, and then robbed me.

The bull grazed slowly toward his left, one slow step at a time while his mouth worked, gradually turning his left flank to me. With a sixty-five-pound bow I could make a fifty-yard shot with a fair degree of accuracy, but an arrow travels much slower than a bullet, and there is no guarantee your target will still be there by the time your arrow arrives where it's going. If your target moves, instead of piercing its heart, your razor-sharp broadhead might slice clean through its belly, causing a slow, painful death. I needed to get at least twenty paces closer to take the shot.

I had a tall spruce maybe twenty yards to my left and, keeping flat on the ground, I crawled yard by yard, over the shrubs and stones, toward the cover of that tree. It took a long minute, but the burning hollow in my gut made it seem like an agonizing half hour.

The great beast had started moving slowly to its right now. I still had a shot, but if I was going to take it, it had to be now, because within seconds he would have turned his left side away from me.

I nocked the heavy, wooden broadhead, stepped out from behind the tree, leaned into the bow and drew till my thumb touched the angle of my jaw. I sensed, rather than saw, the trajectory of the arrow, and in that moment a rifle exploded into the still morning and the roar of the shot echoed across the valley, bouncing off the sides of the hills.

The elk looked up, its body tense as a spring. Next thing it had bounded and was racing across the plateau toward the cover of the trees, north and east. I didn't hesitate. I sprinted after it, covered twenty paces until I could see where it was headed, and settled into a steady run.

A scared deer, gazelle or elk is fast, but they will rarely run for long periods of time. Instinctively they know that predators operate with explosive bursts of speed, which burn themselves out pretty fast. So when the elk's run started to slow, after thirty seconds or a little more, he had covered over three hundred yards, but I was catching on him, staying downwind and out of sight. Man is one of the very few predators who will stay on a single prey relentlessly, sometimes for days on end, until he takes him down.

The bull elk had reached a gentle, wooded slope that rose to higher ground above. In the trees there was an opening that led to a kind of passage that wound up to the higher ground. There he stopped and sniffed the air, then started to graze again. I didn't stop. I kept going at a gentle jog. At forty paces I slowed to a walk, but, as he was looking away from me, I didn't seek cover. I kept walking. I still had the arrow nocked and drew it nine inches. After twelve paces I stopped, drew to my ear, sensed the trajectory and loosed the arrow.

A second shot rang out across the valley. I swore violently under my breath and broke into a sprint as the arrow struck home inches behind the heart. The bull sprang and kicked and bounded up the passage through the trees, with the barb buried deep in its side.

It took me fifteen or twenty seconds to cover the distance. A third shot rang out and I scrambled up the passage through the woodland.

When I got to the top, there was another plateau, smaller than the one below, and there, three paces from where I stood panting, was the bull, lying on its side, dead. Approaching down the slight hill at a slow, heavy run were two men dressed in camouflage. They carried high-powered rifles with telescopic sights. When they saw me, the only change to their demeanor was a complacent smile.

The one in the lead was in his fifties, well groomed, with permed gray hair and a slight paunch. He had a ranger's camouflage hat and a sleeveless camouflage jacket that had probably cost him three hundred bucks. He was wearing jeans and cowboy boots, and touched the brim of his hat with two fingers as he approached.

"Howdy? Good morning to you!"

His pal, lagging slightly behind, was darker, more muscular. His haircut had cost him about five bucks, maybe less, about the same as his peaked camouflage cap. He was smiling, but the smile was for himself, and his eyes watched me with care. The guy with the perm came right up with his hand extended.

"Rex Trent, Trent Enterprises. That was a bold shot, shame it just missed the mark." I shook the proffered hand with little enthusiasm.

"It was on target," I said. "Your shot scared him and he bolted."

His mouth smiled but his eyes leered. "Shoulda used a rifle. That's the problem with a bow. Slow delivery. With this bad boy," he held up his Seekins Pro Hunter, "I never miss a shot." He pointed at my elk. "Got this baby clean between the eyes."

I let my eyes travel over him and his pal, then looked past them at where they had come from. I let my eyebrows shrug.

"By my reckoning you should have two more elk lying somewhere." He frowned at me, not catching my meaning. "I heard three shots," I explained. "One of them hit my elk. Where did the other two go?"

He didn't think that was funny and his face told me so. After a second he gave a laugh that was on the dry side of humorless.

"You call it your elk, but I'm afraid I'm gonna have to disabuse you, son. See, it was my shot that killed the animal, therefore my claim is good."

I didn't bother pretending to smile. I gave him the deadeye instead. "You said it was a bold shot, Mr. Trent, which means you were watching. And that means you fired deliberately to scare my prey. In spite of that," I pointed at the feathers protruding from the animal's chest, "the wound was fatal and the animal would have died within seconds. Your shot may even have been post-mortem. The bull is mine."

"You're new to Sulfur Springs, ain't ya, son?"

"I'm not your son, Mr. Trent. I've been here a few

times, but I stay away from people."

"Well folks round here know me, see? They know me because, well..." He turned to his pal and they both laughed. "Because I own the town, huh, Jacob?" He turned back to me. "Just about everything you see in and around Sulfur Springs is either mine or it's a national park. So I guess you could say I'm like some kind of old-fashioned feudal lord. In the sense, like, that whatever I say goes."

I gave a single nod and gazed around, wondering if I was going to have to hit them.

"So," he smiled amiably, "I don't want to get into a disagreement with you. We'll just say that the damned elk is mine and leave it at that." He cocked his rifle and turned to his pal. "Earl, go get the truck so we can load this bull in the back."

I let my eyes rest on his and held them a moment. I spoke quietly. "The bull is mine."

The smile faded and he jerked his chin at me. "You look like a city boy to me. Things ain't changed around here for two hundred years. Still cowboy territory, and we don't worry so much about the law as we do about what we say... And what *I* say, *is* the law."

I went very still and held his eye for a long moment. "That bullshit might have worked back when Clint Eastwood still had hair. But things have changed since then. Different rules apply. So let me get something clear in my mind. Are you threatening to kill me?"

Jacob pulled back the bolt on his rifle with a loud clunk, put it to his shoulder and trained it on my gut. Trent laughed out loud.

"Hell, no!" he said. "Why, that would be illegal, right, Jacob? And what the hell would we do with the body in this wilderness?" All the laughter drained out of his face, like it had suddenly been punctured. "Walk away, boy, before this gets ugly."

I nodded. "Sure." I pointed at the bull. "But the bull is mine. That arrow is mine." I pointed at him. "And you owe me for that bull."

He laughed, low and soft. "Yeah, city boy? Well you have your lawyer call my lawyer and we'll see what we can work out."

They both laughed loud at that, like he'd said something original and funny. But by that time I was already walking back the way I'd come. I thought about turning and skewering them both, but you can't just kill people because they annoy you. You can't even kill them because they threaten to kill you. Because if we all did that, society would fall apart, and it would be a world of anarchy ruled over by people like Rex Trent. Sometimes you just had to walk away and either forget, or choose your own time and place to visit them again on your own terms.

I got back to my camp a couple of hours later, and as I scrambled up the hill to where I had left my blanket and my rucksack, my cell buzzed in my pocket. I pulled it out and knew it was the brigadier, Alex "Buddy" Byrd, head of operations at Cobra.

"Yeah."

"Good morning. We need you back in New York. How soon can you be there?"

"Couple of days."

"Good. Don't dillydally. We're in a hurry."

"I'm on my way."

I hoisted my rucksack on my shoulder and started down the far side of the hill. It was a half mile as the crow flies to where I'd left my truck, but over that terrain, along the weaving path, it took me over an hour to get there. I slung my stuff in the back of the truck and after that it was a four mile drive down a dirt track, following the course of the canyon, to the intersection with the I-70, and then another half mile along Route 6 to Sulfur Springs.

Once there I paid up at the motel, loaded my stuff in my truck and drove back toward the intersection. As I passed the Roast Buck Eatery, at the exit to the town, I saw a white Ford pickup in the parking lot. It had a bull elk in the back with a feathered barb sticking out of its ribcage. I glanced at it and slowed, wondering about going in to settle matters, but dismissed the thought and accelerated away from the town.

At the intersection I turned right and east and hit the gas. I had two thousand miles to cover, and twenty-nine hours of driving to get through. With four hours' sleep, make that thirty-three. And I still hadn't eaten.

TWO

I got to New York the following evening and went straight to my small, blue, clapboard cottage on Shore Drive, on the Eastchester Bay in the Bronx. I parked my truck down the side of the house and lugged my bags inside. With the door open, I paused a few seconds in the small entrance porch, to smell the air and listen. It was a habit. But the house felt and smelt as it had when I'd left it a couple of weeks earlier. I hung up my jacket, kicked the door closed, carried my bags into my living room and dumped them on the floor.

In the open plan kitchen, separated from the living room by a breakfast bar, I leaned on the sink and spent a moment gazing across my neglected lawn at the dark bay. In the distance, a couple of ghostly, narrow sails bobbed and leaned, white on the black water.

I opened the freezer, pulled out a couple of burgers and threw them in a hot pan. While they fried I cracked a cold beer and thought about nothing in particular, except for wondering what was wrong with me, that even in my spare time I needed to kill. I had come from hunting animals to relax, to hunting people for work.

I dropped my burgers into a couple of buns with

some tomato sauce and carried them upstairs with my beer and my bags. I opened the window onto the dusk and set about eating the burgers while I unpacked my bags.

By the time I'd finished, dusk had turned to evening, and small lights were glimmering over the dark water. I went to drain my bottle but it was empty.

Then the doorbell rang.

I took the plate and the bottle and descended the stairs. As I came down into the living room I could see the silhouette of a man against the glass in the door, backlit by the orange streetlights outside. I pulled my P226 from the drawer in the dresser and slipped it into my waistband behind my back. Before letting go of it I called out.

"Who is it?"

"Special delivery from Brigadier Byrd."

I pulled the Sig from my belt again, held it behind my back and opened the door with my left hand. He was standing sideways on, wearing a trench coat and a fedora, like a character from a Bogart movie. He had a cigarette in his mouth and he was leaning into the flame from a match. He turned and raised an eyebrow at me, and spoke as he shook the match and released smoke from his mouth.

"Harry Bauer?"

"Yeah. Who are you?"

"Captain Russ White, US Air Force. May I come in?"

"You got some ID?"

He reached in his coat and pulled out a brown leather wallet. In the transparent flap was his Common Access Card. I took it, pulled it out and had a look. As far as I could see he was who he said he was. I handed it back and stood aside.

"Come on in, Captain."

He stepped through the door, took off his hat and smiled. "Any objection to first names, Harry? I'm not big on formalities."

"None. You want a beer?"

"Sure." He grinned. "But I'd prefer a Scotch if you have one."

I took his coat and gestured at a chair. "I have one. Ice?"

He lowered himself into the chair. "Two rocks."

I went to the kitchen, took two tumblers and a bottle of The Macallan from the cupboard and filled a cereal bowl with ice. Then I carried the whole lot to the living room and set it on an occasional table between his chair and mine. I don't like coffee tables. They are designed to trip you up and graze your shins.

I poured in silence, gave him two rocks of ice and had mine neat.

"Cheers." He raised his glass and sipped, then smacked his lips and sighed. "The Macallan, a rare treat. A crime to put ice in it, but bad habits die hard."

I nodded, gave him a moment and asked, "How can I help you, Russ?"

He took another sip and regarded his glass like he was particularly proud of it.

"Ever heard of Zak Lee?"

"No. Who is he?"

"Heilong Li, Westernized his name to Zak Lee. He's a Chinese chemist, emerged from obscurity some five or six years ago to become head of viral research at UCP, that's United Chinese Petrochemicals, an umbrella company that handles about fifty percent of Chinese chemical and medical research and development, under government control and supervision, naturally."

"We don't like him?"

"Not a lot, no. At a conservative estimate we figure he is directly responsible for somewhere in the region of one hundred and twenty thousand deaths in Africa alone: Senegal, Cote d'Ivoire, the Congo, Gabon, Angola, Namibia, and South Africa, possibly other places too. Women, children… Men go without saying."

"What do you mean he is responsible for their deaths? How?"

He shrugged. "The west coast of Africa is like his personal testing lab. Testing on human subjects in China is not impossible, but it is difficult. It is a restrictive regime, not anarchic at all. President Xi Jinping is a man with a lot of power, and a lot of personal privilege, but his power comes from the system. The system is supreme in China and he must operate within it.

"So what UCP does, and the system turns a blind eye, is pay large bribes to West African regimes that *are* anarchic, where the system is simply an extension of the man in power, and they are granted permission to experiment on live human beings, whole villages and towns, where basically nobody gives a damn what happens to the people."

I didn't answer. I sipped from my glass while he rattled the rocks in his. He set his glass down and sighed. "He turns up, usually in person but sometimes it's his students and assistants. They are supported by armed guards and they force an entire population to take a so-called vaccine, or a cure for some local disease." He gave a dry laugh. "Of course the objective is not to kill these people. Labs don't make money by killing their customers. The purpose is to establish what the side effects are of the products they are researching, before feeding them to people who *do* matter. So in some cases entire villages have died in a matter of a few weeks. In others the majority of the subjects have gone blind.

"In one case, in the village of Massonde, four hundred miles southeast of Luanda as the crow flies, five hundred and fifty by Angolan road—and the last fifty of those through dense jungle—these *doctors*, for want of a better name, were sent in, protected by armed thugs in uniform, to provide vaccines against the flu. Within forty-eight hours half the town had become psychotic, hallucinating, screaming, running naked through the village square..."

He shook his head. I said nothing, watching him, waiting. He pointed at the bottle and made a question with his eyebrows. I said, "Sure, don't ask. Just help yourself. What happened?"

He spoke as he poured. "The soldiers mowed them down. And anyone who showed symptoms was systematically shot. The town is now a graveyard."

I nodded. "You said there might be other places outside Africa."

"Sure, Latin America, other parts of Africa, remote parts of Mongolia, the Far East... We suspect, but we can't be one hundred percent sure of our facts."

"So you'd like me to pay him a visit."

He smiled, gave a short laugh. "You spent a lot of time with the Brits, right?"

I returned the smile. "A bit, yeah."

"You have their flair for understatement. Yeah, we'd like you to go and blow the bastard's brains out."

"Good. Consider it done. I'll need all the intel you have, obviously."

"Obviously. But it's a little more complicated than that. He's here in New York. So it's important it looks like an accident, or at the very least a mugging or an act of terrorism…"

"You want deniability. That goes without saying."

"Yeah, but there's more, Harry. Zak Lee is here talking to a UN delegation, a delegation from the European Union, and there are US representatives meeting with him too. The brigadier would really like to know what they're talking about."

I frowned. "I thought that wasn't our job. That's what the Feds are for, or the Firm."

"Sure," he sipped, "but let me ask you something. When the big unknown here is China's chemical warfare capability, and the man who's responsible for developing it is in New York, at the United Nations, talking to American companies that are part of the military industrial complex, do you feel relaxed and comfortable leaving things to the CIA and the FBI?"

I nodded and sighed. "I guess not."

"It's a bit like having Dennis Rader break into your house, and you don't do anything because it's the cops' job."

"I get the point. So what does the brigadier want me to do?"

"He's convinced, and some of his advisors agree, that Lee's research has reached a critical point and he may be mobilizing resources to deploy it."

"You mean he fears he's preparing a dirty bomb?"

He shrugged. "That's partly what we need to find out. A bomb is simply a means of delivery. The problem is, the brigadier fears he may actually have something to deliver. If he has, then we need to know what, and where, when and how he plans to deliver it. The consequences could be very serious."

"And you say I have a gift for understatement." I drained my glass and set it on the table. "OK, so I need to know who my targets are, their exact location and any other intel."

"Your primary target is Heilong Li, Zak Lee, your secondary target is Yang Dizhou, no Westernization. He is Zak's personal assistant. He is also a very accomplished scientist and was Zak's student and disciple for many years, then became his assistant. He takes care of business for Zak. He has to go too.

"They're staying at the Oriental Suite, at the Mandarin Oriental, on Columbus Circle. Chinese taxpayers to foot their comrades' bill at fourteen grand a night, power to the people, comrade."

"They don't make Communists like they used to. So who else is on the list?"

"He has a number of meetings scheduled at the UN, plus a couple of private meetings with US scientists from Colombia at the hotel, which I suspect is just cover, and then a couple of dinners with bankers and industrialists from the petrochemicals industry. It's a busy schedule."

He reached in his pocket and pulled out a manila envelope which he handed to me. I opened it and inside were a couple of A4 documents stapled together. I examined them and saw that it was a list of times and dates showing where Lee was going to be, and what he was going to be doing while he was there. There were also a couple of photographs, one of Zak, the other of his assistant.

Zak was in his mid-sixties, bald as an egg, very thin, with hollow cheeks and large ears. He was tall, maybe six two, with a long, thin neck, long thin arms and big, bony hands.

Yang was shorter, thick set, with heavy, bottle-base glasses, receding gray hair and a pencil moustache. Somebody must have told him that was a good idea. I asked without looking up, "He in the same suite?"

"Yeah, and May Ling, the personal assistant's personal assistant."

I glanced at him. "I don't kill women or children. I'm funny that way."

"Relax, that's company policy. Besides, she's not on the list."

"So what about these delegates he's meeting with?"

"OK," he drained his glass and crossed one leg over the other, "that's part of your brief."

"What is?"

"Decide which ones to recommend for termination. You run your list by the brigadier, and the management decides which ones to execute."

I nodded and looked back at the pictures.

"OK. This is going to be expensive. I'm going to need serious expenses. I'm going to need to get inside and recon this place. I need to be invisible..."

"Sure." He reached in his jacket again and pulled out another, fatter envelope. In it was an expensive leather wallet containing five thousand bucks, a driver's license in the name of Auberry Winchester, a Centurion Amex and a Black Visa. "You have absolute operational autonomy," he said. "Do what you have to do. Keep the brigadier in the loop as much as you can, but he likes you and he trusts you, so you have pretty much a free hand." He grinned. "Don't let him down."

"I won't."

He sighed, put his hands on his knees and levered himself to his feet.

"Thanks for the whisky. A rare treat."

I let him out and stood smelling the damp, night air as I listened to his steps receding down toward Barkley Avenue. A few seconds after they had faded I heard the soft hum of a motor, which in turn blended into the night, leaving only the distant call of a foghorn, and the desultory chatter of a bird, fooled by the streetlamps into believing it was day.

I closed the door and went back inside. I picked up the papers he'd given me. Auberry Winchester. I smiled. It was like something out of Scott Fitzgerald meets P. G. Wodehouse. I'd have to go clothes shopping for blazers and cravats. But first I'd have to digest and memorize Zak Lee's schedule for the next few days, and do some observing from a distance. My window of opportunity was small, and I was starting from zero, but it was as important to go slow and steady at this stage, as it was to act lightning fast when the time came.

Zak Lee's first appointment was the next morning, Monday the 30th, ten fifteen at the United Nations building. I figured I didn't need to follow him inside because there was no way I was going to make the hit in there, but I could follow him there and follow him back, see what route he took, what kind of transportation he used and what his security was like.

A guy like him might have real tight security, or he might choose to keep a low profile. He wasn't exactly famous, and the people who might want to kill him were probably too poor to leave their villages, let alone their countries. Either way I didn't want to make assumptions. It was better to keep an open mind. We'd see tomorrow.

I scanned his schedule again and saw he had a lunchtime engagement in his rooms with a Professor

Moricone from Harvard, and then a dinner appointment at nine PM. This appointment, instead of being in his suite, was in the restaurant. That struck me as curious. Either he was not at all shy, or he had a purpose for arranging a public meeting. He must know there were people in the international intelligence community who'd be watching him. I filed that away under "answer later."

So between lunch and nine I'd have a few hours to buy an expensive wardrobe, an expensive watch and expensive shoes. I figured I should get an expensive haircut, too. Expensive people notice that kind of thing. Finally I figured I should hire an expensive car for the week. That made me smile. What the heck, Cobra might need it again for another job in the future. It might be cheaper just to buy one.

This hit had definite pluses to it.

THREE

I was up at six the next morning, went for a ten-mile run, spent an hour training in the backyard and had a breakfast of spelt waffles and honeycomb at nine thirty. Then I showered and dressed and went out to my old beat-up 1999 VW Golf GTI. It was the kind of wreck people made a point of not noticing, but under the dented, scuffed chassis, there was nothing wrong with the tweaked engine or the suspension. I had done some work and jacked it up from a hundred and fifty brake horsepower to two hundred and fifty by taking out the old engine and dropping in an Mk6. I'd had to tweak the suspension and the wheels too, but it had worked out nice. The 1999 model only weighed two thousand eight hundred pounds, compared with the three thousand four hundred of the Mk6, so with the extra power and torque it was doing naught to sixty in four seconds, which was nice.

I climbed behind the wheel, stuck the old-fashioned key in the ignition and enjoyed the low growl and rumble of the engine. Personally I like a stick shift because it gives you more control over the engine and the revs. You drop from sixth to third at a hundred MPH and your revs go through the roof. If you need a burst of speed or power, you can do that with a stick shift. With an automatic you're stuck with what the car thinks you ought to be doing. And if it's a German car, two gets you twenty the car will think you should be obeying the rules.

And the trouble is, a lot of the time I'm breaking the rules, doing stuff I ought not to be doing.

It was a half hour drive from my house to Columbus Circus. I approached down the West Side Highway and West 56th, then turned north onto 8th Avenue. I followed the circus round to West 60th and parked outside the post office, where I had a good view of the entrance to the hotel, and the hotel underground parking. There I killed the engine, adjusted the mirror and settled in for a wait.

It wasn't a long one. At fifteen minutes to ten a black Audi Q8 emerged from the hotel underground parking. A moment later two men exited the hotel and walked quickly toward the Audi. They were Heilong Li and Yang Dizhou. The chauffeur climbed out to open the rear door for them and at the same time a guy the size of a small barn got out of the front passenger side and stood staring up and down West 60thth Street, like he really didn't like West 60th Street at all. He and the driver were both Chinese, with real short hair, dark suits, dark shades and wires in their ears. They were about as conspicuous as my car was invisible.

Once their charges were in the vehicle, they climbed back in and took off. I followed them at a leisurely pace onto Columbus Avenue and down West 57th, all the way to Second Avenue. There they turned south as far as East 40th, where they finally turned onto First Avenue and then into the United Nations compound and underground parking.

As events go it wasn't much, but it told me something important. That was the most direct, obvious route they could have taken to get to the UN, and they had not been a bit shy about it. They had been bold to the point of being showy, and were making no effort at all to be discreet. Which meant that either they did not expect trouble, or they didn't care if they got it. Either way it suited me fine.

I decided not to waste time following them home. I had their schedule and I was keen to get my shopping done. So my first stop was Hickey Freeman on Madison Avenue, where I spent just short of ten grand on two suits, an evening suit and a handful of shirts. After that, I went to look for a suitable car at Cooper Classics on Perry Street, in the Village. I called before I went. When the sweet girl on the other end answered I told her, "Hi, what's the most expensive, cool car I can walk away with this afternoon?"

She took a moment to answer, then laughed and said, "The car I'm in love with right now is a replica."

"A replica?"

"Of the AC Cobra. Factory five, Oxford blue period color, silver Le Mans stripes, cream leather upholstery, VX220 seats, ProCharged four twenty-seven CI SBF stroke engine putting out seven hundred and fifty bad-ass horsepower, stainless-steel headers, four-barrel Holley, Carter fuel pumps, fully lined engine bay in polished alloy, Edelbrock rocker covers, electric power steering, high torque starter motor, ProTech shocks all round, electroplate brake calipers, Smiths instruments, period radio, power steering drives like a dream, complete build portfolio. Man, I'm getting horny just telling you about it."

A Cobra? How could I say no? I smiled into my voice and told her, "Yeah? I think you just sold it. Hold it for me, will you? I'm on my way."

It was a very sweet ride and worth every one of the fifty thousand dollars I paid for it. And when I turned up at the Mandarin Oriental that evening, that replica kit car was going to look just as sweet sitting next to the Bentleys and the Ferraris as it did in the showroom at Cooper Classics. In fact, my only worry was whether the brigadier would let me keep it when the job was done.

I arranged to collect the car later that afternoon and took my purchases home in the VW, along with Dashiell Hammett's *Glass Key*, which I had a feeling I might need at dinner. Once home I made a reservation for a week at the Mandarin, packed a suitcase with a false bottom with all the things I thought I might need, showered and dressed, and made an appointment at the Pall Mall Barbers at 10 Rockefeller Plaza. By the time they'd finished with me, I not only had a name out of a P. G. Wodehouse novel, I looked like a character out of a P. G. Wodehouse novel too.

I'd taken a cab from Throggs Neck to Manhattan for my restyle and a wet shave. One hundred and twenty bucks lighter, I had then taken a cab to Coopers and collected my Cobra. From there I had finally rolled up at Columbus Circus in my gleaming automobile, tossed my keys to the valet, allowed a buttons to take my case and strolled into the foyer to check in.

Once registered, the buttons led me to my room, threw open the curtains, showed me where everything was and stood smiling and expectant at the door. I took fifty bucks from my wallet and handed it to him.

"Say, I heard there was some kind of Chinese scientific delegation here. Am I right?"

He smiled and gave his head a little dance. "Well, it's not exactly a delegation. That's Mr. Heilong Li. I'm never sure which is the first name and which is the surname, they do it the other way around over there. But he's here with Mr. Yang Dizhou and a couple of assistants, on business at the United Nations. 'Course, we get a lot of people here from the UN, because it's very handy for them, just down the road as it is."

"I imagine so." I gave a small laugh. "That's a dangerous business!" I said. "A guy like you who's a little bit awake could pick up a lot of useful gossip on the airwaves."

He gave me a careful smile. "Dangerous is the word, sir. Gossip is a double-edged sword. You're not wrong that there are clients who are willing to pay serious bucks for snippets of information. But you start playing that game and in no time at all you start losing people's trust. And then you're screwed, if you'll forgive my French."

"Sure, I get that. Trustworthiness is one of the five most valuable commodities. But it is, at the end of the day, a commodity that can be bought and sold. And a guy who knows how to work the market can choose his customers and sell *them* his loyalty and trustworthiness. Am I right?"

I was watching him carefully. There was only one thing I was really interested in right then, and it was whether he looked uncomfortable. He didn't. He looked wary, but he didn't look uncomfortable at all. He had been here before and he had negotiated these particular rocks with success.

He gave a small shrug with his eyebrows. "I guess

that's true, sir. For me personally, it would take a lot for me to betray a confidence, or something I had overheard from a customer. I'm no saint and I guess if the price was high enough... But the price would have to be very high, or it would have to be a matter of national security or something like that. It's not just that I could lose my job, there is also the issue of self-respect, right?"

I nodded and tried to look sage while I did it. "I hear you." I pointed at him like my hand was a gun. "And I like what I hear. National security is never more at risk than when it is in the hands of diplomats."

He nodded, and there was a hint of resignation and obedience about it. "Yes sir."

I leaned my backside against the desk that was up against the wall and folded my arms.

"Diplomats," I said, "and big business interests, like the big pharma and petrochemical companies. I, personally, have seen senior management and CEOs of large multinationals, who would have sold their own mothers down the river for a lucrative contract, and these guys were already worth several million dollars apiece." I gave a short, dry laugh and his eyes told me he really wanted to get back to his job. I ignored what his eyes said and drove on. "They would have sold their mothers, but in some cases they actually *did* sell their country down the river for huge payoffs from hostile nations. You know what line of work I'm in, kid?"

"I have no idea, sir, but I am guessing it is something patriotic."

"You're not wrong. You're a bright kid. What's your name?"

"Bobby, sir."

"Well, Bobby, I won't tell you what my job is because then I'd have to kill you…" I laughed noisily and he made a real effort to laugh with me. When I was done I made a real serious face and told him, "But you should know that I am involved in issues of national security and I am here precisely for what you observed, this hotel's proximity to the United Nations. Now, I am well aware of how useful an ambitious young man like you, who cares about his country, can be. So I would like to make an ally of you…" I knew damned well that buttons in luxury hotels have high expectations and don't work for peanuts. So I peeled another fifty bucks out of my wallet and handed it to him. "…and ask you, if you see or hear anything, anything at all, that you think might be of interest to me, let me know."

I held up both hands and made a motion like I was slowing him down. "Now, I am not going to ask you to make an evaluation of intelligence and decide what is useful and what is not. That is not your brief, and it is not a skill I would expect you to have. You just give me anything that comes up concerning Heilong Li and Yang Dizhou: change of schedule, heightening of security, sudden change in his breakfast menu, a call girl who stayed the night…" I spread my hands. "You hear me, right?"

"Yes, sir."

"And not only will you get to feel good about yourself, young man, but you will also find that Uncle Sam can be very generous when he is grateful."

"I have nothing right now, sir. But I will keep my ear to the ground and let you know if I hear anything."

"Addaboy."

At the door he hesitated a moment and turned back to me.

"There is one thing, but I don't know if it's of any

importance."

I had my wallet halfway to my jacket pocket. I paused. "Let's find out."

"Well." He made a face of uncertainty that was almost a wince. "We're pretty used to a high level of security here at the Mandarin, as I'm sure you know, sir. But the setup in the Oriental Suite goes a little beyond what you would expect."

"Yeah, how's that?"

"Well, inhouse hotel security is pretty tight. We have the latest in alarm systems and video surveillance, plus security guards and detectives. Most people who are security conscious add to that a bodyguard and, or, a couple of men at the door." He shrugged. "If you're on the top floor of a Manhattan skyscraper, nobody's going to come in through the window, right? Not unless it's Ethan Hunt."

"OK, so?"

"So Professor Li has two men on the outside of the door, two men on the inside of the door, plus his personal chauffeur and bodyguard, and then he has two men on the roof above his suite. And that is all in addition to the hotel's own electronic security system, which is cutting edge."

I thought about it a second, then nodded. "OK."

His face told me he didn't want me to miss the point so he went on.

"I mean, that's a lot of security, right? But the vehicles he uses are part of the hotel's own fleet. They're top of the line and bulletproof glass, but I'm pretty sure he could get something more…"

I smiled. "I get it. It's a good observation." I pulled a C note from my wallet and handed it to him. "Anything else, keep me posted."

"Of course, Mr. Winchester."

The door closed and I sat a while with my ass against the desk staring at a point six inches above the floor, but seeing only Heilong Li's two guards outside the door, two inside the door and two on the roof. And Ethan Hunt, what film was it? I shifted my gaze to the dark window, with the sparkling lights of the city outside the black glass, and tried to remember for a while.

It didn't really matter. The important thing was the six guards, and where they were placed: two outside, two inside and two on the roof. I smiled to myself, then went and had another shower, and dressed for dinner.

At eight thirty I went down to the cocktail bar, stopping briefly for a chat with Bobby the buttons, and ordered myself a martini, dry. Just for the heck of it I told the barman I wanted it shaken, not stirred. He must have heard it before because he didn't flinch. He just said, "Naturally, sir," and went ahead and shook me a martini dry. By the time he'd finished I had located Heilong Li and Yang Dizhou. They were sitting at a table in the corner with two men and a woman, none of whom looked Chinese. The woman was in her forties, attractive, blonde, well-dressed in an expensive, dark blue suit with diamonds that appeared to be real around her neck and in her earlobes. Her eyes were a pale blue that looked dangerous and her makeup was discreet but effective. I figured that probably summed her up. She was quiet, watching, listening, holding a gin and tonic but not drinking it.

On her right was a big man, six two or three, running to fat. His head was big and enhanced by jowls. His eyes peered suspiciously from pouches and his large lips moved constantly, like he was savoring the air. I estimated his weight at an easy three hundred pounds. Even his thousand-dollar suit couldn't make him look elegant. For all I knew, he might have had a beautiful soul, but he looked like a greedy, arrogant slob. Make that a greedy, arrogant, dangerous slob.

The third guy with them was in his sixties and you could see he worked out and ran his two miles every morning before breakfast. He was lean, well-dressed and wide awake. His gray hair had cost as much to cut as I'd spent on my handmade shoes. And his handmade shoes had probably cost as much as my suit. He had ruthless and predatory written all over him and I had a bad feeling that what was going down among cocktails at that table, among those five people, might have wide-reaching repercussions for a lot of other people, other people who could not afford thousand-dollar, handmade shoes.

As I pretended to read messages on my phone, a waiter from the restaurant entered the bar, approached Heilong Li and bent to mutter in his ear. Li's only acknowledgment was a brief nod. Then he smiled at his guests and said something, and they all rose and left the bar.

FOUR

I sat at a table close enough so I could eavesdrop, but far enough away to be inconspicuous. I ordered a salmon, beetroot and avocado salad to start with, with a glass of dry Manzanilla, and a T-bone steak with a half bottle of claret which I told the wine waiter to recommend for me. While I waited I had another martini and sat and pretended to read The Glass Key, while I listened carefully to my prey.

For a moment I was back in the hills above Sulfur Springs, lying motionless in the shadows of the pines, smelling, watching, listening, while the bull elk grazed peacefully unaware that death was grazing with him in the meadow.

But it was a moment, no more, and I put the thought out of my mind. You can't think that way when you're putting together a hit. Your thinking has to be here, and now.

Heilong Li was doing most of the talking. He had the calm authority and arrogance that comes with believing you are invulnerable. His English was almost accent free. He was saying:

"What we can offer you is a license limited by territory. And the territory must be within the geographical and jurisdictional limits of the United States. You are free to set your own price, but CF Inc. takes a cut of between ten and twenty percent. The higher your price, the higher the percentage, with fifteen percent falling somewhere in the mid range."

The fat guy laughed noisily and drained his cocktail. As he set his empty glass down on the table he belched. "And China comes in playing hardball. You're dreaming and you know it. For starters, why the hell should you limit us geographically? Why the hell shouldn't we have Western Europe too? We can distribute there as easily as anybody. In the second place, fifteen percent, kiss my sweet fanny. You'll take seven percent and be grateful we don't just go right ahead and develop our own vaccine."

Heilong Li and Yang Dizhou exchanged a few inscrutable words, and though they were expressionless and incomprehensible, the contempt was palpable. Once he'd allowed the fat guy to palpate it for a while he turned to him and spoke.

"Mr. Gutermann, we are of course delighted to entertain you as our guest. However, our purpose tonight is to speak about business, and the time we have at our disposal is limited…"

He left the words hanging and smiled amiably as he watched Gutermann's cheeks flush red. The woman stepped in by rattling the ice in her glass and, before sipping, then said, "Mr. Heilong, Peter raises a reasonable point as far as I can see. Our resources are among the best in the world. There is nothing to stop us developing a vaccine ourselves, with no need to pay what are, after all, exorbitant license fees."

Heilong Li screwed up his face in what turned out to be a silent laugh.

"Exorbitant. My English nanny used to say, 'Is as does!' 'Is as does!' I would say to her, 'Nanny! That is not fair!' She would reply, 'Fair is as fair does!' I would complain, 'Nanny! This food is not good!' She would reply, 'Good is as good does!' I never did know what it meant! Then, one day, after she was dead, I realized what it meant…" He leaned forward, leering at the woman. "You know what it meant, Ms. Goldbloom? It meant, 'I have the power, so fuck you!'"

His laughter was shrill and startling, like the spasmodic shrieking of a parrot in a tropical rainforest. In a curious echo to Gutermann's reaction, Ms. Goldbloom's cheeks colored a delicate pink. The third guest's voice was quiet and measured.

"Don't you think you're overstating the case, Mr. Heilong? After all…"

But Heilong Li was already shaking his head, holding out the palm of his left hand in front of the man's face in a bizarre, "talk to the hand" gesture.

"Please, Mr. Browne, let's not waste any more time. The big issue here, which you are carefully trying to ignore, is the fact that I can develop my products a *thousand* times more quickly than you, because I have experimental resources that you have not. I have the vaccine, and I know, as you know, that it will take you years to develop it to a point where you can get FDA approval and start marketing it. So what you need to be asking yourselves is not how much money will you lose with my licensing agreement, but how much will you lose if you don't jump on the wagon right now? It is a simple choice. You have to choose between losing fifteen percent and losing one hundred percent." He gave another one of his parrot shrieks. "We can sit here and pretend to argue, but you know that in the end either you accept my terms, or somebody else does."

Two waiters approached my table. One carried my salmon and avocado salad, the other a chilled glass and a bottle of *Manzanilla*. He set down the glass, poured and went away. Meanwhile a gang of waiters had descended on Heilong Li's table and the conversation had died away.

I carefully set my bookmark in my book, smelled and sipped my wine and set to on the salmon, then returned to reading while I chewed and sipped. By the time I had got halfway down the page there was a pop and a moment later the flock of waiters had left and the table of five was tucking into a bottle of Pol Roger and five dozen oysters. They ate in silence and I phased out everybody else in the dining room until all I could hear was the clatter of shells on china, the desultory slurp of oysters being sucked from those shells and the clink of crystal flutes.

I ate too. If camouflage in the mountains was remaining motionless in the shade and undergrowth, here it was eating and drinking as one of the herd. Eventually, Mr. Browne leaned back in his chair and dabbed his mouth with his handkerchief.

"We are familiar with your...," he hesitated a moment, then gave a small shrug before picking up his glass, "your exceptional facilities, Li. And I for one am not going to pretend that we have anything comparable on this side of the Pacific. I will say, however, that I am by no means sure the FDA will approve your vaccine..."

Li didn't let him finish. He restrained a splutter of amusement into his champagne flute and waved his left hand at Browne across the table.

"My dear Browne, please, that is the least of your worries. The FDA will approve it. The president himself will take care of that."

Browne arched an eyebrow at him. "Yours or ours?"

Li said something to Yang Dizhou in Chinese and they both laughed. Shortly after that three lobsters were brought to the table along with two more bottles of champagne. My plate and glass were cleared away and my T-bone steak was delivered with a bottle of *La Fleur de Petrus*, Pomerol, 2014, which he had opened earlier to allow it to breathe. He poured me half an inch which I swirled around like I knew what I was doing, sipped, thought about it and nodded. He poured me another two inches, bowed and went away on quick, silent feet.

I stroked the T-bone with my knife and it opened up, succulent and slightly bloody on the plate. It was exquisite and I sat back to savor it and the wine while Li started to talk again.

"It is very rare, Browne, very rare, that a person should find himself completely out of options." He nodded a few times. "But it happens. The man who falls out of a window twenty stories above the ground is out of options. The woman who is in the path of a high-velocity bullet is out of options. If that asteroid the doomsayers are always talking about ever shows up, we will *all* be out of options." He laughed, but nobody else at the table did. "The fact is that sometimes karma catches up with us and becomes fate, destiny, whatever you want to call it. And when that happens, we run out of options. This..." He opened his hands like he was opening a large book and gestured at them all around the table. "This is where you are at right now. You are not completely out of options, not exactly. But you have only two options left. Only two. They are, accept my terms, or walk away."

Gutermann had been lost in his own fat world of sloppy, oral delight, chewing and sucking on hunks of lobster which he held with short, conical fingers. Now he picked up his napkin and wiped his face with it.

"And if we walk away?"

Li shrugged. "It makes no difference to me. I have cornered the market. Your antitrust legislation does not affect me. You are convenient to me so that I can break into the North American market, but if you do not like my terms somebody else will." He suddenly leaned back and let out his strange, parrot-like laugh again. "Yesterday Hillary was on the phone to me, begging for a piece of this action." The laughter faded from his face and he reached for another piece of lobster. "But they are a spent force. I would rather work with you. So I offer you this opportunity. However, if you will not work with me, she will."

It was the woman, Goldbloom, who answered. She sighed loudly and shook her head. "There's only one thing I hate more than getting screwed over, and that's wasting time. That's what we're doing here right now. I don't know if we are out of options, but I am damn clear what our best option is. We will take over distribution of your vaccine in the USA and Canada, on your terms, but there is one condition I will impose, and this is not negotiable."

Li didn't answer, but he looked at her with the kind of inscrutable expression that usually precedes a great deal of pain. She held his gaze for a count of three while she sipped her champagne. Then she told him what her condition was.

"We need access to your testing labs."

"No."

"Think long term, Li. Make long movies in your head. You have the upper hand today in this negotiation, but you know that down the line, someday, you will need our good will. We need access to your testing fields, and that is the condition. Otherwise I will personally make sure the FDA does not approve your vaccine. Take it or leave it."

I had to smile. He was quiet for a long while. Finally he said, "Through our agents and supervised by our agents."

She shrugged. "You got yourself a deal, Li."

They all raised their glasses and toasted. I read on about the political corruption in America back in the '20s and '30s. Their conversation shifted to more mundane subjects like illegal hunting in African nature reserves, the latest shows on Broadway and prostitution in Bangkok. I ordered a black coffee and a Macallan, and sat and thought while I pretended to read.

I hadn't learned a lot more than I knew already. I had added detail, but not much more than that. Except that there was a deal going down; a deal in which a corporation represented by Gutermann, Goldbloom and Browne would be granted exclusive distribution rights across North America for a vaccine manufactured by the Chinese. The brigadier had asked for information, if I could get it. I wondered if this was the information he was after, and whether I should now focus on the kill. I turned a page and stared unseeing at the print.

Something told me the brigadier would not be satisfied. He would want more. He would want to know, a vaccine against what? Either way I would need to get into the suite. Whether it was to collect intel or kill these bastards, I would have to get inside. Like Li had said, sometimes you run out of options. Killing him inside the UN was out of the question—security was too tight and getting away would be almost impossible. That left the route from the hotel to the UN complex, and on that route the risk of collateral damage was unacceptably high. That left the hotel and the suite. As there was no way to predict his and Yang Dizhou's movements within the hotel, my only realistic option was to break into the suite. Whether I did that to get information on the deal, or to kill them, at this stage made little difference. I had to get in, and then I had to get out.

I sipped some coffee and followed up with a slug of whisky which I rolled around my mouth for a while, enjoying the thought of how much Cobra would be paying for that sip.

There were six possible points of access to the suite, and most of those could be eliminated straight away. I could enter through the floor, through the ceiling or through one of the side walls from a neighboring room. All those four options would entail some form of demolition and could therefore be eliminated immediately. That left just two points of access: the front door and the window.

Going in through the front door would mean avoiding hotel security, which I had already been told was cutting edge, neutralizing the guards on the outside, opening the door, then neutralizing the guards on the inside. That would leave the bodyguard and the chauffeur, and May Ling. Though they would have to be faced sooner or later whatever my point of entry was.

Which left the window. Entering through the window, if done correctly, could mean getting direct access to Heilong Li and Yang Dizhou without having to tackle the guards on the door. But it would also mean approaching up, or down, a sheer steel and glass wall, fifty-four floors above ground level.

An interesting prospect.

I called the waiter, signed my bill and took my book up to my room. There I tossed it on the bed and dialed a secure number on my cell. It rang twice, then the brigadier's voice spoke.

"Harry, tell me."

"I'm at the Mandarin. I followed Heilong Li and Yang Dizhou to the UN this morning and I've just had drinks and dinner about fifteen feet away from them."

"I hope you're being discreet. This is not Afghanistan."

"Yes, sir. I will also remember to brush my teeth before I go to bed."

"What have you learned?"

"He had dinner with three people aside from Yang Dizhou. A big slob called Gutermann, a woman in her forties name of Goldbloom and a guy in his sixties, name of Browne. They discussed a licensing contract for a vaccine..."

I reported the content of their conversation and he was quiet for a while. Finally he said, "There was no mention of what this vaccine was for."

"None. I know you said you wanted intel, now I'm wondering whether this was the intel you were after, or whether you want more. You stressed to me once that we are not an intelligence gathering agency. Our job is to execute people."

"That's quite true, Harry." He said it like he'd never thought of it that way before.

"So you want me to execute these bastards or you

want me to find out what color panties they wear?"

"Let me ask you a question. In your honest opinion, do you think they have electronic files in their suite relevant to this vaccine?"

"Of course."

"Then I think we have little choice but to collect it. But don't let that take precedence over your primary mission. Execute them and collect whatever intel you can find in the form of documents, paper or electronic."

"OK."

"Have you a plan yet?"

"Yes."

"When do you plan to execute it?"

"Tomorrow night, when I'm not weighed down by a T-bone steak and half a bottle of 2014 Pomerol."

"I see you're making good use of the company expense account."

There was no trace of sarcasm in his voice and that made me smile. I let the smile show in my voice. "Camouflage, Brigadier."

"All right, I'll be waiting for your report. Be careful."

He hung up and I stood looking out at the night, with the constellations of New York City lights scattered against the black sky. I'd be careful. I had no other option. I was out of karma and in the hands of fate, climbing down the sheer face of a glass and steel building, fifty-four floors above Columbus Circus.

– END OF EXCERPT –

To see all purchasing options, please visit:
www.blakebanner.com/dying-breath

ALSO BY BLAKE BANNER

I have a huge catalog of eBooks online, but am slowly turning them all into paperbacks. If you'd like to see what I have in paperback at this very moment, then please visit the following site.

www.blakerbanner.com/books

Thank you once again for reading my work!